Ron Ellis started life a[...] and DJ during the Mer[...] up as Promotions Manager at Warner Bros. Records and hitting the New Wave charts in 1979 (as Neville Wanker & The Punters). In the 80s, he was a salesman, lecturer (in Creative Writing), DJ, music journalist, landlord and teashop proprietor. The *Sun* voted him the man with the most jobs in Britain (eleven at one time).

Currently, Ron is running a course for Liverpool University on 'Pop Music in Britain 1945–80'. He reports on Southport FC matches for the national *Non League Paper*, the *Southport Champion* and runs a property company in London's Docklands. He also does the odd bit of acting, photography, public speaking, broadcasting and DJ-ing in between writing crime novels.

Ron lives on Merseyside with his wife, Sue. Their two daughters have moved to Canary Wharf where they are pursuing careers in marketing and fashion.

To discover more about Ron Ellis and his novels visit his website at www.ronellis.co.uk.

'An incredibly intriguing tale . . . The book is simply but cleverly written, starring a wonderful cast of peculiar characters. It keeps you on your toes just as well as it keeps you turning the pages . . . great entertainment'

Pop Factory

The Singing Dead

A Johnny Ace Mystery

Ron Ellis

HEADLINE

First published in 2000
by HEADLINE BOOK PUBLISHING

First published in paperback in 2001
by HEADLINE BOOK PUBLISHING

10 9 8 7 6 5 4 3 2 1

ISBN 0 7472 6602 6

Printed and bound in Great Britain by
Clays Ltd, St Ives plc

HEADLINE BOOK PUBLISHING
A division of Hodder Headline
338 Euston Road
London NW1 3BH

www.headline.co.uk
www.hodderheadline.com

To all the sales staff
without whom the books wouldn't be in the shops

Chapter One

Friday 6 August 1999

'Lot thirty-five, a Baby Belling electric cooker. Will someone start me off at five pounds?'

We were in the auction rooms in town – in the centre of Liverpool. Not many landlords go to the auctions nowadays, not since the new regulations came in regarding gas and electrical equipment, beds and soft furnishings. Half the stuff they have for sale you're not allowed to use any more. Also, people's expectations have risen over the years. You can no longer get away with Victorian furniture, faded Axminster rugs and iron bedsteads. Prospective tenants demand fitted kitchens, fitted carpets and fitted wardrobes, not to mention double glazing and central heating, or they'll go elsewhere. Soon they'll be wanting jacuzzis and sunbeds. Who'd be a landlord nowadays?

I'd seen the cooker at the preview the day before. The oven was covered with thick rancid grease and one of the rings looked decidedly dodgy, but there was a plug at the end of it.

'Fifty pence,' I called. Someone had to start the bidding. Thirteen-amp plugs were 59p in Woolworth's so I figured that if I got the cooker for 50p, I'd be 9p up on the deal.

Leslie Lomax, the auctioneer, regarded me with a sardonic sneer. 'Wouldn't the bank give you the loan, Mr Ace?'

Lomax had exceptionally short legs, which meant his face barely reached above the podium. Like most undersized men, he felt this need to compensate, in his case by taking the piss out of the punters.

'One pound,' broke in a voice, saving further comments. It was Vinny Hall who owns a few student houses in Liverpool 17.

'Did I hear two pounds?' asked Lomax, but nobody owned up. 'One pound fifty, then? What's the matter – someone stolen your piggy banks?' As most of the audience could have bought and sold him twice over, the remark was fatuous to say the least.

'Looks like it's yours, Vinny,' I grinned.

'I only bid to help you out of the shit with that wanker,' he complained. 'Never mind, I suppose I could cut the plug off and use that. What are you here for?'

'Lot 39, that old Grundig reel-to-reel tape recorder. I found these very old tapes that I recorded years ago at some of the old Cruzads gigs and I've got nothing to play them on.' In the Merseybeat days in the sixties, I'd played drums in The Cruzads. We never made the big-time but we kept going well into the seventies till discos took over and I swapped the drum sticks for a mike.

'I've not seen one of those machines for years,' Vinny said reflectively. 'You should pick it up for next to nothing.'

But Vinny was wrong. There was another bidder – just the one, a tall, dark man with a frown who looked like Boris Karloff on a bad day. I started the bidding at fifty pence again. Within three minutes we were up to sixty pounds.

'Sixty-five am I bid?' Leslie Lomax could hardly keep the excitement out of his voice. He'd probably expected it to fetch twenty quid top bat and here we were, me and Boris, still right in there, matching each other bid for bid.

'Ninety-five, I hear. Will you make it a hundred, Mr Ace?'

I nodded – I don't know why. I do sometimes get carried away at auctions but never before for a battered old tape recorder that was out of date even before cassettes were invented.

'One hundred and five from the gentleman.'

Go for broke, I thought, and scare the bastard off.

'A hundred and fifty.'

A shocked silence hit the saleroom. 'Has Johnny Ace been drinking?' I heard someone whisper.

Leslie Lomax peered over his podium, raised his shaggy white eyebrows at the stranger, but only for a nanosecond before bringing down his gavel with a decisive thud.

The stranger's, 'One seven five,' died on his lips. He started to gesticulate but Lomax's voice overrode his protest. 'Sold to Mr Ace for a hundred and fifty pounds.'

They're an odd lot in the auction game. They're never over-keen on strangers wandering in on their territory, and some auctioneers will go out of their way to favour a regular customer – especially if there's a back-hander in it for them. For all his sarcasm, Leslie Lomax looked after his own.

The man glared angrily then turned and walked briskly out of the saleroom, pushing his way through the crowd in his haste.

'One hundred and fifty pounds.' Lomax repeated the figure, probably to convince himself it was true. He could hardly keep the glee out of his voice. The sale had started well for him. 'For that price I'd want a CD player and a built-in coffee-maker,' commented Vinny. 'What's the betting, after all that, it's broken?'

'Probably.'

There was nothing else I wanted in the auction so I paid for my prize lot at the desk and went over to the porter to collect it. You're not supposed to remove purchases until after the auction but I had a lunch date and didn't want to hang around any longer. The unit was portable enough for me to carry it away without disturbing anyone and, besides, the porter knew me.

'Paid a bit over the odds there, didn't you, Johnny?' Tony was holding up a piece of porcelain for inspection and whispered out of the corner of his mouth.

'These are fetching two grand in Hong Kong, Tony,' I lied.

'Don't forget the box,' he said. 'There's a couple of tapes in it.' With his right foot, he reached under the table and nudged a cardboard box along the floor.

I picked it up and stuck the machine inside it, on top of the two tapes. 'Thanks, Tony. See you around.' I slipped an envelope containing two fivers into the pocket of his brown overall, one for

3

him, one for Leslie. Porters and caretakers keep the wheels of the world turning so it pays to keep them sweet.

After that I drove straight over to my office in Aigburth Road where my Property Manager, Geoffrey Molloy, was looking after Roly.

I acquired Roly in a street brawl six months ago. He's part-lurcher, part-deerhound – not the ideal combination for an urban dog – and he is extremely boisterous, but he has one saving grace which always seems to get him out of scrapes. He has a winning smile.

'You got it then, boss?' Geoff enquired when I marched in with the tape recorder. Roly stood on his hind legs and licked my face in greeting.

'Yes, but I had to pay over a ton for it.' I was curious about that. Why should anyone want to give so much money for an obsolete machine in not particularly good condition?

I plugged it in and switched it on. The deck lit up so I knew that at least something worked. Taking one of the reels of tape from the box, I threaded it through the appropriate slots and turned the knob to 'play'. The tape wound noisily round, the motor struggling to revolve; a loud hiss indicated the commencement of the recording. Geoffrey and I stood waiting in expectation, to be met with a thin wail of sound not dissimilar to a cow in labour.

'Whatever is it?' asked Geoffrey.

'"Some Other Guy".'

'Eh?'

'It's a Leiber and Stoller song. It was a hit in America for Richie Barrett in the sixties. Most of the Liverpool groups played it but it was The Big Three who had the hit over here.'

'This isn't them though?'

'God, no. I've no idea who this is. The tape came with the machine.' I fast-forwarded it and found more wailing. 'Criminal, isn't it?' I said.

'Is that the same song?'

I listened carefully. 'No, I think this is "Over the Rainbow".'

'Sounds the same as the other one to me. Is there no name anywhere on it?'

'Don't know but I can soon find out.' I wound the tape back and removed it from the machine. There was some spidery writing on the label that I could hardly read. I took it over to the window and peered at it closely. 'It says "Bobby and the Voxtones, the Iron Door, April 1962".'

'Never heard of them,' said Geoffrey.

'Nor me, but there were over three hundred groups in the city back then.' We'd played the Iron Door a couple of times ourselves back in 1961.

'What happened to them, The Voxtones?'

'Dunno. Probably politicians or brain surgeons by now.' It was a reasonable bet that they hadn't made it in show business if this horrendous noise was representative of their talents. I switched off the tape recorder and put it back in the box, along with the other reel. 'I hope our tapes sound better than that.'

Geoffrey was not old enough to remember The Cruzads, so wisely declined to comment. 'There's a message for you,' he remembered. 'Jim wants you to ring him.'

Jim Burroughs was my partner in Ace Investigations. For some time, I'd been thinking of turning my hobby as a private eye into an official business and finally, after much deliberation, I'd taken out a lease on first-floor premises, down the road from the Town Hall in Dale Street, and opened up in business.

Jim, meanwhile, had been offered an early retirement package by Merseyside Police, where he was a Detective Inspector, and he didn't need much persuading to come into the venture with me. The idea was that Jim ran the office and did all the phoning and paperwork, whilst I went out doing the investigating.

So far, there hadn't been too much of it. A missing teenager, subsequently found safe and sound by the police, a couple of companies wanting surveillance to prevent staff pilferage, and a woman asking us to provide video evidence that her husband was having it away with her younger sister.

5

The last assignment I turned down as it wasn't a field I wanted to get into, but I quickly realised from the nature of the company jobs that the sale of various CCTV and bugging equipment could probably be as lucrative as the investigation work itself.

However, I felt that was something that I could leave to the future when I was more established so, for the time being, I passed on enquiries of that nature to an old friend of mine, Eddie Smeddles, who ran a security firm in Seaforth. Eddie agreed to pay me a fair commission on any orders he secured from my leads so everyone was happy.

All of which meant that I was left to get on with letting my flats and doing my daily record and phone-in programme on local radio while I waited for a suitable case to come along. Could this one be it?

I picked up the phone and dialled my other office.

'Hi, Jim. You rang?'

'Johnny, can you get down here? I've got something that might interest you.'

'Don't tell me it's a case at last?'

'Don't get too excited,' Jim's stolid voice warned. 'Nothing might come of it – but if the client is kosher, then we're talking about murder.'

Chapter Two

It took me twenty minutes to reach Dale Street in the traffic and then another ten to find a parking space, which gave Jim plenty of time to brew up.

Once inside and out of the glare of sunshine, I gratefully settled myself in the visitor's armchair in front of the large mahogany desk. It's a large and well-cushioned chair, made of soft brown leather, one of those comfortable chairs that you sink into and can't get out of again. The idea is that it helps the client to relax which, in turn, encourages him or her to unburden themselves. Or so Jim tells me and he's been on enough police psychology courses.

Jim came in from the adjoining kitchenette, handed me a mug of strong tea and settled himself into the imposing swivel chair at the other side of the desk. Years of police service had kept his back ramrod straight, and the steel-grey hair cropped close to his head showed little sign of receding.

Roly, who had come in the car with me, settled on his blanket under the desk. It had been hate at first sight between the pair of them, but Jim was slowly getting used to sharing canine-minder duties with Geoffrey and had even been known to give the animal the odd pat when he thought nobody was looking.

'The client is a Mrs Skidmore, a Penelope Keith type, very middle-class, lives in Formby. She reckons somebody killed her husband.'

'What did he die from?'

'Car accident a month ago.'

'Someone ran him down deliberately?'

'No, he was driving his own car. He didn't make the bend coming down Parbold Hill.'

'What did the inquest say?'

'Accidental death. No other vehicle was involved. The coroner put it down to lack of concentration, saying he could have dropped off for a second. It was one-thirty in the morning, see. He'd been to a charity sportsman's dinner in Standish.'

I raised my eyebrows.

'Not what you're thinking, Johnny. According to his wife, Bernard Skidmore wasn't a drinker.'

'Which means, if he wasn't used to it, a couple of whiskys might well have slowed his responses?'

'Who knows?' Jim shrugged. 'But his missus reckons the car had been tampered with.'

'In what way?'

'Her theory is that a pipe could have been cut, causing the brake fluid to leak out so when he pressed the pedal there'd be nothing there.'

'And *had* it been tampered with?'

'Couldn't tell. The whole thing went up in flames on impact. Saved the crematorium a job – he was already ashes. Maybe a cable was cut, we'll never know.'

'But the coroner was satisfied it was an accident?'

'Mainly because there was no motive. Mrs Skidmore worshipped the ground he walked on, he had no big debts, there was no malarkey going on with other women, and he didn't leave enough money to make it worthwhile for anyone to top him.'

'Life insurance?'

'I asked that. Only a mortgage protection policy.'

'What did he do for a living?'

'Civil Service. He worked at Smedley in Birkdale as one of the bosses in the census office – births and deaths registration.'

'Anything dodgy from that angle?'

'I can't see it. It's a dead man's shoes type of job.'

'I was thinking more of an office affair, Jim. Jilted mistress, maybe, or jealous husband.'

'According to his wife, he only had eyes for her.'

I hummed the tune.

'The Flamingos, 1959,' snapped Jim. He joined in the chorus and we both laughed. 'Never was a hit in Britain,' he said.

'Not for them, but Art Garfunkel covered in 1975 and it got to No. 1.'

'Smartarse,' said Jim.

'It's my job to know these things. Anyway, what about the late Mr Skidmore? If he wasn't doing it with his secretary and there was no big insurance scam going on, why in hell's name does she think somebody booked him for the pine box?'

'The accident was out of character. He was a very careful driver. Also, the week before he died he was nearly run over and she thinks that might have been deliberate.'

'What happened?'

'A car swerved onto the pavement in front of him in London Road and he only escaped by jumping into a shop doorway.'

'Not very convincing, is it? Probably just a maniac driver. There's a lot of tossers on the roads these days.' Jim gave me a hard look. He'd passed comments about my own driving often enough.

'About this brake pipe,' I said. 'Who had access to the car?'

'Just about anyone who wanted it. He parked it in the road outside Smedley every day so it would be easy enough for somebody knowing his movements to get at it.'

'Not that likely, I wouldn't have thought, not on a public road. Had he had it serviced or anything recently? The garage may have broken the pipe accidentally.'

He looked doubtful. 'Unlikely.'

'Actually, thinking about it, if someone did cut the brake pipe, I imagine it would need to have been done on that particular night, whilst he was inside the hotel having dinner.'

'Knowing he'd be going straight over Parbold Hill.'

I frowned. 'It all seems rather flimsy, Jim. I mean to say, attempted murder! Had he fallen out with anyone likely to harm him?'

'According to his wife, he was liked and respected by everyone

9

who knew him. He hadn't an enemy in the world except . . .' Jim's voice changed slightly.

'Except what?'

'Skidmore was a magistrate and his missus reckons he could have been killed for revenge. Some criminal he'd put away.'

'Possible, I suppose.' But I felt as sceptical as I sounded.

'Well, it's the only lead we've got so I'm going to obtain a list of all the people who'd been up before him in the last six months.'

'Seems a reasonable first step. Has this Mrs Skidmore told the police of her suspicions?'

'Elspeth's her first name. No, she says she doesn't want to waste their time. I think she's frightened of making a fool of herself.'

'Very wise of her.' Nowadays, you'd have to bugger the Chief Constable's daughter on the Cathedral altar during the Christmas Day service to excite the attention of the constabulary.

'Quite, but she seemed pretty convinced, Johnny, and she's prepared to pay. Anyway, I told her you'd call round and see her.'

'Why not?' I rang Mrs Skidmore at work, in Littlewoods Pools head office, and arranged to call at her house that evening after I'd done my radio show.

'We'll see what comes of it,' I said to Jim, 'although I'm not hopeful. Right now, I'm off for lunch.'

At one-thirty, I was meeting my girlfriend Maria at Lucy in the Sky. When I made my way down to Cavern Walks, she was already in the café waiting for me. Maria looks a lot like Cher except all her bits are her own. She's tall and slim and the lemon top and skirt she was wearing contrasted with her long black hair.

'Did you get the tickets?' she asked immediately.

I took them out of my wallet and handed them to her. 'Here they are. October the second, back stalls.'

'Is he taking you somewhere nice, love?' Margie came over with a bowl of soup for Maria.

'A concert at the Bridgewater Hall in Manchester.'

'Oh, it's supposed to be nice there.'

Maria smiled. 'It is, and they're playing Mozart's *Jupiter*

Symphony which is one of my favourites.'

I was glad that Maria was looking forward to it. There'd been a time a few months ago when we hadn't seen much of each other. Maria had mistakenly believed I'd been sleeping with one of my clients and it had taken some time before we'd got back to where we'd been in the relationship.

It was difficult enough for her to accept that for the whole three years I'd known her, I was still seeing Hilary, who was my lover of twenty years' standing. Another woman on the scene would have been just too much – for me as well. I had enough trouble balancing the two of them and yet I knew I needed them both. In some strange way, they complemented one another. Plato might have called it an enigma.

'I'll have the soup as well,' I told Margie. 'What is it?'

'Bacon and lentil.'

'Brilliant. That'll do me.'

'Stop yer soft-soaping, kid. Listen, have you got your season ticket yet?'

'Certainly have, Margie. They should do better this time, especially now they've signed Kevin Campbell.'

'Hey now, don't you forget Franny Jeffers. He's better than Michael Owen, him.'

'Everton,' I explained to Maria, noticing the blank look on her face. 'Margie's a fan as well.'

Maria started to tell me about her morning at Picton Library, where she worked. When I'd heard enough about the staff shortages and performance tables, I acquainted her with news of my latest case.

'I don't suppose it will come to anything,' I concluded. 'I think this Mrs Skidmore's overreacting.'

'I don't know,' said Maria. 'Women have gut feelings about things like that. Does she seem a hysterical type of woman?'

'I'll tell you that when I've met her.' My foot touched Maria's under the table, and I gave her my special smile. Her cheeks went Barbara Cartland pink.

* * *

11

In the event, Mrs Skidmore was far from hysterical. I called round as arranged that evening when I'd finished my radio show and found a woman in her early fifties, conservatively dressed in a calf-length beige skirt with a high-necked cream blouse.

She invited me into the lounge of her detached house in The Evergreens, on a newly built estate in Formby, and repeated to me the circumstances of her husband's brushes with death that she had already recounted to Jim Burroughs.

I waited until she'd finished before asking her, 'Are you sure there's nobody at all among your friends and acquaintances who might have a grudge against your husband, whether real or imagined?'

'Nobody, Mr Ace. Don't you think I haven't been racking my brains? Yet I can't think of anyone at all who would have wanted him dead.'

'Forgive me for asking,' I began, knowing I was on delicate ground, 'but has there been any suggestion of . . . er, marital impropriety on either side?'

I knew what Jim had told me but I wanted to hear the denial from her when I had the chance to look into her eyes.

She wasn't shocked, nor was she offended. 'Nothing like that. Bernard and I had a very happy marriage and a fulfilled one, if you take my meaning.'

I did. Her voice was deep and controlled which gave an air of authority to her words.

'I also appreciate, Mr Ace, that the spouse is the first suspect in a case like this but I can assure you that I loved my husband and had no desire to kill him.'

She suddenly seemed ready to cry. All right – I was prepared to take her word for it. For the time being.

'My partner tells me that you think his death may have been connected with his work as a magistrate,' I said gently. 'Did your husband mention anyone who might have held a grudge against him?'

'Never, but it's the only explanation I can think of.'

'I could understand it if Mr Skidmore had been a judge, but he was just a local magistrate dealing with relatively minor crimes.'

'I know Bernard,' Elspeth Skidmore said quietly. She used the present tense. 'He was murdered.' She said it as a statement of fact. 'I will pay you well to find out who did it.'

I couldn't argue with that. I told her I'd take an advance of £500 and work on the case for a week or so. If I found nothing incriminating at all, I would let her know there was no point in going on. She gave me a list of their friends that I might want to talk to and I promised to do my best.

Chapter Three

After my visit to Formby, I drove back towards the city. It was Friday night and Jim Burroughs' group had a gig at the Bamalama Club.

The Bamalama is a blues club on the fringes of Toxteth. In the fifties and sixties it would have been called a *shebeen*. The clientèle is mostly black, apart from the white hookers and a sprinkling of musicians who appreciate the music and like the atmosphere.

I don't quite know how Jim had persuaded Jonas, the owner, to put on a band of middle-aged white men at all. Surely there were enough genuine elderly black blues-men still knocking around the globe to give a bit of authenticity to the proceedings? But The Chocolate Lavatory had landed the weekend spot and I'd promised to go along to give my support.

I arrived in time for their opening set. After much prompting from myself, Jonas had finally agreed to take in a stock of Scrumpy Jack cider so I didn't have to drink the disgusting beer they served up at the Bamalama.

'Not seen you for ages, Johnny.' Shirley, the barmaid, smiled at me. 'You been avoiding me?'

Shirley and I used to have this thing going but, a couple of years ago, I bought the house she lived in, in Princes Avenue, and decided it would be better to keep our relationship strictly business in future. Besides which, the new boyfriend she'd acquired about the same time didn't look the type to argue with.

'I've finished with that Rodney, you know,' she continued, reading my thoughts, as she handed me my drink. 'You'll have to come round again to inspect your flat. I decorated the lounge a few months back and it's looking real nice.' When she smiled, her white teeth shone against her black skin and I remembered nights we'd spent in her patchouli-scented bedroom.

'Hey, Shirl, two beers over here, girl.' I was saved from replying by the queue of people fighting to get served at the bar and I made my way to a table near the stage to listen to Jim's band.

They were playing a familiar repertoire of sixties' rhythm 'n' blues favourites, 'Hi Heel Sneakers', 'If You Gotta Make a Fool of Somebody', 'You Better Move On', and the like. The same act, in fact, that they were doing in 1961. So much for progress.

They finished with a rousing version of 'Some Other Guy' and afterwards I followed them to the cramped dressing-room at the side of the tiny stage. On the way, I caught sight of Kenny Leatherbarrow, one of Merseybeat's failed musicians, another alcoholic casualty of the sixties. He was sitting alone in a corner, his fingers drumming in time on the table, minutes after the music had finished. He saw me and waved.

Jim was still singing to himself as I closed the dressing-room door behind us.

'Funnily enough, I heard that song earlier today,' I said, '"Some Other Guy".'

'Oh yes?' He wiped the sweat from his face. I didn't reckon his musical career was doing his angina much good. Good job he'd not attempted the Chuck Berry duck walk or he could have been ready for one of those pig's-heart transplants by morning.

'Yeah – by a group called Bobby and The Voxtones. It was pretty awful, I can tell you. Even worse than your version.' I explained about the auction and the tape recorder.

'Sounds odd. Just an ordinary tape recorder, you say?'

'Yes, one of those Grundig reel-to-reel jobs. Do you remember them at all – Bobby and the Voxtones?'

Jim removed his blue lurex shirt, gave himself a quick rub-down and put on a Blondie T-shirt. It was hard to believe he'd recently been a serving police officer of high rank.

'Dimly. I think we were on at the Cavern with them one night, with The Hideaways. Or maybe it was The Pattern People – remember them? Used to do Mamas and Papas stuff.'

I did. They later joined up with a singer called Joan whose daughter, Melanie, is now one of The Spice Girls.

'Have you still got the tape?' asked Jim.

'Yes, it's over at my place. Why don't you come back and have a listen?'

Jim looked nervously at his watch. 'We don't finish till one-thirty. Rosemary'll kill me if I'm not home by two.' Jim's wife had assumed the role of his gaoler since the onset of his coronary trouble. 'Why not bring it to the office in the morning?'

'OK.'

'Coming for a jar, Jim?' The drummer from The Chocolate Lavatory was leading the rest of the band to the bar. He nodded to me and I tagged along with them.

'Not tempted to take up the sticks again, Johnny?'

'No way, Pete. I'm sticking to playing records these days, not making them.'

I stayed for a couple more drinks and we discussed the current music scene, about which none of the group knew very much. Pop music seemed to have ended for them in the sixties. Eventually, the conversation dried up and I took the opportunity to tell Jim about my meeting with Mrs Skidmore.

'Do *you* reckon there's anything in what she says?' he grunted.

'There's five hundred in it for us for starters,' I said. 'As for her old man being murdered, I don't know, but she seems pretty convinced. When are you getting that list of offenders from the court?'

'Monday, all being well. Think it will tell us anything?'

'It's all we have. There doesn't seem to be much amiss in his private life.'

I took a long swig of Scrumpy Jack. It was getting pretty hot in the club. The Bamalama hadn't got round to air conditioning. At one time, Jonas used to leave the fire exit door open for ventilation but people started coming in that way to avoid paying so now he locks it. God help us all if ever there's a fire.

I left before the band's second set. I'd heard enough. Why on earth did they still do it? Why not grow old gracefully? Mind you, Tony Bennett was still going strong at seventy and singing the same numbers he did in the forties. P.J. Proby and Tom Jones were sixty and back in the charts, so who could begrudge The Chocolate Lavatory their Indian summer?

I drove back to my flat in Waterloo Dock and collected Roly for his late-night walk. We strolled past the new Crowne Plaza Hotel and up to the Pier Head. It was still warm, even at one in the morning, and it looked like a hot weekend was on the cards. Not ideal weather for the opening of the soccer season. Luckily, a slight breeze blew in from the river to counteract the humidity.

Back home, I brought out the old Grundig tape recorder again and threaded the tape through. On came the now familiar whine of Bobby and the Voxtones. It didn't improve on hearing it again.

I wound it back and took out the other tape lying at the bottom of the box. There was no name on this one but written on the label were the words *My Songs, 1961*, with a cartoon of a stick man penned alongside. Curious, I put it on the machine and waited to see what came out.

Again, the quality was not good, with plenty of tape hiss, but this time, instead of a group, there was just a solo voice backed by acoustic guitar.

As I listened to it, a shiver ran down my spine. I realised now why somebody had been prepared to pay over the odds for this elderly machine and its two obscure tapes. The song was new to me but the voice I recognised immediately. It was unmistakable.

It was the voice of John Lennon.

The next morning, Saturday, I lay in bed as usual, listening to Kenny Johnson's *Country Music Show*, which begins at 10.00 a.m. on Radio Merseyside. Kenny and I go back to the days of the Black Cat Club in London Road when he was Sonny Webb and the Cascades and I was The Cruzads' drummer.

And, presumably, Bobby was fronting The Voxtones.

Kenny had a new CD out and was playing a couple of tracks from it. Had they been recorded by a Texan with a cowboy hat they would probably have got into the Billboard charts but America takes little notice of British country bands. Ask The Hillsiders or Cheap Seats.

I decided now was the time to phone Jim Burroughs and let him know what I had found.

'John Lennon!' he exclaimed. 'Are you sure?'

'Positive.'

'Christ! What are the songs like?'

'Some of them are pretty good. Not up to "Yesterday" standard, but not bad. Put it this way: if they were released today they'd attract a few cover versions.' Which is as good a criteria as any by which to judge a song.

'Any new John Lennon album would sell several million,' said Jim. He sounded as though he was still in shock.

'Of course, but the point is, the tape itself is what the collectors would be after – the fact that Lennon actually owned it.'

'I wonder who it belonged to before you bought it?'

'And why did they put it into a crappy little furniture auction in Liverpool instead of sending it to Sotheby's?'

'Perhaps they didn't know what was on the tapes. Thought they were just selling an old tape recorder.'

'But someone knew,' I pointed out. 'The guy who was trying to buy it at the auction.'

'You didn't know him?'

'No, but I'd recognise him again. He was a dead ringer for Boris Karloff.'

'How come he gave up bidding at a hundred and fifty pounds if he knew it was worth hundreds of thousands?'

'The auctioneer was too quick for him. Brought his gavel down a bit smartish before Boris could get his next bid in.'

'The old cartel scam, eh?'

'Not really. Leslie Lomax just likes to look after his regulars.'

Jim paused, then: 'I hope Boris, as you call him, hasn't found out

19

where you live or you could be in for a midnight visit.'

I looked down at the large brown creature sprawled under the grand piano. 'Roly'll soon see them off if they try it. Get down to the office, Jim, and I'll bring the tape over.'

'Hang on, I'm not up yet. I had a late night in case you'd forgotten. Give me an hour.'

I hung up the phone and found my copy of *The Best of Cellars* to check the list of groups that had played at The Cavern in the sixties. There was no mention of Bobby and the Voxtones. I then went through Spencer Leigh's *Let's Go Down The Cavern*, the Merseybeat bible which lists over 200 groups, but drew another blank.

I rang Spencer at home to see if he knew anything about the group but he was away at some weekend insurance convention. His wife, Anne, said she'd get him to ring me.

I gave up. On the radio, Frankie Connor was just starting his brilliant sixties show. Frankie probably played more times than anyone at The Cavern, with the Hideaways. 'C'mon, Roly,' I called, 'time to go to work.'

Roly jumped up, wagging his stump and panting enthusiastically. I gathered the box with the Grundig and the tapes and we set off for the office.

I was surprised to find we had a visitor.

A swarthy, heavily-built man in his late thirties wearing a pair of beige chinos, a navy Maine blouson and a light blue shirt sat at the desk opposite Jim. He had black hair, permed and moussed, and small crinkly eyes that darted about the room constantly as he spoke. His suntan was pure Costa del Crime and I'd have put money on him to go the distance with a young Ronnie Knight.

'Johnny,' Jim stood up. 'Glad you got here. This is Owen Jenna. My partner, Johnny Ace.'

I put the box down on the floor and we shook hands. Jenna's handshake was firm and he looked me straight in the eye.

Roly sniffed his trousers briefly and gave a quiet growl before making for his blanket.

'Glad to meet you, Mr Ace. I hope you will be able to help me.'

'Mr Jenna is trying to find his wife,' Jim explained.

Something clicked. *Susie Jenna*. It had been a big news story over three months ago. A local housewife, she'd gone out to the supermarket one Saturday morning, leaving the two kids, three and five, with her husband. She'd never returned.

Owen Jenna, looking strained and tired, had appeared on various TV newsreels begging her to come back, tearfully repeating how distraught he was and how the children missed her. He insisted they had enjoyed an idyllic relationship and he was worried for her safety.

It didn't take long for the papers to uncover the cracks in the Jenna marriage. Neighbours reported regular fierce rows between the couple; he'd once had an affair with a woman at his office (she sold the sordid details to the *Sun* when the missing wife story became news); and Mrs Jenna had made two previous abortive attempts to leave him. Photos were printed showing bruises on her face with the implication that these were inflicted by her husband.

The police duly arrested Mr Jenna but, despite an excavation of the couple's home and garden that would have done credit to a team of archaeologists, his wife's body was not found.

Rumours abounded. After carrying out surveys using infra-red cameras borrowed from the Army, Merseyside Police discredited the theory that Mrs Jenna might be buried beneath the newly built roller-coaster, the Traumatiser, on Southport's Pleasureland.

Underwater frogmen similarly failed to find her body anywhere along the coastline from Formby Points to Banks, and neither did it come to light in the pinewoods beyond the Jennas' semi-detached home in Freshfield. Every rubbish dump and piece of waste land in the area had been searched without success.

Posters featuring Susie Jenna's thin sad face were displayed in nearly every pub and shop in the area without producing even one genuine lead.

Airports, railways and ferries had no record of Mrs Jenna travelling out of the country – indeed, her passport was still at home – and every hospital in the country was contacted to no avail.

BBC's *Crimewatch* did a reconstruction of her alleged last trip but, apart from giving work to a few resting actors, it achieved nothing. And then, one month after his wife had gone missing, Owen Jenna announced that he had received a letter in his wife's handwriting saying she was going to Greece and would not be coming home. The postmark was Liverpool.

'I hope this lets me off the hook,' he told the police, who had made no secret of the fact, without putting it into words, that they believed they had the murderer in front of them. 'She must be alive to have written this.'

Forensic experts confirmed the writing was genuine but said it could have been written at any time and posted by Mr Jenna himself. It was subsequently pointed out to Mr Jenna by the senior investigating officer that the card could have been written by Mrs Jenna under duress and posted to himself by Mr Jenna after he had murdered her.

So Owen Jenna was *not* off the hook, yet neither was there enough evidence to charge him, so he walked the streets a free man but increasingly the target of hate-mail and abuse. Careless of the effect on his two young children, angry locals had broken his windows, pushed dogdirt through his letterbox and had vandalised his car while it stood in his driveway. Someone had sprayed his garden wall with the words *Murderer, you won't get away with it* in bright red paint. The police told him they had no men to spare to give him the round-the-clock protection he asked for and proceeded to book him for having an out-of-date tax disc on his car.

I didn't care much for the man, although perhaps I was biased. I'd kept up with the case and, like most people, thought he was guilty. It was just a matter of waiting for him to make that vital mistake.

'I didn't kill her, Mr Ace.' His voice sounded angry but restrained. 'And I know she isn't dead.'

'Then why do you think she doesn't come forward?'

'Who knows? Amnesia maybe. Or perhaps she's abroad and hasn't seen all the publicity.'

'Come on, Mr Jenna.' I tried to keep the cynicism from my tone. 'Her passport's still here so she must be in the country and her picture's been in the papers more times than Tony Blair's.'

'She could be hiding away on purpose to discredit me.'

'That won't wash. She'd never let her children suffer. Everyone says she was a good mother.'

'Everyone, as you put it, is just her cronies,' he snapped. 'Always saying how devoted their little Susie was.' He rose to his feet. 'That bitch was out clubbing it every weekend, never got in before three and four. And housework? Forget it. I did everything around the house – made the kids' meals, took Wayne to school and Kylie to nursery. Thank Christ my mother's moved in now to help with the kids, or I'd have to give up my job and all.'

'Makes me wonder why you want her back,' I said quietly.

'So the police will stop bloody harassing me – *that's* why I want her back,' he said heatedly. Did he protest too much? 'As long as she's missing, I'm their only suspect. They're not interested in looking for anyone else.' He took out a packet of Regal and started to light one.

'I'm sorry, Mr Jenna,' I said immediately. 'This is a no-smoking office.'

'What?'

I pointed to Roly, seemingly asleep on his blanket but with one eye open. 'He's asthmatic. We daren't risk it.'

Jenna glowered but put the cigarette away.

'What makes you think we can find her when the police with all their resources haven't?' I asked him.

He laughed bitterly. 'They're not looking any more, are they?'

Jim hastily intervened. 'Mr Jenna has given me a cheque for a thousand pounds, Johnny, as a retainer.'

'You'll get another grand when you find her, plus all expenses, of course.'

I thought it over. 'OK, I'm prepared to listen but if you're so sure she's still alive, where do you reckon she might be?'

'If I had any idea of that, don't you think I'd have brought her back?'

It was a fair enough answer. I listened as he trotted out the same story that I knew well from the media coverage.

'How do you think it feels for me?' he finished.

I thought about it. If he had killed her then I imagined he would be feeling pretty nervous, terrified of making that one fatal slip that the police might pick up on. Would somebody find the body? Had he given something away when questioned? It would be hard for him to remain calm. He'd be forever waiting for that knock on the door.

On the other hand, if he hadn't killed his wife, where was she? Had someone else harmed her? Had she really gone away to punish him? Could she still be alive, maybe held prisoner?

I concluded that, either way, Owen Jenna couldn't be feeling too good and told him so.

'So, have you decided?' he asked. 'Will you find her for me?'

I looked across at Jim. He said nothing but quietly waved the £1000 cheque in the air.

'We'll give it a go, Mr Jenna,' I said. I even shook his hand as he left, and the guy looked marginally more cheerful.

'It's weird,' I remarked to Jim when Jenna had gone. 'We have two new clients with entirely opposite aims. For Mrs Skidmore we're trying to make out there's been a murder when the chances of foul play are remote, and for Jenna we're trying to prove there's been no murder when the world and his wife thinks there has.'

'Badly expressed but I follow your drift,' agreed Jim. 'And furthermore, just to make it harder, we've no idea if either of them is telling us the truth.'

I sighed. 'True. Anyway, before we discuss our two cases, just listen to this. This is an even bigger mystery.' I pulled the Grundig out of the box, set it up on the desk and fed in the tape I'd brought.

'Bloody hell,' breathed Jim when the first verse had finished. 'It's him, all right. Lennon.'

'Of course it's him. With acoustic guitar. And all songs we've never heard before.'

'What are you going to do with it?'

'I'm going down to the auction rooms to find out who put it into the sale.'

'Why bother, Johnny? It's yours now – you bought it legit. Put it into Sotheby's yourself. You'll make a packet.'

'I'm curious, Jim.' To me, this was more of a mystery than either of our two official cases. 'The date on it's 1961. Where did it come from after all this time? There's something very strange here and you know me, I always want to know the reason behind everything. That's why I've started this investigation business. Being just a radio presenter and landlord isn't enough.'

But I'd spoken too soon. A minute later, the phone rang. It was Ken, my producer at the radio station.

'You're in trouble, boyo. Creegan wants to see you in his office pronto.'

'Hang on, Ken, it's Saturday.'

'It wouldn't matter if it was Christmas Day, he wants you in now and I don't think it's to give you a rise.'

Chapter Four

I'd been expecting it.

Eric Creegan was the station manager. I remembered him when he was Rocking Ricky Reegan, a jumped-up little prat who'd risen to local radio fame in the punk era of the late seventies.

As a presenter he was crap, pouring out a stream of meaningless comments in an affected mid-Atlantic squeak, but he was adept at ingratiating himself with the bosses and consequently was known for some time around the station as 'Browntongue'.

When the politically correct bandwagon had started rolling in the mid-eighties, Eric had been quick to jump on it and, as it gathered force throughout the industry, he'd allowed it to catapult him to the heights of management.

Needless to say, my own show with its controversial phone-in and unusual records was anathema to Eric's acquired prejudices and only the high ratings had kept me on the air. So far.

On Thursday's show, however, I'd played the wrong track by mistake from a David Allen Coe CD and a song went out that should never have been heard on the public airwaves. I knew, if anyone had twigged, I'd be in for a rocketing. It wouldn't be the first time.

'What's your problem?' I asked Creegan when I arrived at the cramped, untidy cell he called an office. Posters advertising various station events were plastered round the walls.

'You can't go on slagging people off on the radio like this, Johnny.' He was pacing up and down, hands behind his back.

I hadn't a clue what he was talking about. 'Which people are these?' I asked. I had to move my head to follow his progress round the room. It was like being on the centre court at Wimbledon.

'Your comments last night about the Everton chairman. "If the fans had their way, Peter Johnson would be first in the queue outside the Birkenhead Jobcentre tomorrow morning *and who's to say they are wrong*." Those were your exact words.'

'What's wrong with that? That's what a lot of the fans are saying.'

'Maybe, but it's not your place to echo their feelings.'

'Of course it's my place. That's what my show is about, reflecting the opinions of the man and woman in the street, and those people are entitled to ask why the team ended last season lucky to escape relegation yet again.'

I think my vehemence took him aback. 'Er, quite,' was all he managed to reply.

'*And* with borrowed money, as it turns out, so the club are now in financial shit as well. Look, has somebody out there complained?'

Creegan bit his lip and made a tactical switch. 'And playing *that* record too, that was unforgivable.'

So someone had heard it.

'I hold my hands up to that but it was a genuine mistake. The tracks were mixed up on the CD and I played the wrong one by accident. It could have happened to anyone. At least it wasn't on a children's programme.'

'I don't think "cum stains on the pillow where she once laid her head" would have been suitable listening even after the watershed. We had several complaints. One lady this morning said her seven-year-old son was singing it on his way to school.'

'I took it off when I realised.'

'Only after the first verse and by then it was too late – the damage had been done. In future, I'm insisting you stick to the station playlist. No more of these obscure records of yours and I'm stopping the phone-ins too.'

'On what grounds?'

'Too controversial.'

'Controversy is what makes radio exciting and pulls in the listeners.'

'What was it you said last week? "All judges should be made to live on sink council estates for a month to let them see what real life is like". Are you telling me you really believe that? Was that your idea?'

I certainly do believe it and, furthermore, most listeners agreed with me.'

'You're encouraging the wrong type of listener.'

'Eh?' Wrong type of listener? It was as bad as British Rail and the wrong type of snow. Where do these people come from? 'Bollocks,' I said angrily.

'Well, I'm sorry.' He stood up from his leatherette office chair and tried to look dignified but it only made him pompous, especially in striped braces and a brown suit. 'I'm adamant. You stick to the station policy or . . .'

'Or what?'

'Or we give your show to Shady Spencer. He's very popular, is Shady. No outlandish statements, inoffensive music.'

'Shady Spencer thinks Max Bygraves is at the cutting edge of pop.' It was hard to believe that in his Rocking Ricky days, this pillock in front of me had been a staunch supporter of The Sex Pistols. What is it they say about reformed sinners?

'And he writes those nice poems. The listeners like those.'

I walked two steps menacingly towards him. 'In that case, you let them have him. You can stick your pigging show . . .' I stormed towards the door, 'where the gerbils go. Tell that to your rhyming friend.' I slammed the door behind me.

But I wasn't giving up without a fight. I went straight round to the *Daily Post* office to have a word with a friend of mine in Editorial.

'Brilliant stuff, Johnny,' he said, when I'd told him the story. 'I'll try for Page One but we'll definitely make a big story out of it. Can you do a photo if I get a photographer round in an hour?'

'Sure. About six? Pity we can't take it outside the ground.'

'Digital photography now, Johnny. We'll take it at your place and superimpose you against a background of Goodison Park from our files.'

29

'Wonderful, Marty.'

The article appeared on Monday morning. I read it in The Diner in the Royal Liver Buildings where I'd gone for my breakfast. RED CARD FOR JOHNNY raged the headline. THE MAN THEY'RE TRYING TO GAG.

'Sorry about Page One, Johnny,' said Marty, when I rang to thank him. 'The meningitis epidemic beat you to it.'

I said it was understandable.

'The idea of the raincoat and trilby was a good one,' he said. 'Makes you look like a newshound from the *Los Angeles Times*.'

'Saw you in the paper trying to look like Humphrey Bogart,' remarked Jim Burroughs, when I presented myself at the Dale Street office later in the morning. 'What are you going to do without the radio programme? Will you try City?'

'No commercial station would employ me in these days of political correctness, Jim. They're too accountable to their advertisers. Besides, they're into music, not personality presenters. No, I'm banking on a groundswell of public opinion that will force that dickhead Creegan to reinstate me.'

'You'll be lucky. You've gone too far this time.'

'We'll see.'

I'd taken the weekend off. On Saturday night I took Hilary to the cinema to see *Notting Hill*, in which Rhys Ifans was brilliant, and on Sunday I watched the Blues hold treble-winners Man United to a draw, a result which augured well for the forthcoming season. Now I was ready to do some work.

'Time we got started on these cases, Jim. Has that list of sentences come through from the magistrates' court?'

'I've got it here.' Jim handed me a folded sheet of A4. 'The majority of them are fines and community service sentences. To start with, I think we should just go with the six people Skidmore sent to prison in the six months before he died.'

'Is that all? It doesn't sound many.'

'The beaks don't send many people down, Johnny. Most of the

so-called crimes dealt with in the magistrates' court are motoring offences, non-payment of council tax, petty theft, shoplifting, drunkenness, that sort of thing. The big stuff goes to the crown court.'

'What happened to the short sharp shock?'

'Went the way of public flogging and the stocks. Anyway, Skidmore did manage to put six villains away.'

'Anything out of the ordinary about any of them?'

'I've made a few notes alongside. Mostly stuff I've got from the local papers plus a few odds and ends I picked up.' Jim glanced down the form. 'A nineteen-year-old shoplifter got twelve months, six for each of two offences.'

'Any previous?'

'Lots. She *was* nineteen, Johnny. They start at ten these days. By the time they're twenty they're old lags. She had all the gear with her, apparently, the demagnetisers and the tinfoil-lined shopping bags.'

'OK. Who's next?'

'Another girl. Three months for assault. Broke her best friend's nose in a fight over her lover.'

'Lucky man. I wish women fought over me.'

'The lover was also a woman.'

'Oh.'

'Par for the course these days,' commented Jim, who had an inevitably jaundiced view of modern society, shaped by his years in the Force. He continued, 'Bloke here got six months for careless driving.'

'Seems a bit steep.'

'The man he ran into died and he didn't stop. He was picked up by the police the next day. A witness took the number.'

'Lucky he wasn't done for manslaughter. He can't complain about six months. He'll be out in four or less.'

Jim's voice picked up. 'Here's a possible one. Bloke called Dickson, got sent down for slashing a fellow bouncer outside a nightclub. A likely case for retribution there. Probably a gang connection or drugs.'

'Promising.'

'And another – a drunken brawl in a pub. This offender seemed to be the ringleader in a family feud.'

'And families stick together at times of trouble.'

'Precisely. So the law gets the blame.'

'What's the last one?'

'A botched burglary.'

'Much stolen?'

'Nothing. The owner of the house was woken up by this loud crash. He went to investigate and found Chummy lying unconscious in the hall. Turned out he'd fallen downstairs and knocked himself out. By the time he came round the cuffs were on him.'

'You did well with all that information, Jim.'

He tapped his nose knowingly. 'Friends in high places.'

'Some of them will still be inside, I take it?'

'Two, that's all. The burglar and the driver.'

'Which rules them out. So that leaves four suspects who might have had it in for the late Mr Skidmore?'

'Right. I've managed to get their names and addresses and I've written a few notes beside each one.'

'That was quick.'

'Some of us work weekends, you know.'

'Great.' I realised what a good move it had been for me to take Jim into the business. As well as having all the right contacts, he was totally methodical and thorough.

He handed me the list. 'You should be able to get round to most of them today.'

'You're hoping to rule them all out, aren't you, Jim?' I'd caught the dismissive tone in his voice.

'Not hoping, Johnny, but expecting. I think that Mrs Skidmore's clutching at straws. Won't accept her husband died by his own bad driving.'

'Just what I think too.'

'Not least because there's always two or three magistrates sitting on the bench at any time so why kill one and not the other?'

'That's a point. I take it no other local magistrates have met untimely ends in the last six months?'

'I checked. They're all still with us and no reports of any attempt on their lives. Like I say, Mrs Skidmore's so-called evidence is decidedly spurious but she's paying us to investigate so we must give it our best shot.'

'Don't worry, Jim, I will, but first of all I'm going up to the auction rooms. I want to find out who the Boris Karloff look-alike really is.'

Chapter Five

Leslie Lomax remembered the Grundig tape recorder very well, not least because he'd been duly reprimanded by his boss after the unsuccessful bidder had lodged a complaint.

'Can't help it if I didn't catch his glance,' he said. 'He should have shouted louder.' And he gave me a broad wink. Instead of his usual brown suit, he was wearing a Gyles Brandreth-style cardigan that could have come from the props department of *Joseph and the Amazing Techni-coloured Dreamcoat*. It clashed horribly with his spotted green and yellow tie. Obviously, he reserved his suit for auction days.

'Who was he?' I asked casually. 'I don't recall seeing him at the auctions before.'

'Neither do I. They had his name at the office because he bought something else at the sale – some dinner plates, I think it was. Cronkshaw he was called.'

'Do we know who put the tape recorder in the sale, Leslie?'

He looked at me keenly. 'Why this strange interest? You've collected the machine, haven't you?'

'I'm curious as to its history, that's all.'

He looked unconvinced but led the way to his office, a room cluttered with bric-à-brac and dusty ledgers and lit by a fluorescent light in an old-fashioned metal holder. He took a large stiff-bound volume from the top drawer of a huge oak desk and found the relevant entry.

'The Grundig tape recorder was put into the auction by a Mr Edgar Marshall.' He swivelled the book round to show me. I peered at the spidery writing and made a note of the address Marshall had given. It was a street in Old Swan.

'I remember him bringing it in,' Leslie said. 'Spindly-looking chap, a bit down at heel. Reminded me of Peter Cook in his E.L. Wisty role but without the raincoat.'

'How old?'

'Late fifties, I'd say, and didn't look like he'd had an easy life.'

I looked at the entry again. 'No reserve on it, I notice.'

'Not on something like that. Until you and our friend Mr Cronkshaw started, I hadn't expected it to make more than twenty pounds. What was the attraction?'

'Well, for me I just wanted something to play my old reel-to-reel tapes on. I can't answer for Mr Cronkshaw.' But I had a bloody good idea.

'Thanks, Leslie,' I said and slipped a fiver into his waiting hand.

'Pleasure to be of service, Mr Ace.'

I left the auction rooms and drove down Kensington until I came to the street in Old Swan where Edgar Marshall lived. I parked the RAV4 at the corner and walked past a row of two-up two-down Victorian houses, most of them in a poor state of repair.

No. 2 was at the end of the cul-de-sac. When I was about fifty yards away, the front door opened and a tall man came marching down the path. I recognised him immediately: it was Boris Karloff alias Cronkshaw. I quickly crossed over to the other side of the road and walked with my head down until he'd passed.

This was something I hadn't expected. I gave him time to reach the end of the road, then I turned and followed him. Marshall could wait until later.

By the time I made the corner, Cronkshaw was way up the road. I quickened my stride, but suddenly he broke into a run and jumped onto a No. 10 bus that was heading for the city centre. The bus pulled away before I had a chance to reach it.

I ran back for my car and chased the bus into town. It stopped at every stop and I stayed behind it but Cronkshaw didn't alight until we came to the Playhouse Theatre, right in the middle of the city centre. I was defeated. I was in a queue of traffic surrounded by double yellow lines and there was no way I could abandon the car. I could only watch helplessly as Cronkshaw disappeared into St John's Shopping Precinct.

'Shit,' I said. Roly, who'd been comatose on the back seat since the start of the journey, opened one eye querulously then shut it again.

I drove up to Dale Street and along to the Pier Head. I couldn't be bothered to return to Old Swan. That could wait. I needed to turn my attention to the Skidmore case. I stopped at a red traffic-light and took the opportunity to study the list that Jim Burroughs had given me.

The first name was that of Noreen Bowyer, who lived in Jermyn Street, just off Princes Park. 'You're in luck,' I said to the dog. 'Time for your morning walk.'

I drove along Princes Avenue past my house where Shirley lived. For a moment I was tempted to call in and see her but I knew what that would probably lead to, so I carried on driving straight to the park.

There weren't many people around. I sat down on a bench, watching Roly recklessly chase a large Rottweiler across the grass, and tried to work out the reason for Cronkshaw being at Edgar Marshall's house.

The obvious explanation was that he was on the same trail as myself. He wanted to know where the tape had come from and if there were any more from the same source. Yet how did Cronkshaw know that the John Lennon tape was in the sale? He wouldn't have been able to listen to it in the saleroom and there was nothing on the cover to indicate who the singer was. Yet he must have known it was there, otherwise why bid so much for what was ostensibly an old tape recorder?

I knew old radios could fetch good prices these days but not old tape recorders – at least, not that much.

The only other explanation I could think of was that Cronkshaw was at the auction on behalf of Marshall to get the machine back.

Maybe Marshall had realised he'd left the Lennon tape in the box by mistake. But then, why not go down himself and withdraw it from the auction? Or at least extricate the tape from the box.

Screams and a loud barking interrupted my thoughts. A woman in a long black dress was holding a small Pekingese above her head, seemingly to prevent Roly, who was doing his impression of an Olympic high jumper, from eating it.

'Is this animal yours?' she shrieked as I ran up to her.

'I'm afraid so,' I admitted, grabbing Roly's collar and snapping on his lead.

'It ought to be under control. It's wild.' She put her own creature on the ground where it promptly relieved itself on the grass. Roly moved across to sniff and, to the lady's disgust, left his own mark beside it.

I dragged the reluctant dog back to the car and drove the short distance back to Jermyn Street and Noreen Bowyer's house. The front garden was overgrown and the rotting wooden gate hung on one hinge, I noted as I walked up the litter-strewn path and pushed the bell.

The girl who answered the door was about nineteen. She had a Gothic look about her, white face, gaunt expression, anorexic figure, several rings inserted through various portions of her face and tattoos on both shoulders.

'Yeah?' she said, leaning against the doorway, a cigarette in her hand.

'I'm looking for Noreen Bowyer.'

'Not from the DSS, are yer?'

I said I wasn't.

'What do yer want then?' She didn't ask who else I might be representing.

'Can I come in?'

Reluctantly, she stood aside and I walked into the front room where another girl was sitting in front of a television set playing a computer game.

On the screen, a robot wielding a machete was methodically

mowing down a group of soldiers in the jungle, in vivid red Technicolor. And they ask why kids are so violent nowadays!

'You've been in prison recently.'

She sat on an upright chair beside a table filled with empty breakfast dishes, leaving me standing in the middle of the room. 'What's it to do with you?'

'I'm from the Prisoners' Release Society. We just call on people who've recently returned to the community to make sure they are managing, back in society.' It sounded authentic social services speak. She didn't ask for any ID.

'I'd manage better if you gave me a giro, otherwise you can pig off.' She took a long drag at her cigarette and blew the smoke out in front of me.

'Assault, wasn't it?'

'That's right. It was me what she beat up.' It was the other girl who spoke, without turning round. She had cropped ginger hair and wore a leather jacket. Her finger remained pressed on the button as more soldiers were obliterated on the screen.

'That's Sheila,' said Noreen. 'She lives with me now.'

'I see.' I tried to work it out. This must be the best friend who had supposedly been chatting up Noreen's lover, only now she appeared to have taken over the role herself. 'This was your first time inside, wasn't it?' I asked, trying to sound sympathetic. 'Was it bad?'

Noreen shrugged. 'It was all right. I knew some of the girls in there.'

'Who was the magistrate that sent you down?'

'I dunno. Two old geezers and some stuck-up woman who was a right pain.'

'Were you expecting to be sent to prison rather than being fined?'

'Never thought about it. Couldn't have paid the fine anyway, not with what the DSS give me.' She stubbed out her cigarette and replaced it in her mouth with a wad of chewing gum. She had a stud implanted in her tongue.

She caught my gaze. 'Not seen one of these before? Here, have a good look.' She stuck out her tongue right in front of me. 'Like it, do yer?' She resumed her chewing.

'It's a good job you don't go out with men,' I said. 'You could rip some poor sod's dick open giving blowjobs with that.'

'Funny.' She curled her legs up beneath her on the chair. 'Look, what am I getting out of all this?'

'Nothing, I'm afraid. Like I said, we just make sure—'

'Yeah, well, you can make sure somewhere else, right?' She was becoming agitated, chewing as furiously as a demented Sir Alex Ferguson did when Man United were losing.

I didn't argue. Without realising it, she had given me all the information that I'd been seeking. She wasn't intent on wreaking revenge on Bernard Skidmore.

I walked to the door as she jumped aggressively to her feet and I was down the road in the RAV4 almost before she'd had time to slam the gate after me.

The next name on the list was Lenny Dickson, who lived in Seaforth, but I decided he could wait until after lunch. I drove towards the river, stopping on the way to buy some fish and chips at a takeaway in Park Road.

I ate them at the far end of the Albert Dock car park, sitting on a seat overlooking the Mersey, well away from the tourists. I threw Roly the odd chip as he sat patiently beside me, and opened the can of Scrumpy Jack that I always keep in the car.

A few small boats moved up and down the river against the background of the Wirral coastline. It was hard to imagine the great ocean liners and bustling docks of the earlier part of the century.

Feeling pleasantly full now, I turned my thoughts to the Skidmore case. Noreen Bowyer, I felt, could be crossed off the list. It was obvious she held no particular grudge against any of the magistrates. Bernard Skidmore hadn't even registered with her.

However, so far it hadn't been a very successful morning. Maybe the afternoon would bring more promising results.

On paper, Lenny Dickson looked a much more likely candidate for revenge. He'd taken a knife to the doorman outside a city centre disco so he was obviously no stranger to violence.

I chanced that, being a night-worker, he'd be in during the day, and I was right.

Lenny lived in a flat halfway up a tower block behind Seaforth and Litherland station. The room was sparsely furnished and tidy, but lacking anything of the owner's personality. There were no flowers, no photographs and certainly no woman's touch. Dickson had been in the middle of watching a Jerry Springer show on an old Rediffusion TV when I called. They do say that whatever time of day it is, there is always a Jerry Springer programme on some channel or other and I can believe it.

I didn't go with the 'Prisoners Release' line this time as I figured, with the disco connection, that Dickson might recognise me. The story I gave him was that I'd been asked to organise a dance at the Grafton Rooms for this charity and I was looking for doormen. They don't like to be called bouncers any more.

'Oh yes?' he said suspiciously, but moved aside to let me in. My name hadn't seemed to register with him at all.

'Are you still in that line of work?'

'I'm in Security.' I noticed he was wearing a black shirt and matching slacks that might have passed as a uniform with some companies.

'Whereabouts?'

'I move around,' he said cautiously. 'Depends where the work is. Who put you on to me?'

'Jimmy Turner.' Turner was the man whom Dickson had put in hospital.

'Are you having me on?' His face contorted into a snarl.

'What do you mean?'

'That bastard would never give you my name. He ran off with my fuckin' missus.'

'You're joking?'

'I soon fixed him though, good style. Hospital job.'

'Badly hurt, was he?'

41

'Lucky he wasn't dead. I stuck a knife in his neck. Bled like a stuffed pig he did.'

'Come to think of it, he was wearing a scarf when I saw him.' That seemed to please Lenny. He laughed out loud. Not a nice sound. 'Did they do you for it?'

'Six months in Walton but it was worth it.'

'Was it?'

'I just wish I'd have finished him.' He went back to the matter in hand. 'Hey – if you're booking the Grafton, they'll have their own doormen, won't they?'

'I never thought of that.'

'That toe-rag probably knew that, that's why he put you on a bum steer. Just to remind me he was still around.'

'Could be.' I was glad of the excuse to get away without further questioning. 'Sorry to have bothered you, then.' I stopped at the door. 'Bit harsh – prison, wasn't it? Must have caught the bench on a bad day.'

'Whatever. Like I say, it was worth it. I'd do it again.'

'Has she not come back, your wife?' Looking at the bleak room, I knew the answer.

'Shacked up with Turner, isn't she? Women! They're all gobshites.' He suddenly looked at me closely. 'Hey, I've just realised. You're Johnny Ace – the fellow that's on the radio every night.'

'That's me. Listen to the show, do you?'

'Not me. I have the telly on myself, but I know you're on, like.'

Not any more I wasn't. It seemed strange, driving back into town, not to be going to the radio station. I wondered how long my ban would last. Would I indeed ever get back on the air? If not, would there be a slot for me on Radio Merseyside?

There were two more names on Jim's list. Sean Ince had been charged with assault after a pub brawl in which half his family had been involved, together with members of the notorious O'Shea clan.

I knew both families vaguely. They'd been around Liverpool for years, always involved in some scam or other. Sean was the youngest, in his late teens and grandson of Wild Paddy Ince, the head of the

42

family. Most of them went in the Masquerade Club from time to time so I decided to look in later and see if I could catch up with Sean there.

The fourth name on the list was Irene Tidd, the habitual shoplifter.

I drove back to my flat to sort out the night's itinerary. First of all, I rang Jim at the office to inform him that we could rule out two of the names on his list.

'As I expected really,' he replied. 'What happened with the Lennon tape?'

I told him about losing Cronkshaw.

'Didn't you go back to see Marshall?'

'It was out of the way. I'll call tomorrow.'

There were half a dozen messages on my ansaphone, all to do with my 'sacking'. Five were from well-wishers offering sympathy and support, and one was from Marty at the *Daily Post* to say they'd had several phone calls and e-mails from listeners disgusted at my dismissal. So far, so good – but no offers of other jobs. No word, either, from Creegan but I didn't expect that, at least, not so soon.

I made myself a pot of tea and rang Hilary on the Ward. She's a sister at the Royal Liverpool Infirmary.

'What time do you finish tonight?' I asked her.

'Ten, why?'

'Do you fancy the Masquerade for an hour?'

'If we can have something to eat first.'

'It's a deal.' I arranged to pick her up outside the hospital after her shift. That gave me a couple of hours to pay a visit to Irene Tidd.

At six o'clock, I switched on the radio to listen to *The Shady Spencer Show*. I wasn't impressed. It was pleasant enough but painfully bland. I'd heard more exciting music in elevators. He played James Last-type records and his phone-ins revolved round such gripping items as the amount of cholesterol in a pound of butter. Shady was not a man to court controversy. However, I imagined that Ken, the producer, might be relieved to have a life free of comebacks and complaints. He always said I was a shit-stirrer. God, even Ken could turn against me.

* * *

Tidd lived on the edge of Sefton Park, in a huge Victorian house now divided into ten units by the adroit use of chipboard and plywood. Hers was a bedsit on the back of the first floor, little bigger than a broom cupboard. It would have probably fetched half a million in Knightsbridge.

There was a sink in the corner, next to a Baby Belling cooker, but most of the space was taken up by a metal single bed. There were no signs of affluence to suggest that Irene Tidd was a successful shoplifter; in fact I suspected her prison cell might have had the edge in comfort. She certainly hadn't been in a hurry to leave it, her parole having been rescinded after she attacked a warder with a fork in a dispute over the quality of the prison dinners.

Irene was nineteen and looked thirty. Her hair was mousy brown and brushed back in rats' tails. Her skin was greasy and her fingernails were bitten to the quick.

I was back with my Prisoners' Release Society story but she didn't seem concerned to know where I was from. She lit a cigarette and sat on the edge of the bed while I went through my spiel. At last I got round to the point of the interview.

'Do you remember the magistrates who were on the bench the day you were sentenced?'

She thought for a moment. 'There was three of them. Two old fellas and one about forty. I'd seen them all before.'

'Had you?' I was surprised. For a minute I'd forgotten she was a regular visitor to the magistrates' court.

'Yeah, all the time. You get to know them all. Old Skiddy, he isn't so bad. Feels sorry for young girls in trouble, specially if you show him a bit of leg.'

I wondered how Mrs Skidmore would handle that piece of information.

'The young one I hadn't seen before, he looked a bit nervous. He might have been new. The other old one, Gibson, I know him. He has this carpet shop in London Road. My mate used to work for him, a right tyrant he was. He was the one what put me inside, you mark my word.'

'You think so?'

'I'd bet on it. But he's not the worst, you know. There's this woman, Maud Small – "Tiny" they call her. A big, stuck-up cow she is. Fart in front of her and she'll send you to the crown court tor perjury.'

'You didn't know Bernard Skidmore outside the court at all?'

'Skiddy? Nah. I saw him leaving with his wife once. A right prim beggar she was. I felt sorry for him.' She looked hard at me. 'What exactly was you after with me?'

'Mr Skidmore has died,' I said, 'in a car accident. It was suggested his car might have been tampered with so I'm looking for people who might have a motive.'

'Revenge, you mean, for putting them away? As if you would. I mean, the poor bastard. He looked like he could have done with a good shag, did old Skiddy.' She laughed. 'I'd have given him one if he'd have asked.' Looking at her, I thought it was doubtful that the late magistrate would have wanted to take her up on the offer. 'And now someone's done for him.' She sighed at the injustice of it all.

There was nothing more for me to say. I thanked her for her assistance and returned to the car where Roly was waiting patiently.

'C'mon,' I said. 'Time for your training.' We headed for the park and I threw a large branch for him to retrieve. He ran after it, stared at it quizzically for a moment, then ran back without it, wagging his stump happily.

'If I ever get a job as a gamekeeper,' I told him, 'you'll have to go.' After a while, I gave up with the games and let him chase round on his own whilst I walked up to the Palm House and back.

Work had started on renovating the Palm House to its former Victorian splendour. At the rate it was progressing, I feared it might not be ready by the next millennium never mind this one.

Mrs Skidmore's suspicions were becoming less credible by the minute. I'd eliminated the third name on the list, which left just one possible suspect for the supposed revenge murder of our friend Bernard Skidmore.

Chapter Six

Wild Paddy Ince's grandson was the last hope, otherwise Mrs Skidmore's theory looked like being the non-starter Jim Burroughs had always suspected.

At a quarter to ten that evening, I left Roly to guard my flat and picked up Hilary at the Infirmary. We stopped off at the Shangri La for a Chinese meal before driving down towards the Pier Head and the Masquerade Club.

'They've started Beach Nights on a Monday,' she said, 'did you know?'

'What are Beach Nights?'

'It's all this Ibiza thing. Dance music, sunshine and holiday atmosphere. You'll see. It's supposed to be brilliant.'

She was right. The Masquerade was normally as dark as a crypt – probably, the regulars thought, to obscure the dilapidated and filthy state of the décor and to prevent people from counting their change at the bar. Now, however, bright spotlights shone out like artificial suns from the newly painted yellow and blue walls. Plastic palm trees reached to the ceiling and striped canvas awnings lined the bars. Dance music blasted from the speakers at ear-splitting volume.

The barmaids were dressed in matching yellow and blue bikinis and Vince, the head barman, appeared to be wearing only a loincloth that reached almost to his knees.

'Optimistic, isn't it?' I commented, gesticulating towards the garment.

'Not at all, Johnny,' Vince smiled pruriently, 'as several of my close friends would tell you.' He winked at Hilary, who laughed.

'Your usual, is it?'

We took our drinks over to the door where Tommy McKale was chatting to Dolly in the paybox. Tommy, who owns the club, is an ex-Mr Universe contender and successful racketeer and not someone to be trifled with. Several men who have crossed him are reputed to be lying on the bed of the Mersey. He's stockily built with Brylcreemed black hair and shoulders that Charles Atlas would have died for.

'You've really gone to town on the place, Tommy,' I said.

'Got to keep up with trends to bring the kids in, Johnny. We still get the regulars in the top bar, of course – the gangsters, whores, druggies, policemen and weirdos that we've always had. They're our bread and butter. These kids are the pus on the boil as the saying goes.'

'I think the saying is actually the icing on the cake,' I murmured.

'Whatever. The thing is, the kids also bring in a few extra old perves who like to have a blimp at the meat market.'

'I noticed that everyone's half dressed in here,' I said. 'Have you turned the heating up again, to sell more drinks?'

'It's the fashion,' said Hilary. 'Bare midriffs and cleavages are in at the moment.' She herself wore a leopardskin crop-top, leather trousers and stiletto boots, with a good two-inch gap between the top and the pants to display the diamond in her navel.

'She's right,' agreed Tommy. 'The lads want to show off their muscles and the girls want to display their tattoos. Even Dolly's got dressed up.'

I turned to look in the paybox. Dolly had on a bright yellow and blue halter top and short flared skirt with sparkling silver tights. Dolly is Tommy's grandmother. She's eighty-five. I was relieved to see the halter top overlapped the skirt. Dolly's naked stomach might have been too much for me.

'Christ, Dolly,' I said. 'It's a bit young for you, isn't it?'

'Rubbish,' said Tommy. 'She likes to keep in fashion, don't you, luv? Keeps you young.'

'Except for this thong,' grumbled Dolly. 'It keeps creeping up my bottom. Why don't they make proper knickers any more?'

I wondered if the Queen Mother had a similar problem.

'Are any of the Inces in?' I asked Tommy, before Dolly could reveal any more unnecessary details about her outfit.

'I think Paddy is – why?'

'It's Sean I need to speak to.'

'He's still in the nick, I think.'

'No, he came out a couple of week ago. Good behaviour.'

'Sean always was the white sheep in that family,' said Tommy.

'How come he got put away then?'

'Not the lad's fault really. There was this punch-up in their local, much worse than the usual barney you get when the Inces and O'Sheas get together. Someone was going for the old man with a knife, so young Sean broke a bottle over his head. Nearly killed him.'

'But he only got six months.'

'First offence and no previous. Probably have got away with probation if he hadn't been an Ince. What's it all about, Johnny?'

'A case I'm on. I'm looking for someone who might have had it in for one of the magistrates.'

'The city must be full of them,' said Tommy. 'I'll give you the wire if he comes in.'

I ushered Hilary back to the top bar where the music was quieter. Wild Paddy Ince was sitting at a table with five of his cronies, men in their sixties wearing a mixture of designer training gear, football replica shirts and shell-suits ten years out of date. Paddy himself sported a fur-collared brown leather bomber jacket, faded and cracked with wear. All he needed was the goggles and he could have been a pilot in *Biggles*. They were all drinking pints of Guinness.

'I don't like the look of them,' Hilary said as we found a table a few feet away. 'What do they do?'

'Protection, mainly, but there are rumours about arms and the IRA. Not nice people.'

'Not people you want to get involved with. Are you sure this investigation business is a good idea, Johnny?'

Hilary has never been keen on my private eye work and, in the past, I've always played it down with her. Since I've opened the office, however, she's had to accept that this is what I do although she makes it pretty obvious that she doesn't like it.

'It might be all I have left soon.'

'Have you heard nothing about your radio programme?'

'Not yet.'

'Give them time, they'll come crawling back.' That's what I'd thought but it hadn't happened yet and I was beginning to get slightly worried.

'And how's the lovely Maria these days? You never seem to mention her much.'

Not without good reason, I thought, noting the scarcely disguised sarcasm in Hilary's voice.

'She's all right,' I said guardedly.

'It's over two years now that you've been seeing her, Johnny. If you're not careful, she'll be getting ideas.'

Didn't I know it? But: 'I shouldn't think so,' I told Hilary.

'Take it from me, women like that, they're like ragwort.'

'Ragwort?'

'Hard to get rid of and just as poisonous.'

I said nothing. I didn't want to get rid of Maria. Neither, of course, did I want to get rid of Hilary.

On television last week, on the ubiquitous *Jerry Springer Show*, I'm told they had a man who said he was in love with two women. The conclusion that Springer and the TV audience reached was that he didn't really love either of them. Someone added a rider to that – namely that the only person the man truly loved was probably himself. Maybe that was true of me but I didn't like to think so.

I was saved from further discussion on the subject by the arrival of Sean Ince who, pint of Guinness in hand, had joined his grandfather at the table. He looked across towards us and held up his glass in greeting. I acknowledged him and he came over.

'Sorry to hear about the show, Johnny,' he said. 'It was announced that you'd been suspended but you only repeated what everyone else has been saying for weeks about Everton.'

After the *Daily Post* article, they could hardly have pretended on air that I was off ill. 'Thanks, Sean.'

'It's true. Good result for the Blues though yesterday, holding Man U to a draw?'

I agreed it had been and we spoke for a minute about the match before I broached the subject I wanted to talk about. 'Sorry to hear you got sent down, Sean.'

He looked grim. 'My own fault.'

'From what I hear, you were only protecting the old man. I thought the magistrates were a bit harsh.'

'The family reputation went before me.' He grinned ruefully. 'It won't happen again. I'm off to London next week – going to do a three-year course in computer studies. Put it all behind me.'

I persisted. 'Won't be easy getting a job with a criminal record, though.'

'Don't you believe it. They don't give a shit as long as you know what you're doing. You can write your own salary cheque in the IT field.'

He didn't look like a man bent on revenge.

'I must say, he seems quite pleasant,' remarked Hilary after Sean had returned to his table.

'He'll do well to get away. It won't be easy with a family like that. The peer pressure must be tremendous.'

My night's work was done but we stayed on for a few more drinks and a couple of dances, then went back to my flat.

'That's new,' commented Hilary, pointing to a large wicker basket covered with a red tartan rug standing in the corner of the lounge.

'Roly's new bed. He seems very pleased with it.'

'So he should be. A brand new blanket as well! Better than him sleeping in the bedroom, I'll give you that. I want you to myself in there.'

I didn't tell her that he still slept at the foot of my bed on normal nights. When Hilary was round, he knew better. Hilary was more a cat person and he seemed to sense it. Dogs she tolerated.

'I suppose Maria thinks he's wonderful.'

Maybe it was the way she said it, or just the moment. She slipped it in as she was removing her bra, almost as an aside in a quiet voice, but it hit me like a punch in the kidneys. It was as if Maria had suddenly been thrust into our private world, a world Hilary and I had shared for nearly two decades, and it unnerved me.

I said nothing and we continued undressing in silence but somehow a rift had been opened and, although we made love together with our usual passion, I felt something had irrevocably changed in our relationship.

I remembered the Jim Reeves song 'When Two Worlds Collide'. I'd managed to keep my two worlds apart, but for how much longer?

Next morning, I left Hilary having a lie-in and walked over to the office with Roly to give Jim Burroughs the news about Irene Tidd and Sean Ince.

'Dead ends, both of them, Jim.' I went into the adjoining kitchen and fetched a big marrow bone from the fridge for Roly. He took it over to his strip of blanket to eat.

'Are you sure?'

'Pretty sure, yes, and that's all four out of it.' I went down the list with him. 'Noreen Bowyer said prison was better than a fine and the only magistrate she noticed was the lady anyway and she was a cow. Dickson was more upset at the bloke he'd attacked who's run off with his wife. Sean Ince is on to college and wants to forget the whole thing and Irene Tidd, far from hating Skidmore, would have been quite happy to give him a legover.'

'You're joking. What was she like?'

'A right slapper. Even you would have thought twice, Jim.'

Jim frowned. 'So, back to square one then?'

'I'm not sure. I'm thinking about the two still in prison. They could have arranged for friends or family to do their dirty work. Can you use your contacts to get me in to speak to them?'

'Worth a try, I suppose. Leave it with me. In the meantime, I've put together these notes on the Susie Jenna case.'

I had to marvel at him. His talent for organisation was second to none. If only he'd been on the square he'd have ended up Chief Constable.

'What's your take on that, Jim? Do you think her old man killed her?'

'Our lot certainly do. They've turned half the town upside down and still haven't managed to find a body.'

'What would be the motive?'

'I reckon temper,' declared Jim.

'Temper?'

'We know he used to batter her. This time he hit her a bit too hard.'

'It can't be as simple as that, surely?'

'Well, there was no monetary gain.'

'So why would he batter her?'

'Other men, maybe. He looks the jealous type. If she'd been seeing someone else and Jenna found out, he would have gone ballistic.'

'I can't see her doing it. She wouldn't have dared risk it, she'd have been too scared of him. After all, he's had different women on and off for years and if she ever voiced her displeasure, he'd belt her. She'd learnt to shut up and live with it.'

'Until this last time maybe?' pondered Jim.

'You mean, perhaps she didn't shut up so he killed her?'

'Exactly.'

'So why hire us to find her?'

'A form of alibi. To cast doubt in the minds of those who think he might have killed her. Maybe he hopes it will eventually persuade the police to call off the search and close the case.'

'Which it won't.'

'No unsolved case is ever officially closed but it will certainly go on a back burner as new cases come along. Bound to.'

I told him I'd read over his notes before deciding what to do next. We'd taken a lot of money from Elspeth Skidmore and Owen Jenna, but I wasn't at all certain we would ever be able to deliver the goods.

There looked to be little mileage for us in either case. Also, I had to confess, I found the mystery of the John Lennon tape much more intriguing and there I *did* have something to go on.

'I'm just calling in at Geoffrey's,' I told Jim, 'and then I'll have another go at Edgar Marshall. Page me if anything comes up.'

Tuesday morning was my time for catching up on any outstanding property business although, over the years, I'd been leaving more and more of the work to Geoff.

'I like the sign, boss,' he said as I walked in. *Ace Estates* had been painted across the window of the office.

'Job lot with the one down the road, Geoff – *Ace Investigations*. Adds a bit of class, doesn't it?'

There were no untoward problems, I learned. We had an empty flat in South Albert Road but I could trust Geoffrey to let that.

'Kirkdale should be ready to let by the end of next week,' he said. 'It's looking smart now the decorators are in.'

I'd bought this old terraced house off Hawthorne Road which had previously been occupied by an elderly lady called Violet Parker. I'd been investigating a case involving stolen cameras and the house had become the venue for a gangland shoot-out. Somewhere along the way, poor old Mrs Parker had ended up dead.

'Great. We should have no problem letting that.' I approved the list of outstanding repairs, signed a few cheques then drove out to Old Swan to Edgar Marshall's.

The little cul-de-sac was devoid of cars today: everyone must be at work. This time, I drove right up to the house. However, there was no answer to my ring. I knocked loudly on the door in case the bell wasn't working. Still no answer. Then I peered through the letterbox but all I could see were the stairs in front.

A headscarved old lady came out of the adjoining house. She had a humped back and was bent nearly double so that the shopping trolley she was wheeling came almost up to her shoulder. 'Not seen Mr Marshall, luv, have you?' I asked.

'He'll be at his garage,' she said in the grating voice of a bronchial bittern.

'Where's that?'

'Only two streets away.' She started to give me directions but they quickly took on the dimensions of a scenic tour so I quickly told her I had an *A-Z*.

I said, 'I didn't know he had a garage.'

'Oh yes. He's had it as long as he's lived here, over twenty years. He was here when we came and that was in 1976. He always mended my late husband's cars.'

I thanked her, got back in the RAV4 and made the short trip to Edgar Marshall's garage, which turned out to be a run-down detached building at the corner of a similar cul-de-sac to the one I'd just left. There was no sign of activity. The garage was guarded by steel shutters below a fading painted sign saying *Marshall's Motors*. I knocked on a glass-fronted side door but there was no reply and no sound of any activity within.

I gave up and returned to Dale Street. 'No joy,' I told Jim. 'Marshall wasn't in. It turns out he has a garage down the road from his house but that was all shut up.'

'Perhaps he's moved away?'

'I'll go back tomorrow,' I said.

'Well, I've got a bit of news for you,' said Jim. 'Spencer Leigh rang with some interesting information. You'd asked him about Bobby and the Voxtones?'

'That's right. That was the group on the other tape.'

'Well, listen to this: guess what Bobby's real name is?'

'Go on.'

'Edgar Marshall!'

'It all fits in,' I said slowly. 'Trust Spencer to know everything. And who were The Voxtones?'

'He doesn't know all their names but I mentioned Cronkshaw and he thought they might have had a drummer called Albert Cronkshaw.'

'It could explain how Edgar Marshall came to have the tape, if he was on the beat scene in the sixties.'

'Do you think he pinched it from Lennon or what?' said Jim.

'Who knows? Probably he nicked it, otherwise he'd have sent it to somewhere proper like Sotheby's. Everyone knows how much money there is in pop memorabilia these days.'

'He's hung on to it for a long time, hasn't he? Nearly forty years. I wonder what made him put it in the auction?'

'It must have been a terrible mistake.'

'Where would you advertise something like that? It's twenty years since I bought the *Melody Maker*. I've lost touch with today's sounds.'

As if I didn't know. The Chocolate Lavatory were hardly at the cutting edge of pop. '*Record Collector*'s the obvious place,' I told him. 'Or maybe *Mojo*.'

'*Exchange and Mart*?' added Jim. '*Loot, Quid's In*?'

'Yes, any of those. But surely he would have got a reply from an advert like that. "Unissued John Lennon tape." God, if the tabloids had got wind of that . . .'

'I still don't remember them properly, you know,' said Jim, 'Bobby and the Voxtones.'

'Neither do I, but there were hundreds of groups around in those days. Some only lasted a week or two and many of them never played outside their church hall youth clubs.'

'Or their own front rooms.'

'Were there any other calls, Jim?' I'd been hoping that Ricky Creegan might have rung to apologise and give me my job back.

'No.'

'I'll get back to the flat then.' Roly reluctantly surrendered his bone and I fastened his lead on to his collar to walk him back home.

Hilary had left her usual lipsticked note on the dressing table mirror. *Bye, babe. Ring me. XXX*. I made myself a BLT sandwich, opened a bottle of Scrumpy Jack and settled down to read Jim's notes on the Susie Jenna case.

It was all much the same as I'd read in the newspapers, together with most of the population. She'd simply walked out of her home and into oblivion. There had been numerous sightings, especially after *Crimewatch*, but of Susie Jenna there was no trace.

Numerous psychics, clairvoyants and mindreaders had been wheeled in, some by the police, some by Owen Jenna, and one by a national newspaper. Several of them said she was dead and gave the location of the burial plot whilst others maintained she was alive and well and living in either the West Indies, Melbourne or Stoke-on-Trent. Take your pick.

The children were still with their father and grandparents whose picture had appeared in several papers, pleading on behalf of their grandchildren for their mother to come home. I wondered about Susie Jenna's parents. They hadn't been mentioned at all. Perhaps they were dead. I made a note to check.

It was mid-afternoon when Jim Burroughs phoned. 'The Skidmore case,' he said. 'I've fixed the prison visits. Nigel Abram's at Kirkham open prison and Frank Harriman's in Altcourse, that new privatised place out at Fazakerly.' Jim wasn't one to hang around.

'Any special time?'

'Both between nine and five.' He gave me a reference number to quote in each case.

I looked at my watch. 'If I leave now, I should have time to see Harriman this afternoon.'

'Good luck.'

'Before you go, Jim – Susie Jenna's parents,' I said. 'I can't see anything about them in the files yet Owen's mother and father are all over the newspapers doing the loving grandparents bit.'

'As far as I know, Johnny, they're both dead. They divorced when Susie left school. The father went to live in Canada and died out there. Her mother married again and went to live in London, and I believe she was killed in a motorway pile-up.'

'No brothers or sisters?'

'No. She was an only child.'

'Right.'

'Anything significant that I should know about?'

If there was, it hadn't hit me. 'Not really. I'll muse on it. Right now, I'm off to visit Her Majesty's Guesthouse.'

Chapter Seven

Altcourse was one of the first prisons to be run by a private security firm. At first, there had been some public disquiet about safety in such institutions after a couple of well reported cock-ups when prisoners escaped whilst being transported from the courts but, as far as I knew, things at Altcourse had settled down well.

After a complicated routine of form filling and searching, I was conducted through a series of double doors to a large hall where I waited for the prisoner to be brought to me.

Frank Harriman was a slightly built lad, not much more than twenty, with a pale skin and hard eyes. He had a way of looking at you that I found faintly disturbing, like meeting the Yorkshire Ripper for the first time. He reminded me of psychopaths I'd met in Ashworth Hospital when The Cruzads did gigs there in the seventies.

A bulky prison officer sat within earshot.

'Who are you?' was Harriman's first question.

I told him I was investigating another crime and that he might be able to help me. He said he would try. He was anxious to persuade me that he was not a regular offender and knew no other criminals. 'I'm not a really a burglar, you know.'

'But I thought you broke into someone's house. What else would you call it?'

He looked suddenly cagey. 'It wasn't like that, not housebreaking for the sake of it. This bloke had something I wanted.'

'Couldn't you have offered to buy it from him?'

'I'd no money. At least, not the amount he was asking. I'm on the dole.'

'And you wanted it so badly that you thought you'd steal it? What was so special about it?'

His voice rose; he was obviously excited to be talking about his quest. 'Are you into music at all?' I said I was. 'Well, he had this tape he was trying to sell, a very rare tape.'

And suddenly, I knew what was coming next.

'It contained these new songs by John Lennon that nobody had heard before. Do you realise the significance of that?'

'I think I do. It must have been worth a fortune.'

Harriman scoffed. 'Who cares what it's worth, it's the music that matters.' He leaned forward eagerly. 'I'm a collector, see. I've got practically everything The Beatles ever recorded, photos, fan club magazines, original copies of Bill Harry's *Mersey Beat* magazine, you name it, right back to the Hamburg days. I've even got Brian Kelly's autograph – the bloke who used to run Litherland Town Hall.'

I was impressed. 'Did you already know the man who owned the tape, the one you burgled?'

'No.' He looked shifty but the story slowly came out. He had been working at a second-hand shop in West Derby that stocked records and musical instruments. One day this man had rung in offering a rare Beatles tape for sale. Harriman took the call and told him to bring the tape into the shop for a valuation.

The man hadn't shown up but fortunately Harriman had dialled 1471 and made a note of his phone number. After a few days had passed, he rang him offering to call round and inspect the item and had thus acquired the man's address.

'He lived in this little house in Old Swan,' Harriman told me. 'He played me the tape and I knew it was genuine but he was asking thousands.'

'Did you ask him where he got it?'

'He said Lennon gave it to him years ago. Apparently, he used to play in a group himself and one night they were on at The Cavern with The Beatles. That's when he got the tape.'

'What was his name?'

'He never said and I was so excited about the tape I forgot to ask.'

'But he wouldn't sell it to you?'

'I told you, he wanted thousands and some bastard would have bought it who didn't give a shit about The Beatles, just to make money.' His voice rose in anger. 'I knew I had to have it.'

'So you went back to steal it?'

'Yeah.'

'And got caught. Fell downstairs, didn't you, and woke him up?'

'That was crap. He woke up while I was in the room and he recognised me. He went for me with this axe he kept by the bed. I legged it and that was when I fell down the stairs and knocked myself out but nobody believed me when I told them he'd attacked me.'

'And this axe had disappeared when the police came?'

'Of course.'

'And you ended up in prison.' I remembered my reason for calling on Harriman was supposed to be more to do with Bernard Skidmore than Edgar Marshall. Did the youth hold a grudge? 'Seems a bit harsh for your first offence.'

'They sent me down because I was carrying an offensive weapon. I'd taken this iron bar to prise open the window to get in but the bastard said I'd attacked him with it.'

'And did you?'

'No, I told you. He stitched me up proper. He must have seen the bar on the floor by the window where I'd broken in and put it in my hand whilst I was out cold.'

'Ready for the police to find?'

'Yeah.' He snarled viciously. 'I should have killed the bastard.'

I had to say I admired Edgar Marshall's way of handling the situation. If he'd dared harm Harriman in any way, he'd probably have been locked up himself for assault. Worse, Harriman might have sued him for compensation for his injuries. In a society where McDonald's have to pay compensation when someone spills their cup of coffee and scalds themselves, anything is possible. Also, of course, locked up, Harriman would not be able to re-burgle Marshall's house.

'Do you feel you were badly done to, ending up in jail instead of community service or a fine?' I wondered if his unnerving presence had influenced the magistrates in their sentencing.

'Too right I do. Like I told them, this was a one-off. I'm not a fucking burglar.'

'So mad you'd want to get your own back on the magistrate who put you away?'

'What you talking about?' Again, a flash of cold hate in those eyes.

'A magistrate has been threatened.' I didn't say he was dead. 'Bernard Skidmore. That is why I'm here. He was one of the three people on the bench at your trial.'

Harriman spat out of the corner of his mouth. 'Wouldn't know him from Adam. I couldn't give a shit who they were. OK, I'm angry about going to prison but all I really care about is that fucking tape and God knows where that is now.'

I wasn't going to enlighten him. One crime had already been committed because of this tape. How many more would follow?

Maria had invited me round for a meal at her Blundelsands flat so I drove there straight from the prison. On the way I caught the end of Shady Spencer's show on the car radio. He was asking listeners whereabouts they'd be watching tomorrow's eclipse of the sun from. Wow! He then followed up with a Richard Clayderman record. Riveting stuff. Would there be anyone left listening by the end of the week? I asked myself.

I'd not seen Maria since our lunch the previous Friday so, during the meal, I started to acquaint her with the details of the two new cases.

'I know all about Susie Jenna,' she said. 'It's hardly been out of the papers for weeks.' We'd eaten the roast duckling in lime with fennel, parsnips and sauté potatoes, and had moved on to Maria's speciality dessert that she called a Bomb, her own concoction made with whipped eggs, crushed macaroons, cream and a liberal quantity of sherry.

'And what's your opinion?'

She nibbled at a macaroon. 'It's got to be the husband, hasn't it? Why else would they dig up half of Southport?'

'I suppose so.'

'You're not sure?'

'It's just me being naturally argumentative. I'm playing devil's advocate like I do on the show.' Or did. 'When everyone says he's guilty without really knowing anything about it, then all my instincts tell me to prove otherwise.'

'It's the rebel in you,' she said fondly. 'You can't stop yourself, can you, Johnny? That's why you ended up getting kicked off the radio. Have they not begged you to come back yet?'

It was a sore point. 'No.'

Maria caught my tone. 'Ooooh. Hurts, does it?'

'I just know I do a better show than Shady Sodding Spencer.'

'Everyone knows you do. Let's move on to your other case.' Maria was nothing if not diplomatic. 'Last time I saw you, you were going to see that woman who thought her husband's accident wasn't one. What happened about that?'

'Mrs Skidmore, you mean?' I told her about the interviews with the various suspects. 'I'm afraid it looks like it was an accident after all.'

'Afraid?'

'If it was an accident then there's no case to solve.'

'Not a brilliant start for the new business, then?'

'No, but I have got something for you to listen to that you'll find interesting. It's in the car. You'll never believe it.'

'Eat up first.'

There was a small portion of Bomb left on the plate. 'I couldn't manage another spoonful,' I said.

'Nor me. I'll give it to Roly.' Roly pricked up his ears at the sound of his name and followed Maria into the kitchen, his stump wagging feverishly.

I carried some plates into the kitchen and put them in the sink. 'Go and sit down,' ordered Maria. 'I'll open another bottle of wine and bring it through.'

I felt I could get used to being waited on like this.

'You've got him a bowl,' I said, observing Roly slurping his Bomb from an earthenware vessel inscribed in big black letters with his name.

'Well, I thought, why not? You've got your big mug with *Johnny* on it so why shouldn't Roly have his own bowl?' She stroked his head and he turned round and licked her hand.

'I'll just go and get this tape.'

'I take it you're staying the night,' she said. 'Only I wouldn't want to encourage you to drink and drive.'

'Of course I am.'

I went to the RAV4 and brought back the Grundig that I'd hidden behind the back seat. By the time Maria returned with the wine and glasses, I'd set it up ready. 'Have a listen to this and tell me who it is.' I switched it on and waited for the initial hiss followed by the familiar voice.

Maria closed her eyes. After four bars she was tapping her fingers; after eight bars she exclaimed, 'It sounds like John Lennon!'

'Well done.'

'I didn't know you were a big John Lennon fan.'

'I'm not. I mean, I don't dislike him but he's not one of my favourites. I'd rather listen to Eddie Cochran or Larry Williams or Sam Cooke. They were the originals. Lennon did write one good song though, I'll give him that.'

'"Imagine", you mean?'

'Yes. I'd like to have heard Otis Redding sing it, though.'

'It's funny, isn't it, Johnny? All the singers you like seem to be dead.'

'Their records live on, though. Look at Bing Crosby. He may have gone years ago but he'll be singing "White Christmas" for ever. It's a form of immortality.'

'More like those Hammer horror movies,' said Maria. 'Except that, instead of the undead we have the singing dead.'

'And now John Lennon's one of them as well.'

'Strange how so many of them were murdered or killed in plane crashes.'

'It's a dangerous life, rock 'n' roll.'

We listened to a bit more of the song. 'Not a very good recording, is it?' said Maria. 'Where did you get it?'

'In an auction.'

'I don't think I've heard that song before.'

'You haven't. Nobody's heard any of these songs before.' I recounted the whole story and Maria became quite excited.

'It'll be worth a fortune, Johnny. Are you going to sell it?'

'Not till I find out where it's come from and how it got there.' I smiled ruefully. 'It's the rebel in me again.'

'What a coincidence, that man in prison being the one who broke into this Edgar Marshall's house. I wonder how many other people know about the tape?'

'I've no idea.'

'There could be others, so you'd better be careful. If it's that valuable, they'll stop at nothing to get hold of it. When are you going to see Marshall again?"

'Tomorrow, after I've been to Kirkham prison to see the last of the Skidmore suspects.'

'Take care, Johnny. I don't want you ending up like John Lennon.'

'I said rock 'n' roll could be dangerous.'

How dangerous, I didn't quite realise.

Chapter Eight

Kirkham was forty miles away on the Preston to Blackpool road. The trip next morning took me an hour and a half, the traffic being particularly heavy on the A59 through Penwortham, a stretch that seemed to suffer perpetual roadworks.

Maria had offered to keep Roly as Wednesday was her day off and she thought she might take him on the beach. 'If you're sure,' I said and arranged to pick her up at eight and take her for a meal.

'I take it you'll both be staying again. Perhaps I should get Roly a basket as well as a bowl.'

'I think he's quite happy sharing the bed.'

I'd read through Jim's notes again over breakfast and realised that my initial reaction, that Nigel Abram had got off lightly with a six-month jail sentence, was somewhat harsh.

Abram was a twenty-nine-year-old accountant who worked for Price Waterhouse Coopers in town but had a few of his own clients with whom he dealt from home. It was a familiar story. Serve your time with a big firm, build up a list of clients until you can afford to make the break, then set up on your own.

He'd never been in trouble, was a member of West Lancs Golf Club and was married to a primary-school teacher. They had two children who attended their mother's school.

The dead man, a part-time taxi-driver called Des Harward, had stepped off the pavement straight in front of Abram who, according to his statement, was unable to avoid hitting him. Abram's big mistake had been to panic and drive away without stopping. Unfortunately for him, an alert passer-by had witnessed the accident and taken his registration number. He was picked up by police within the hour.

In the accountant's favour was the fact that Harward had just come out of a pub and was well over the limit when he staggered into the road, all of which gave credence to Abram's story. The witness had corroborated this at the trial. Nonetheless, the magistrate had said that, in view of the fact that a member of the public had lost his life, he felt bound to impose a custodial sentence.

The magistrate was Bernard Skidmore.

I was ushered through various locked doors and reception desks till I reached Abram's cell where I explained to him the reason for my visit. 'I'm doing a radio programme on the effects of prison on non-criminals and I wondered if I could talk to you about your own experience.' I'd rehearsed the line a few times and thought it sounded plausible.

Nigel Abram was a tall, slim man, his dark, neatly-parted hair falling across his forehead. He looked more like a lawyer than a jailbird, but then I remembered Jim telling me that Kirkham had a fair number of accountants and solicitors within its walls, mostly there for fraud.

Abram didn't speak for a moment, then: 'I'm not sure I want that,' he replied stiffly. 'The fewer people who know about it all, the better.'

'The accident was well reported in the media,' I pointed out. 'Besides, I don't need to use your name or describe the actual incident, I can just refer to you as a young professional man.'

I could refer to him as anything I wanted. There wasn't going to be a programme but he wasn't aware of that.

'What exactly did you want to know?'

'How were you treated? Were you in a cell with hardened criminals? Did it alter your views on prison as a punishment? That sort of thing.'

He thought for a second then started to talk. Keeping quiet about his ordeal must have been a strain for him because now he seemed only too pleased to have somebody listen to him. He went on for several minutes during which time I gave occasional nods and grunts to keep the narrative flowing.

Apart from the obvious loss of liberty, the shame and any financial repercussions, the actual stay in jail had not been too traumatic for Nigel Abram. 'In a strange way, I'm glad of it,' he said. 'It has helped assuage the guilt I felt for taking another man's life, however accidental it was.'

'How were his family about it?'

'Very bitter. I think they'd have preferred me to have been hanged.'

'They were in court?'

'Yes, they were, but I'd already been round to see them shortly after the accident – against my barrister's advice, I may add. Like I say, I felt guilty and I suppose I was looking for some sort of redemption, but I certainly didn't get it.'

'No?'

'They didn't want to know. Threw me out, almost physically. I think that if it had been up to them, I'd have been sent to the electric chair. This was why, in a way, I didn't mind the sentence. If I couldn't be forgiven, I could at least be punished.'

This was the perfect lead-in for my Big Question. 'You didn't feel resentment, then, at being sent to prison rather than being fined?'

'My barrister had warned me it was on the cards. In a way I was lucky, insomuch as I was charged with Careless Driving, not Dangerous Driving, which meant I didn't have to go to the crown court where the sentence could have been a lot longer.'

'All the same, it can't have been pleasant hearing some man on the bench take away your freedom.'

'No, but like I said, I was almost resigned to it and I knew that I'd be out in a few weeks with parole. The firm had already agreed to keep me on.'

'Good of them.'

'Maybe, but I'd not done anything criminal.' He seemed philosophical yet self-assured about his ordeal.

'How does your wife feel about it?'

'She thinks I was lucky I didn't get a longer sentence.'

No resentment there. 'Well, thank you for your time,' I said and assured him once again that his name wouldn't be mentioned on air. We said our goodbyes and I didn't expect to see Nigel Abram again.

How wrong could I be?

On the journey back to Liverpool, I had plenty of time to think, and it did seem as if the Skidmore case had run into a dead end. Far from showing a desire for revenge, the six so-called suspects had displayed a complete lack of interest in the magistrates who'd convicted them.

Jim Burroughs would believe his pessimism about the case was vindicated but I was more interested in telling him about the coincidence of Harriman and the Edgar Marshall burglary.

As I drove past Aintree Racecourse and into Warbreck Moor Lane, I noticed people standing on the pavement outside the shops holding cardboard sunglasses to their eyes, watching the eclipse of the sun, the most over-hyped event of the year after the Millennium.

It didn't do much for me. Apparently, Cornwall had been expecting a huge influx of people to see it but, in the end, hardly anyone had turned up and speculators expected to lose thousands. I couldn't see people asking in years to come, 'Where were you when the Total Eclipse of 1999 took place?' It wasn't even dark enough to switch the car lights on.

Coming up to the ring road, I decided on a quick detour and turned into Queens Drive to Old Swan. I could try my luck at catching Edgar Marshall before I went to the office. After meeting Harriman, there was a lot more I wanted to talk to Edgar about.

I went straight to the garage, rather than to his house, and this time it was open. On the forecourt, a young lad of about nineteen wearing oil-spattered overalls was working on an old Ford Escort.

'Excuse me.' He looked up from beneath the bonnet, his face smeared with grease. 'I'm looking for Edgar Marshall.'

'He ain't in.'

'What time are you expecting him?'

The lad's hands continued moving round the engine. 'Dunno. He comes in when he feels like it.'

'Might he be at home?'

'Could be.' His head ducked down, the conversation over for him.

I persisted. 'When did you last see him?'

'I think he went away for the weekend. He ain't been in since.'

'You were closed yesterday.'

'No, we was open.'

'I called yesterday morning but the shutters were down.'

'I'd have been out on a breakdown.'

'I'll try him at his house.'

I thanked him and drove the short distance to Marshall's front door. I rang the bell: no answer. When I peered through the letterbox, I saw a bundle of letters on the floor behind the door. Suddenly, it wasn't looking good.

Harriman said he'd gained entry to Marshall's home by prising open a ground-floor window. I tried the side gate, found it unlocked and went round to check out the back.

My guess was that, after the burglary, when Marshall had moved the tape out of the house rather than risk being broken into again, he might not have bothered to secure the premises.

And I was right. The window-frame that Harriman had forced had not been repaired and I was able to open it without too much trouble. I climbed inside and made my way through the kitchen into the small front room, which was empty. The house seemed unnaturally quiet.

I called out but there was no reply. Slowly, I walked up the steep stairs and into the front bedroom. All my instincts were telling me to expect the worst – and I found it.

The thin curtains afforded ample light for me to take in the horrific scene. Lying on a double bed, half-covered by a turquoise candlewick bedspread, was the thin lifeless body of a man whose age I put somewhere in his mid-fifties. A vicious gash across his throat accounted for the proliferation of dried crimson bloodstains on the bedclothes and over the front of his pale blue pyjamas.

One look was enough. I ran downstairs to ring Jim Burroughs to tell him what had happened. Then I dialled 999.

If the body on that bed was Edgar Marshall, then one thing was for sure. Bobby wouldn't be singing with The Voxtones any more.

Chapter Nine

'So what do you think the motive was, if it wasn't theft?' asked Jim Burroughs.

It was late afternoon and I'd finally made it back to the office, having given a statement to the police who'd arrived shortly after my emergency call from Marshall's house.

Naturally they weren't too happy that I'd broken into the premises. I explained to them that I was calling at the house regarding repairs to my car, having been sent there by the assistant at Edgar Marshall's workshop. When nobody had answered my ring, I'd gone round to the back of the premises where I noticed that the back window had been forced.

Assuming there had been a break-in, I had been anxious to make sure that Mr Marshall was unharmed so I'd climbed in through the said window and subsequently had come across the body in the bedroom.

The policeman was not impressed at my public-spiritedness. 'A bit presumptuous, wasn't it, breaking into a strange house when you didn't know the man personally?'

'I'm actually an enquiry agent,' I told him, showing him my business card. 'I suppose it was professional curiosity.'

'Do I assume that you were visiting Mr Marshall as part of an investigation you're undertaking, then?'

'No,' I answered truthfully. 'I was merely calling to have my car repaired.' I saw no reason to mention Harriman or the John Lennon tape.

As Marshall had obviously been dead a good while, they could hardly accuse me of having just killed him, although they did say they would want to speak to me again.

In the meantime, Marshall's assistant was brought round from the garage to identify the body as that of his boss. The lad looked terrified and upset.

I stuck around long enough to ascertain that nothing appeared to have been stolen – there were credit cards and cash lying around – and that Marshall had probably been dead for well over twenty-four hours.

Which meant Cronkshaw could have committed the crime when I saw him leaving Marshall's house on Monday morning.

'Well, Johnny?' Jim Burroughs broke in on my musings. 'The motive?'

'Frustration, possibly, Jim. They broke in, he told them the tape wasn't there so they killed him out of spite. Strange thing was, there didn't seem to have been a struggle. He was just lying on the bed almost as if he'd been asleep.'

'Perhaps he was.'

'No. He was awake when he was killed. His face had a look of shock mixed with terror. He'd obviously not been expecting his guest to turn on him.'

'You mean it was someone he knew?'

'He'd hardly let a stranger in his bedroom, would he, like I said, he was in bed. My guess is the visitor had somehow got hold of a key.'

'And the place didn't look like it had been turned over?'

'Oddly enough, it didn't. His killer must have believed him when Marshall said he hadn't got the tape. Either that or he was disturbed.'

'If Marshall told his assailants you'd got the tape . . .'

I didn't need telling. 'I know. If he gave them my name, they'll be after me now and they'll probably want to kill me too.'

'Some people like killing,' said Jim.

I knew what he meant. Harriman had that look about him but, luckily, he was in jail. Which meant, of course, that he had a cast-iron alibi for Marshall's death.

'Certainly some of these collectors are obsessive,' I agreed, 'but Lennon did tend to attract nutters.' I told him about the meeting with Harriman in Altcourse.

'What a coincidence,' Jim said. 'That's two people we know of who've been after that tape. I wonder how many more know about it?'

'God knows,' I said, 'but it seems pretty certain that one of them killed him for it.'

'What about Cronkshaw?'

'Can't see it. After all, he knew Marshall hadn't got the tape any more because he was at the auction. He's more likely to be Marshall's accomplice. They played in the same group, and we presume it was Marshall who sent Cronkshaw to retrieve the tape?'

'I guess so.'

'On the other hand, I can't rule him out altogether. They could have had a bust-up over something. I tell you what though, if Cronkshaw didn't kill him, he'll be shitting himself when he hears that Edgar's dead in case he's next on the list.'

'We need to get hold of him, Johnny. He's our only lead.'

'He'll probably want to talk to me just as much. After all, he must know I've got their tape.' For a start, Leslie Lomax would give out information to anyone who slipped him a bluey.

'That's right. And you're too high profile in this city for him not to find you. By the way, what happened to the other tape, the Bobby and the Voxtones one? You never played me that.'

'It's at Maria's, with the John Lennon one,' I said.

'You said it was bad.'

'Yeah, it's pretty dreadful, but now that he's dead, perhaps we could release it as *The Bobby and the Voxtones Memorial Album*.'

'You're sick. No wonder they threw you off the radio. Nothing new on that front, I suppose?'

'No,' I said shortly.

'Right.' Jim knew when to shut up. 'Anyway, forget about Marshall for the moment and let's talk about the jobs we're actually being paid for.'

'No luck at all with the Skidmore case, I'm afraid. The last two suspects were a waste of time. Harriman was only interested in the Beatles. He didn't give a shit about the magistrates. As for Abram, he reckons they did him a favour. He says he deserved his stretch for running down the taxi-driver so the sentence came as a sort of divine retribution.'

'Total dead end, then?'

'Looks like it, unless Mrs Skidmore was wrong when she said there was nothing untoward in her husband's private life.'

'I didn't get the impression she was lying.'

'Neither did I, Jim. Christ, she's the one paying out the cash so she obviously wants us to get a result.'

'So?'

'But I do think it's possible that he could have been conning her. Mrs S. may well have trusted her Bernard a hundred per cent whilst all the time the cunning bastard could have been pushing heroin, shagging his secretary, fiddling his expenses, interfering with scoutmasters and doing whatever else behind her back. Love is blind, Jim. Didn't the Yorkshire Ripper's wife say she'd no idea he was a serial killer?'

'If you believe that, you'll believe anything.'

'All the same, Skidmore could have been a skilful deceiver.'

'So what are you going to do?'

'I'm not sure yet.' I needed to check out his friends on the list his widow had given me and find out which of his work colleagues he used to drink with, in the hope that one of them might drop a hint of something untoward.

'And what about Owen Jenna, Johnny? He's going to want to see something for the grand he gave us.'

Susie Jenna was a problem. I'd been through all the files and couldn't see any avenue that the police had not already explored.

'I'm going to ask around, Jim, look up a few old contacts, see what the word on the street is.' It was all pretty vague but I could think of no other way of approaching the case. 'You of all people should know that most crimes are solved by informers. Maybe someone will talk to me who wouldn't talk to the Law.'

'That was before DNA, Johnny.'

'There's no DNA involved when there's no body so I'm going to have a go at some of the usual faces around town.'

And there was no better time to start than the present.

I wasn't meeting Maria until eight so I went back to the flat, changed into jeans, blue check shirt and leather jacket and started walking down the dock road.

Since the docks moved out to Seaforth, many of the old haunts like Frank's Caff, the Sandon Lion and the Dominion have shut down. For a while, in the eighties, a fun pub called Bonkers brought in a young crowd with speciality acts and disco but the craze died and now only a few places are left. It was in one of these, the Bramley Moor, that I found the man I wanted.

He was known as 'Accordion Billy' and it was all I'd ever heard him called. He was now in his late fifties, his skin leathery and engrained with dirt. Most of his life he'd spent busking on street corners, alternating between Liverpool, Belfast and Dublin, living in men's hostels.

He sang mainly Irish drinking songs and, in recent years, he'd followed the fashion and acquired an old, hairy dog to lie beside him on a ragged coat to attract the animal sympathy vote.

He spotted me before I saw him. 'Johnny Ace,' he called out. 'The man's a star an' all. What are you having?'

'I'll get them, Billy.' In one morning outside Marks & Spencer he probably earned more than The Chocolate Lavatory did on an average gig but it didn't show in the state of his torn anorak, dirty T-shirt, crumpled jeans and torn trainers. Even his dog looked mangy and moth-eaten. I was glad I didn't have Roly with me. He might have caught something.

I took over a pint of mild to Billy and joined him at the table, being careful not to step on his accordion which lay next to his dog.

'I seen your picture in the paper,' he said. 'Looking like that Colombo.'

'Yeah, right.' Why did nobody mistake me for Pierce Brosnan? I took a sip of cider. 'Good weather for your business, Billy. Are you doing much?'

He grunted a non-committal reply. 'I see your mate's back on the road.'

'Who's that?'

'Jim Burroughs – The Chocolate Lavatory.' I'd forgotten that Accordion Billy had been in a group in the sixties but then, hadn't everybody in Liverpool? 'I remember them at Garston Baths. They was crap then and I bet they haven't improved.'

'You didn't know Bobby and the Voxtones by any chance, did you?'

'Course I did. Bobby used to run a garage somewhere up by Old Swan. He still does, for all I know.' He sniffed. 'They were crap as well. A parrot with a cracked beak could sing better than him.'

I hoped Billy wouldn't be asked to write Bobby's obituary for the *Liverpool Echo*. It might not read well.

'Tell me, Billy, you know everything in this town . . .'

He caught my conspiratorial tone and leaned forward. His breath smelt of decayed mushrooms. 'Go on.'

'This missing woman that's been in all the papers – Susie Jenna. Have you heard anything?'

'Like what?'

'Like is she really dead or has she done a runner? And, if she's dead, where's the body?'

Billy swiftly downed the last of his pint and handed me his empty glass. 'Get me another drink, will you, Johnny, while I thinks about it?'

I went obediently to the bar. Only a couple of other people were in the pub, they looked like truckers. It was too early for the evening crowd, not that there was much regular midweek trade with the dockers gone. The truckers sat motionless at the bar, their eyes glued to the television in the corner, like the zombies in *The Invasion of the Body-Snatchers*.

Accordion Billy accepted his pint gratefully. 'Very noble of you,

Johnny. Cheers. I hope you get your job back, I do. Now, where was I?'

'Susie Jenna,' I reminded him.

'Ah yes – the missing woman. No, I've heard nothing of her, but would I though? She's not a woman who'd be known in places like this. Too downmarket for her. Did I tell you to buy MFI shares, by the way? There's a take-over in the offing, Johnny. You want to get in there. Well worth a punt, mark my words.'

There had been rumours over the years that Accordion Billy had stashed away a small fortune from his dealings on the Stock Exchange but, if he had, he showed no signs of having spent any of it on himself.

'I lost two hundred on your last tip, Billy. You told me to buy Eagle Trust.'

But his mind had changed track again. 'I'd bet a pound to a whore's titty she's snuffed it.'

'What?'

'The Jenna woman. He'll have fed her to the hogs. It's a better way of getting shut of a body than burying it. With the hogs, it can't reappear you see, except as pigshit and no one's going to be wanting to go sniffing through that. And it's quick too. A few mouthfuls and there'd be nothing left of her.'

I was glad I'd decided against the pork scratchings.

'You don't reckon she's moved away then?'

'You don't disappear these days, Johnny, not with all these cameras about. You can't have a pee in private any more. Even the lavvys are bugged. Chuck Berry got done for that, you know, but everyone does it now and nobody says fuck all.'

'Never mind, it was just a thought.' I rose to go but he placed a hand on my arm.

'That Owen Jenna though. He's been throwing his money around town.'

I sat down again. 'I thought you'd heard nothing.'

'I haven't. Not about her.'

'So where's he been spending it then?'

'In the bookies and down the casino in Renshaw Street. Have you bought into Stanley Leisure, Johnny? You should do. Owen Jenna is boosting their profits big-style.'

'I wonder where it's coming from? He won't have been able to cash any insurance policy until she's officially dead.'

'Who knows? Perhaps he's been lucky with the gee-gees.' He cackled at the improbability of it and took a swig of ale.

I realised I knew very little about Owen jenna, other than that he worked in an office.

Perhaps it was about time I found out more.

Accordion Billy had nothing else of interest to tell me, so I drank up and set off again down the road. Outside the Atlantic, I saw a familiar old bicycle propped up against the window and went inside.

Gypsy Gloria was sitting in a corner holding a glass of Guinness in gnarled arthritic hands. Grey roots betrayed her jet black hair and her face was so lined her cheeks looked like they were encased in a net.

'Hello Gloria,' I said.

Her eyes lit up. They were like sparkling sapphires. 'Johnny Ponny, sit down with me.'

She was tiny, inches under five feet, and she wouldn't see ninety again but she had a vibrancy about her missing in many much younger people.

'I'll just get a drink. Are you having another?'

'I won't say no.' She cackled delightedly.

I went over to the bar. The place was already pretty full. Fading pictures of once-famous acts who'd visited the pub adorned the black and white walls, alongside old theatre posters advertising forgotten stars like Hoagy Carmichael and Frankie Laine.

'All right, Johnny?' Pat, the barmaid, gave me a fetching smile. 'Your usual, is it?'

'Please, Pat, and a Guinness for Gloria.' I looked at two older men in jeans and cowboy shirts tuning up guitars on the small stage beside the door. 'Who's on tonight?'

'Sonny, Sonny Phillips. And anyone else who wants to get up

and do a spot. Ricky Tomlinson was in the other night. Have you seen *The Royle Family*, Johnny?'

'Yeah, it's great.'

'Best show on the telly.'

I knew Sonny from the old days when he used to run clubs in town. Now he goes round the circuit with his guitar playing folk and country.

'What brings you here?' Gloria asked when I rejoined her at the table.

'I saw your bike outside, Glo. Are you still doing the palms?'

'Trade hasn't been so good, Johnny.'

She was a regular at village fêtes and garden parties, her name chalked on a blackboard, *Gypsy Gloria, Fortunes Told*, sitting in a tent with her crystal ball and Tarot cards. When the weather became colder, she moved her operations indoors, appearing in local church halls at Autumn Fairs and Christmas parties.

I wasn't surprised about her drop in business. She was the only fortune-teller I'd ever known who predicted disaster. Instead of the usual promises of trips to exotic lands or winning huge sums of money, startled clients were horrified to learn that they could be already suffering from an incurable wasting disease or were shortly going to lose somebody very close to them. Not the sort of prognostications to bring in much repeat business.

'Sorry to hear that, Glo. Maybe you ought to start telling people they're going to meet the man of their dreams and live in splendour on a Caribbean island.'

She looked at me sternly. 'You can't say what the stars don't tell. Let me read your palm, Johnny.'

I drew my hand away quickly. 'No thanks, Glo, I'd rather not know what's going to happen to me. But you can help me. What can you tell me about Susie Jenna?'

'That girl what's been in all the papers, that's run away?'

'That's the one.'

The old woman took a sip of stout and wiped the froth from her lips with the back of her hand. The skin on her arms was like parchment over her bones. She leaned back and closed her eyes.

'No need to go into a trance, Glo. I'm not asking you to contact the other side.'

She opened her eyes quickly and snapped, 'She's not dead, Johnny, I can tell you that.'

'You don't reckon? What have you heard?' Gloria had been around so long and knew so many people in the city that, in her time, she'd absorbed an incredible amount of gossip. Most of it she remembered in detail despite her great age. It helped her enormously when giving her readings. Often she knew so much about people before she'd met them that many were convinced she really was clairvoyant.

'She isn't dead,' she repeated, adding a low moan which didn't impress me.

'Come on, Gloria, none of this Indian spirit "voice from the clouds" bullshit. What facts have you got?'

She spat at me. 'Unbeliever, Johnny Ace.'

'I know you move in certain circles, Glo. You might have heard something.'

It was reputed that what she didn't make from her predictions, Gloria more than compensated for from her other occupation as a fence. Instead of crossing her palm with silver, many clients would 'pay' her in stolen goods which she would then sell at a considerable mark-up to dealers of her acquaintance.

'I might,' she snorted. 'That's a nice watch you have, Johnny Ponny.'

'You're not having that,' I said. 'Here.' I slipped a bluey into her bony fingers. She slid her hand inside her long black skirt and transferred it to a pouch in her knickers. It was a good hiding-place. Few muggers would be likely to thrust their hands up Gloria's bony legs.

She gripped my wrist and made as if she was reading my palm. 'Susie Jenna had a friend,' she whispered.

'A lover, you mean?'

'No, another woman.'

'And she's with her?'

'You'll need to look beyond these shores.' She let go my hand and pushed it away. 'That's all.'

'But . . .'

'That's all, Johnny,' she said firmly. 'There's no more.'

I thought about what she'd said as I walked back to the flat. Susie Jenna's passport was at her house and she couldn't have left the country unless she had a fake passport. Would she have found it easy to get one? That suggested a lot of planning, not to mention accomplices outside the law. I couldn't see it. It was just the ramblings of a crazy old woman.

Wasn't it?

Chapter Ten

I took Maria to Mr Ho's in Waterloo for a Chinese and, over the meal, I told her about the murder of Edgar Marshall.

'Oh no, that's terrible,' she said, when I'd finished. 'And to think you were the one to find him. I told you that tape could be dangerous, Johnny.'

'You were right and it still could be. Whoever killed Marshall won't stop looking for it.'

'What are you going to do?'

'Find Albert Cronkshaw and see what he can tell me.'

'Do be careful, won't you. I don't want you dead. What about your other cases?'

I brought her up to date with the latest predictions regarding Susie Jenna.

'So let me get this straight,' said Maria. 'One of your contacts thinks she's been eaten alive by rampaging swine and the other says she's sunning it in the Tropics?'

'Doesn't look hopeful,' I admitted.

'The police are still digging round Freshfield hoping to find her body, you know.'

'It'll keep them off the streets.'

'What about your other case, the magistrate?'

'Nothing. A dead end.' On that note I changed the subject and we concentrated on the chicken and cashew nuts in black bean sauce.

'We should take Roly for a walk,' she said when we were back at the flat. 'I went on the beach with him this afternoon but he's been in all evening.'

Roly wagged his inch of tail in agreement so we walked over to the Serpentine and watched the lights of New Brighton across the river.

'I've got something to ask you,' Maria said when we returned to her flat. I was sitting in the lounge glancing through the *Echo* as she brought through two cups of tea and a packet of chocolate biscuits.

'Go on.' From the wariness of her tone, I wasn't sure I was going to like this.

She put the cups down on the coffee-table and sat beside me.

'Kaye and Alex have hired a boat for a week on the Norfolk Broads and they want us to go with them.'

Kaye is Maria's sister and we've had the odd meal with her and her husband but I've never felt comfortable about getting involved with relations. In some way I feel it takes away my identity. I become merely 'Maria's boyfriend'.

'When is it?'

'Not until the second week in September.'

'I'm not sure I'll have sorted these cases out by then.'

'There'll always be cases, Johnny, but you've got to have holidays and you're forgetting Jim. He'll be able to look after things.'

I couldn't argue with that and, suddenly, with Maria's arm wound affectionately around me and Roly sitting within catching distance of a biscuit, I didn't want to.

'What do you say?' she asked, looking into my eyes. 'Shall we go?'

I kissed her gently. 'Why not?'

I didn't regret my decision next morning as I drove into town, although I wasn't sure how I'd break the news to Hilary. I'd never been on holiday with Maria before.

I parked on a meter in Moorfields and walked across with Roly to the office, picking up a *Daily Post* from a newsstand on Dale Street on the way. When I learnt that Aston Villa had beaten Everton the night before, I had the feeling it wasn't going to be my day.

'Any joy last night?' Jim asked me as I walked in. Roly and he exchanged the merest flicker of acknowledgement.

'Not really. All I found out was that Owen Jenna's been throwing his money around. What do we know about him, Jim?'

'They're not badly off. He's got an office job somewhere and his missus stayed at home to look after the children. Gave up work when they were born.'

'That's odd nowadays for a start. Most women are back at work within weeks of giving birth.'

'Perhaps he makes enough money for both of them. What sort of house do they live in again?'

'A semi in Freshfield.'

Jim grimaced. 'Could mean anything out there.'

Freshfield and Formby had started out as farming villages but, once the railway was built between Southport and Liverpool, the first electric line in England, they rapidly spread into a dormitory suburb for upwardly mobile Scousers.

Since the war, thousands more had streamed in as new housing estates covered the old farmland and developers bought up every garden and spare bit of ground that they could find. Consequently, thatched cottages stood in the same roads as rambling Victorian houses, bungalows, pre-war semis, modern mansions and blocks of flats.

I agreed. 'Let's see what their exact address is.' Jim had the Jennas' details stored away as I would have expected.

I read over his shoulder as he took the papers out of the file. 'Freshfield Road. There's a few big semis down there, so let's say he might not be short of a bob or two. The question is, why is he throwing it around suddenly?'

'He works for a car-hire outfit in town,' Jim read. 'Office manager, no less, so he's probably on a good screw there.'

'Not to mention the benefits in kind as the taxman would say.'

'How do you mean?' Jim looked blank.

'His bit of skirt in the office. The woman who sold her story to the tabloids.'

'Ah, I get you.' He frowned. 'This sudden gambling puzzles me. There must be a reason for it.'

'I'll do a bit of nosing around, Jim. In the meantime, I ran into Gloria the Gypsy last night and she said something about Susie Jenna having a woman friend and that she'd gone beyond these shores, whatever that means.'

'Probably New Brighton. You didn't really go to see that old witch, did you? Christ, you'll be brewing potions in a bleedin' cauldron next and swapping your car for a broomstick.'

'I'd called in at the Atlantic and she happened to be in there.' I decided to keep quiet about Accordion Billy and his theory about the hogs.

Before Jim could come out with any more choice comments, the phone rang and I picked it up. 'Ace Investigations.'

There was a pause, then a husky voice said, 'My name's Albert Cronkshaw. I believe you've got something belonging to me.'

I quickly switched on the machine to record and glanced at the call display screen. He was calling from a payphone in the Aigburth area.

'What's that?' I asked.

'Don't mess me about, you know what I mean. The tape from the auction: I know you've got it.'

'You'll have to come here. Do you know where my office is?'

'No.' I gave him the address. 'You'd better have it ready,' he growled, then put the phone down.

I turned excitedly to Jim. 'That was Albert Cronkshaw. He's on his way over here.'

'Do you think he'll really turn up?'

'He has to. He wants the tape.'

'But you won't give it him?'

'What do you think?'

Albert Cronkshaw arrived within the hour. Today, his resemblance to Boris Karloff was even more striking than at the auction. He had dark rings beneath his eyes, his cheeks were white and sunken and he wore a long black coat, even though it was August, as though he'd been auditioning for the lead role in *Phantom of the Opera*.

Unlike the Phantom though, Albert Cronkshaw was carrying a gun.

'Where is it, then?' He stood, revolver in hand, in front of the desk with Jim and me marooned at the other side. 'Well?'

He clicked the safety catch. Roly growled and rose menacingly from his mat, sensing danger.

'Now then . . .' Jim began but I jumped in quickly.

'For Christ's sake, Bert,' I said in a deliberately conversational tone, 'put that bloody thing away before it goes off. I'll make us some tea and we can sort this out.'

He looked puzzled and, for a moment, things could have gone either way. I picked up two mugs from the desk and made a move towards the kitchen. If he was going to shoot me it would have to be now, and in the back. 'How many sugars?' I asked him, to divert his mind from the idea.

The gun wavered. He'd missed his chance. I didn't try to grab it; I just brushed past him and went into the kitchen. Roly lay down again.

'You might as well sit down,' I heard Jim say. Bemused, Cronkshaw put the gun in his pocket and pulled up a chair as I came back into the room.

'Right,' I said, 'the kettle's on, let me take your coat,' and I held out my hands. At first he hesitated then he removed the garment and handed it to me. I stuck it on a hook behind the door and quietly transferred his gun to my own pocket as I did so.

I didn't think Albert Cronkshaw was cut out to be a professional criminal but I knew never to underestimate the danger posed by an unstable amateur armed with a dangerous weapon.

'Where'd you get the shooter from?' I asked him, careful to keep my tone conversational.

His voice was shaky. 'Fellow in a pub in the Dingle. I needed protection.'

'From whom?'

'There's people who'll stop at nothing to get that tape.'

'Like who? Who else knows about it?'

He started to rise angrily. 'You know bloody well . . .'

I cut him short. 'Where did the tape come from?'

He sat down again and reluctantly admitted that it was Bobby's. 'He's had it since the sixties,' he said, and the whole story came out.

It had all started on the night of 23 January 1963.

'I'll never forget the date,' said Albert. 'It was the first and only time we ever played The Cavern and we were all under seventeen.'

Bobby had persuaded Bob Wooler, the velvet-tongued DJ at the Cavern, to give the Voxtones an audition.

'The Beatles were top of the bill. We went on first, before Freddie Starr and the Midnighters.'

'How did you go down?' I asked apprehensively. I'd heard the tape.

Albert shrugged. 'Not bad. Bobby was no great shakes as a singer. Someone said he sounded like a sheep with a cleft palate.'

'So did Adam Faith and it didn't hamper his success.'

'When we did "Money" the girls all started screaming at us.'

'Money' was the song whose success had helped propel co-writer Berry Gordy Junior from the assembly line of a Detroit car factory into pop music's big time with his own Tamla Motown label.

Most of the groups on the Merseybeat circuit played 'Money', though probably few of them as badly as Bobby and the Voxtones. It was another of the tracks on their tape and I figured their out-of-time, out-of-tune wailings owed less to the influence of American rhythm and blues than to excessive consumption of the Higson's bitter served at the Grapes public house on the opposite side of Mathew Street.

'The atmosphere was incredible.'

I remembered it well. The Cruzads had played The Cavern too. The girls wore pinafore dresses and lacquered 'bird's nest' bouffant hairdos and danced the Cavern Stomp beside their handbags. This involved moving their arms up and down in a staccato movement in time to the crashing beat of the music, there being no room in the humid, smoke-filled cellar to move their legs.

The boys sported round-collared jackets, imitation leather slipovers and pointed Italian shoes, and many of them had brushed their hair forwards like their heroes, The Beatles.

'So what happened about the tape?'

'Sorry, yes. The Beatles were late arriving. They'd been recording in London for BBC Radio and their van windscreen had shattered on the way back. We were just packing up our Commer when they rolled up. Bobby was working as a car mechanic in the daytime so he offered to take their van to his garage and mend it for them.'

'And he found the tape inside?'

'In the glove compartment. He was having a nose round and there it was. He took it home in his dinner-hour to have a listen. Twelve new songs written and sung by John Lennon. It even had his handwriting on the box.'

'So Bobby kept it.'

'Yes. He took the van back to them that afternoon and they were off to fame and fortune. He assumed they'd be too busy to notice it had gone.'

'And he was right.'

'He thought the songs might turn up one day on an album but they never did.'

'Did you know about this at the time?'

'Heavens, no. Bobby never confided in us. Anyway, the group broke up shortly afterwards.'

'What happened to the others?'

'Croaky, the lead guitarist, was killed in a motorbike accident and the bass player, Mick, went away to college.'

Albert himself took the advice of his parents and got a 'proper job', though whether being a drains inspector for the Water Board was an improvement on drumming for The Voxtones was, I thought, open to doubt.

'Bobby took the hint and gave up singing. He'd never have made it, I don't think. Apart from his voice, he had these elephantine ears and an acne problem.'

I agreed. 'Not the best attributes for a teenage idol.'

'He served his time as a mechanic and ended up with his own garage. He did well for himself.'

'When did you first find out that he had the tape?'

'Oh, years later. I'd kept in touch with him on and off. I was the only one who did. Croaky had died and Mick went to Australia when he'd finished university. He got a job as a civil engineer or something like that. I remember, his folks had a big farewell party for him at Dovedale Towers. All his old mates were there yet we've never heard from him from that day to this.'

'And you stayed in Liverpool?'

'Never left.'

He'd stayed with the Water Board all his working life, seemingly spending much of his time in sewers. It probably accounted for his waxen complexion. He'd meet up with Bobby from time to time and they'd share a pint and chat about the old days.

A year ago, Albert had taken early retirement. His wife had recently left him for a forty-year-old toy boy, the two children were long gone, so he sold the family home and moved into a small terraced house in Old Swan. He started to see more of his old friend, they both drank in the Old Swan pub, and one day Bobby told him the story of how he acquired The John Lennon Tape.

Bobby had realised that, after John Lennon was shot dead in 1980 and the whole Beatles phenomenon became a multi-million-pound industry, his prize possession was an ever-appreciating asset.

'He said it could be worth a fortune now. He'd seen the prices people paid for Beatles stuff at the Beatles Conventions. He said it was his pension.'

'And he was ready to cash it in?'

'Right. He'd already had this bloke round from this record shop in West Derby. I was there when he came to hear it. Weird bloke he was, a right oddball but menacing with it, if you know what I mean?'

I did. I'd met Frank Harriman and it seemed a fair description.

'And Bobby wouldn't sell it to him?'

'He'd no money, had he? So Bobby fucked him off and the next thing, the bastard broke into his house in the middle of the night and demanded Bobby hand it over.'

'But he didn't?'

'Not likely. Bobby gave him a good battering before he called the law and the bastard went down for six months. Bobby then started buying various music magazines, looking for people advertising to purchase Beatles memorabilia. He wrote off to one of them saying he had this valuable tape of unheard John Lennon songs for sale and, like a fool, gave his address.'

'Why didn't he just take the tape to Sotheby's?'

'I don't know. Probably because they'd say it was stolen and he'd be arrested.'

Perhaps that's what would happen to me.

'So did he get a reply from these people he wrote to?'

'Not a word, but shortly afterwards, his house was turned over again. They trashed the place and left this message sprayed across the kitchen wall. *We'll be back*, it said. Put the fear of God up Bobby. He had to repaint the kitchen.'

'But they didn't come back?'

'Not so far they haven't but Bobby was frightened they might do at any time so he decided to put the tape somewhere they couldn't get at it.'

'But why put it in an auction? Why not just give it to you to keep?'

'I'd not seen him for a couple of weeks so I suppose it didn't occur to him. Probably a spur-of-the-moment thing.'

Or maybe Bobby didn't trust his old drummer.

'Whatever. Anyway, it was safe in the auction rooms for four weeks until the next sale. He'd stuck it in with another tape hidden in the box beneath his old Grundig tape recorder. The plan was he'd buy it back and take it to the Beatles Convention himself later this month. I ran into him the day before the auction and, when he told me about it, I suggested he let me bid for it, then nobody would connect it with him.'

'And he agreed?'

'I think he knew that there was still a risk that they might come back to his home or garage and sooner or later they'd find it.'

It was Bobby's misfortune that I'd wanted an old-fashioned tape recorder and had outbid him, otherwise they would have regained possession of the tape without any trouble. Whether they would have held on to it, of course, was another matter.

'When did you last see Bobby?'

'A couple of days ago. He was furious that I'd allowed the tape to be sold to someone else but I've promised to get it back for him. So will you give it to me so's I can return it?' He looked at me pleadingly. 'I'll give you your £150 back and you can keep the machine.'

I suddenly realised that Cronkshaw was unaware of his friend's death. 'You mean you don't know?'

'Know what?'

'It's in all the papers. Edgar Marshall, Bobby, is dead. I found him myself. I went round to his house yesterday. He was lying in his bed with his throat cut open.'

'Oh Jesus Christ.' Albert swayed in his chair. 'No.'

Jim jumped up. 'I'll make the tea. Looks as though he needs it.' I let Albert sit with his head in his hands until Jim returned with two steaming mugs which he handed to us.

Albert took a couple of quick swigs. I didn't know how he could drink it so hot. He took out a grey handkerchief and rubbed his eyes. I figured half his agony would be concern about his friend and the other half the awful realisation that the same thing could happen to him. I waited a few seconds for him to recover his poise before continuing.

'Have you no idea who this collector was that Bobby had contacted about the tape?'

He had another few sips and shook his head. 'No idea – he never said. When did he die? How? Oh, God.'

I ran over the details of his friend's untimely demise.

'They reckon it was in the last forty-eight hours but they'll know more when the pathologist puts in his report. You realise you'll be a suspect?'

'Me?'

'You were probably one of the last people to see him apart from his killer. He didn't turn up at the garage after the weekend.'

Cronkshaw looked desperate now. 'I never killed him. I didn't know he was dead. Why would I kill him?'

I couldn't believe that he was being so dense. 'If he was dead, you wouldn't have to give the tape back.'

That reminded Cronkshaw that he hadn't actually regained possession of the tape. 'Where is it, anyway?' he asked.

'In my safe-keeping,' I said evenly. 'I bought it legitimately and I'm keeping it.'

'But. . .' he felt for his pocket, realised he'd taken his coat off and stopped.

'Looking for this?' I asked and pointed his gun at his heart. Jim said later that he turned even whiter than an advert for Daz. Certainly he looked scared and I feared for the new office carpet.

'Don't shoot!' he cried. 'It's loaded!'

'Look, Albert,' I said kindly, 'I've no quarrel with you. The tape's mine, right? Bought and paid for. It was never yours, and Bobby's dead now. Come to that, John Lennon's dead too. Maybe I should send it to Yoko but I don't see her needing the money. Perhaps Cynthia or Julian might feel they have a claim on it, I don't know. Or it might end up in a museum. Time will tell but in the meantime it's mine and it's staying mine.'

He made no comment except to say, 'Wasn't a bad tape, was it?'

'As good as some of their later stuff,' I agreed.

He looked at me almost shyly. 'Did you happen to play our tape, the other one in the box? Bobby and the Voxtones? Only, I wondered what you thought of it?'

I could hear the howling vocals in my head as he asked me but I saw no reason to shatter the dreams of his youth. 'Some good tracks, Albert. I liked "Over the Rainbow". Pity you never stayed with it.' Just as long as he didn't go back to it. I could not stand another Chocolate Lavatory experience.

'I've heard your show on the wireless, you know,' he said. 'Didn't you used to be in a band once?'

'The Cruzads. I played the drums like you. You had a nice tight beat on that recording.'

He looked pleased and his earlier hysteria seemed to have subsided. Then he became nervous again. 'What about these people who are after the Lennon tape? They'll stop at nothing.'

'Then I shall need your help to get to them first.'

He clasped his hands together. 'Look, I've made a bit of a prat of myself, haven't I? I want to find the people who killed Bobby.' He paused to choke. 'He's the only friend I really had.'

I stopped him before he became maudlin. 'You say he contacted somebody advertising in a magazine. Which one?'

'He never said.'

'What magazines did he read? I mean, you went to his house sometimes, didn't you? You may have noticed some lying around.'

Albert Cronkshaw frowned. 'I think he mentioned *Record Collector* once.'

'Right. Now you say these men came the week before he put the tape in the auction and that was a month ago?' Albert nodded. 'That takes us to the middle of July. Let's say he placed the advert a couple of weeks before, then we're probably talking about either the July or the August issue.'

'Hang on a minute,' interrupted Jim. 'Isn't this a matter for the police? No reason for us to be involved.'

'If you want a reason, I'd be prepared to hire you.' I turned round to Cronkshaw in surprise.

'What?'

'I want these people to be caught. Let's face it, until they are, then I'm in danger too, aren't I? So, I'll hire you to protect me. What do you charge?'

Anyone could see he wasn't a rich man. People who say there's money in muck weren't referring to sewer cleaners. He'd taken early retirement which meant his pension wouldn't be up to scratch and probably most of it would go on alimony. Divorce usually administered a financial kick in the balls to cast-off husbands.

'Ten pounds a month,' I said before Jim could stop me. 'Payable when we finish the job.' I felt Mrs Skidmore and Owen Jenna could well afford to subsidise him and it gave me an excuse to pursue the only case which was getting anywhere.

'A deal then?' he said and held out his hand. I shook it, avoiding Jim's eye.

'Give me your address and phone number and I'll keep you up to speed with what's happening. Oh, and lock your doors at night, just in case.'

I said it jokingly because I didn't really think Albert Cronkshaw was in any immediate danger.

It was my big mistake.

Chapter Eleven

Later that day, I walked over to Toffs Wine Bar at the corner of Castle Street and snatched a bite to eat before calling in at W.H. Smith's to pick up a copy of the August edition of *Record Collector*. As usual, the shop was packed with lunchtime shoppers who seemed to have mistaken it for a reading room and I had to fight my way through them to reach the shelves.

They didn't have the July issue but I knew somebody who might. I'd seen him a few times in recent weeks standing outside George Henry Lees selling copies of *The Big Issue*. I walked along Church Street towards Central Station and there he was.

'All right, Nudger?'

People say Nudger got his nickname because of his habit of digging people with his elbow to break into their conversation but alternative, and more reliable, sources ascribed it to the prodigious size of his dick.

'Johnny! Good to see you, mate. What's happening with the show?' He was in his late thirties, tall with straggly long hair and boasting the sweet and sour smell of a man who was a stranger to soap. He wore a pair of shabby khaki combats and a T-shirt featuring a photo of Ronald Reagan with the words *Who Am I?* above it and *Please tell me* underneath. I thought it was in poor taste.

'You tell me,' I said. 'Looks like Shady Spencer's in for the long haul.'

'He plays some Almighty shit, that creep. He had Des O'Connor on yesterday. Hey, that was a good wheeze of yours, playing that David Allen Coe track.'

'That's what got me the sack.'

'Oh shit, no. Have they no sense of humour?' He stopped to take some money from a youth wearing a camouflage uniform two sizes too big for him.

'What's with all this?' I asked, as he handed the magazine over. 'I thought you had to be homeless to sell the *Issue*.'

He grinned. 'Course you do, Johnny. Just like you have to be Catholic to play for Everton.'

I didn't argue the point.

'Nudger, I'm trying to get hold of a July *Record Collector*. I thought you'd be just the person to help me.'

Nudger was the ultimate anorak. Not only did he have the largest collection of 45s I'd ever seen, his flat in Mount Street was stacked to the ceiling with music magazines dating as far back as the fifties.

I was amazed he didn't go on *Mastermind* answering questions on pop. He'd have cleaned up. Come up with the most obscure track and he'd tell you who wrote it, who sang it, when it came out and how high, if at all, it got in the charts.

Now here he was, selling *The Big Issue* but I suppose it was better than wandering around in the sewers.

'No problem, Johnny. Pick it up anytime tonight after eight. I'll be in.'

I said nothing about the John Lennon Tape although I knew Nudger would be fascinated to hear it. However, the fewer people that knew about it the better. For now.

I bought a *Big Issue* as a gesture before returning to the office. I find I end up buying at least two copies a week for one reason or another. Good job it's not a daily.

Jim greeted me at the door. 'Owen Jenna phoned.'

'Oh Christ. What did you tell him?'

'You look worried. I told him you'd been to see this hundred-and-one-year-old fortune teller who was able to confirm that his wife was living in tropical luxury with a lesbian lover.'

'Very funny. What did you really say?' I was glad I hadn't mentioned the hogs.

'What could I tell him? I said we were following a couple of lines of enquiry that we hoped would prove fruitful.'

'You should have been in PR,' I said admiringly. 'Did you mention the gambling?'

'No. That's your department but I think he's going to want some action soon.'

'Give it time, it's only Thursday. We've not had a week on it yet.'

'And what was all that ten pounds a month business with Cronkshaw? Now we've got three cases we can't bloody solve.'

Nobody could accuse Jim of looking on the bright side.

'I'm involved in that anyway. I'm the one with the tape, for heaven's sake. And I found Bobby's body. Christ, he's even got me calling him that now. Don't worry, Jim. I won't neglect the other cases and we'll get a result in all of them, I promise.'

To prove my point, I took out the Skidmore file and found Elspeth's list of her husband's colleagues and friends. Eight names were on the sheet; five of them were couples and the rest people who worked with him at Smedley. One of his colleagues, George Cox, was the man who'd been with him at the function in Standish on the night of his death.

I rang him at his works number, since private calls aren't a problem in the civil service, and said I wanted to see him about a matter concerning Bernard Skidmore. He told me I'd be welcome to call at his home any time after five.

Cox lived in Ainsdale. Bernard Skidmore would drive through Ainsdale on his way to Parbold, so why had they gone in separate cars?

The house was a mock Tudor detached in Shore Road. A blue Rover 200, M reg, was parked in the drive next to a new Toyota Yaris when I arrived just after six. It was easy to see where Mr Cox came in the pecking order.

I parked the RAV4 on the road and walked the hundred yards to the front door. Mrs Cox answered the bell and I introduced myself.

'Do come in,' she said. 'My husband's expecting you.' She was

101

small with dark curly hair, thick make-up and an artificial smile. She screamed 'golf club wife'.

Cox himself was sitting in a dralon-covered armchair in the lounge, smoking a Silk Cut and reading the *Daily Mail*. 'Mr Ace is here, dear, from . . . ?' she looked at me questioningly.

'Ace Investigations.' I handed him a card. 'I wanted to talk to you about Bernard Skidmore's death.'

'I'll leave you two to it.' I could hear Australian drawls from a television in the kitchen. Mrs Cox was obviously anxious to get back to *Neighbours*.

Her husband stood up. 'I don't understand. What is there to investigate? Bernard's death was an accident. I've never heard it suggested otherwise.'

'Mrs Skidmore doesn't think so,' I said and waited for the bombshell to hit him.

'Good Lord.' He sat down again. I had him for late fifties but he hadn't worn well. His trousers were having difficulty containing his stomach, broken red veins on his face suggested he liked a tipple and by the sound of his breathing I'd have said he'd have a good chance of winning compensation from Benson & Hedges.

'How did he seem to you on the night he died?'

'In good form. He was very jovial, in fact. We were at this Gentleman's Evening – you know the set-up: had a few drinks, they put on a decent meal, the speaker was amusing, some ex-rugby player.' He didn't mention the two exotic dancers and the blue comedian that I knew were also on the bill.

'You say a few drinks?'

'Nothing over the limit, I hasten to add, because we were both driving. Probably four or five halves of lager at the most. He wasn't much of a drinker at the best of times.'

'Why did you go in separate cars when you lived so close to each other? Surely it would have made sense to have gone together?'

'No mystery. I was coming straight home but Bernard had a call to make in Ormskirk on the way back.'

'Really? That's never been mentioned before.'

'No? Well, I'm sure there's nothing significant in it. Probably something to do with his quizzes. You knew he played in the local quiz league?'

'No, I didn't.' What other activities did Skidmore have of which I was unaware? 'He didn't say who he was calling on?'

'Not to me. He just said I'd better take my own car as he'd likely be back a bit late.'

'So he must have been expecting to spend some time with this person, otherwise, if he was just collecting or dropping something off, you could have waited in the car?'

'I suppose so. He didn't look distressed in any way though. Nothing to indicate he was going to take his own life, poor devil.'

'Oh, it isn't suicide that Mrs Skidmore suspects, Mr Cox. No, you've got it all wrong. She believes her husband was murdered.'

This time he looked really startled. 'Why ever would she think that? Bernard was very popular, hadn't an enemy in the world.'

'I'd heard he was a bit of a ladies' man,' I lied. 'Did he have any girlfriends that you know of?'

George Cox looked horrified. 'Certainly not. Never. On the contrary, I think Bernard preferred a decent meal to anything like that.' He chortled wistfully. 'Don't we all these days?'

I certainly wasn't expecting to swap my nights of lust and wild passion for a chicken casserole when I got to sixty but I didn't argue the point.

'And you say you don't think he had any enemies?'

He rose to his feet again as if he was going to deliver a speech. 'Most people manage to ruffle a few feathers during their lifetime but I can honestly say that Bernard Skidmore was well liked by everybody who knew him, and I'm proud to say that he regarded me as a friend.'

There was no arguing with that. I thanked him for his time and returned to the car.

On the surface, Bernard Skidmore looked as squeaky clean as he'd always appeared to be, but somebody in Ormskirk had been waiting for him to call that night and he had never arrived.

Who could it have been? Did it have any bearing on his death? And how could I find out?

My next call was at Mount Street in Liverpool, a row of houses opposite John Lennon's old art college right in the middle of the trendy Liverpool 8 area which spawned The Mersey Poets and all that pop culture back in the sixties.

Most of the houses are now occupied by people in the arts or from the nearby universities. The Philharmonic Hall, where Buddy Holly sang in 1958, is down the road, and the Everyman Theatre and the famous Philharmonic pub another block away.

An appropriate place for Nudger Ainsworth to live.

'Come in, Johnny,' he greeted me. 'I'm afraid it's a bit cluttered in here. I bought a job lot of vinyl at the record fair on Saturday.'

Around 300 singles and a similar number of LPs stood in the middle of the room. Iggy Pop's 'The Passenger' was blasting out from a machine in the corner but the sound was deadened by the vast amount of clutter. The dust alone must have weighed several tons. Quentin Crisp would have been proud of it.

'I haven't seen one of those for years,' I marvelled, looking at the old stereogram.

'Just a record player in a cheap wooden case on legs,' pointed out Nudger, 'with a radio added. Mustn't forget the radio. Very desirable item of furniture in its day.' He moved over to one of several piles of magazines propped against the far wall. 'The *Record Collector* you wanted, wasn't it?'

'That's right. July's.'

'You don't want any old 45s, I suppose?' he asked hopefully as he started ploughing through his back issues.

'No thanks. I'm surprised anybody buys vinyl now with CDs and mini-discs.'

'They don't. The bottom's dropped out of the market. Except for the very early London-American ones, that is. I got this lot for peanuts. There might be the odd gem amongst them, you never know.' He ferreted about and eventually pulled out half a dozen copies. He brushed them on his sleeve before handing them to me. 'Here's January to August. You might as well take the lot, but do let me have them back, won't you? I like to keep an unbroken set.'

I said I would and he wished me well with the show. 'I miss listening to you of an evening. Nobody else plays the records you play.'

'You'd better write to the station and tell them that.'

Back at the flat, Roly was waiting patiently. He looked towards the hook beside the front door where his lead was hanging. 'We're on the late walk this week,' I explained to him. 'Dinner first.'

I shoved a frozen chicken meal in the microwave, opened a can of Scrumpy Jack for me and a can of Chappie for the dog and put the new Blondie CD on the hi-fi. On balance, I think the evening at Maria's with the duckling and the Bomb had the edge.

When I'd finished the meal, I set about an examination of the *Record Collectors*.

My intention was to look for adverts offering to buy Beatles material, in particular ones that appeared in only one issue. I was working on the assumption that someone who advertised every month was more likely to be legitimate.

I worked my way through all eight issues and eventually came up with just one advert that appeared only once. It was in the July issue and read, *We will pay top prices for Beatles records, photos and any memorabilia. Write today with full details. No time-wasters.* There was no address or phone number, just a PO Box number in Chester. Was this the advertisement that Edgar Marshall had answered to his cost?

I took a plain sheet of paper and wrote offering for sale a tape of songs written and sung by John Lennon and previously unheard by anyone else. I didn't give my name and address, just my phone number, and sealed the letter in an envelope.

'OK,' I shouted to Roly. 'Walk!' and he immediately went over to the door and brought me his lead between his teeth.

We set off along the dock road. Since the Seaforth end was closed off, most private vehicles use Derby Road which runs a parallel route away from the river. We passed no pedestrians and, judging by the lack of cars parked outside the pubs, the licensed trade was having a lean time. I didn't see Gloria's bicycle outside the Atlantic.

Further away from town, there were more signs of activity. *The Bravo Merchant* was in dock, ready to leave for Dublin and, further along, the *Lagan Viking* had arrived from Belfast. On both sides of the road, rows of lorries were parked. Most of them had curtains drawn across their windows as the drivers slept in their cabs, a well-known truckers' scam to make on the expenses.

I posted the letter and we were back in the flat by midnight. I thought of trekking out to the casino to see if Owen Jenna was playing the tables again but decided it could wait till tomorrow night when I was seeing Hilary.

Tonight, back in my own bed again, I needed to catch up on some sleep.

First thing in the morning, I rang Mrs Skidmore before she left for work. 'Do you know anybody in Ormskirk your husband might have been calling on, the night he was killed?' I asked. If he was as straight as she insisted, the question should have held no mystery for her.

'In Ormskirk? Not that I can think of, not at that time of night, why?'

'George Cox said Bernard couldn't give him a lift to Standish because he was going on somewhere afterwards. To visit somebody in Ormskirk.'

'Oh, I see.' She sounded relieved. 'Well, I can explain that. Bernard never liked travelling with George because he chain-smokes, and it used to aggravate Bernard's rhinitis so he used to make excuses to go in his own car.'

I wasn't totally convinced but I let it pass.

'Have you found out anything yet about the people he convicted?' she asked.

'There were only six people that your husband sent to prison, Mrs Skidmore. I've spoken to all of them and none of them displayed any kind of antagonism towards him.'

'What about the others – the ones that were fined?'

'I hardly think a fine, however heavy, would drive a person to murder. But we are trying other avenues. We haven't given up yet.'

What the other avenues were I wasn't sure but I did know I'd soon have to think of some.

After breakfast, I drove out to Keith's Wine Bar in Lark Lane where I hoped I might find Badger, my tenant from Livingstone Drive. Badger was an habitué of Keith's, where he could often be found in the later morning perusing the papers and drinking several cups of caffé latte.

Badger is supposed to be studying for a doctorate at the University of Liverpool but, nocturnally, he moves among the more notorious of the city's glitterati at various charity and showbusiness functions. He might have come into contact with Owen Jenna.

I parked at the Aigburth Road end of the lane and walked down towards Sefton Park, stopping, as I always do, to read the notices in the window of the Mad Hatters Delicatessen.

Mad Hatters is an incredible store, a Liverpool institution. It's run by a girl called Kim who bakes bagels and croissants in big ovens in the shop and sells old-fashioned items like liquorice sticks and spices by the spoonful.

In the window, she displays customers' post cards pleading for the return of lost pets, often with some success. Amazingly, over half of them this morning were proclaimed FOUND in big red letters with touching postscripts like, *Yippee, Scully's home safe and sound*.

Beneath the cards was a harrowing letter concerning a frail eighty-eight-year-old lady who lived on her own nearby and who had been burgled numerous times in the past year. Now she'd nothing left to steal so the intruders had taken to throwing her against the wall instead as a kind of perverted game. The police seemed to be powerless and the writer asked the community for help.

So much for our civilised and caring society at the end of the twentieth century.

I stepped into Keith's and there was Badger, sitting in a corner reading the *Investors Chronicle*. He was easy to spot, wearing a mustard jacket, royal blue shirt and navy slacks.

'Make mine a large Chablis,' he said without seeming to look up.

'Luckily, your rent cheque didn't bounce this month so I might be able to manage that.'

I bought a glass of rosé for myself and joined him at his table.

'Wondering where to put your money, Badger? I heard MFI might be a good bet. A takeover in the offing.' I reckoned the Stock Exchange was pretty much like racing and Accordion Billy's tips were as likely as anyone else's to come up.

'Forget it, I'm sticking to gilts, man,' he said. 'And what brings you up to this neck of the woods?'

'You frequent gambling dens and other palaces of vice. What do you know about Owen Jenna?'

'The Merry Widower, you mean?'

'Not so merry, Badger.'

'Don't you believe it, man. Wifey gone, and he got a nice little bunny tucked away in a hutch in the country.'

'Really?' That was something that hadn't been mentioned before by anyone. 'And what about his exploits on the tables?'

'Ain't short of a few bob, that's for sure. He was at this Variety Club dinner last week, contributing generously to noble and not so noble causes.'

'What's the word on Mrs Jenna?'

Badger sipped his wine slowly. 'No word.'

'You think she's dead?'

'If she is, they could drain the Irish Sea and still not find the body.'

'But Owen Jenna thinks she's alive and he's hired me to find her.'

'Yeah, I heard you were a full-time private eye these days. What happened to you on the radio?'

'Sore point. I hope to be back soon.' Although it was becoming less likely as every day went by.

'That pillock they've got on now, he's a wanker. Plays no dance music, no rap, no hip-hop.'

'He's a Dennis Lotis fan. What do you expect?'

'So you're working for the Merry Widower, eh?' He leaned forward. 'He's got some face, that slimeball. I tell you, he don't want her found. He's happy as a pig in shit.'

'Where did his money come from suddenly?'

'Who knows. Maybe he bought MFI shares.' Badger laughed, showing off a recently jewelled tooth.

'Dig around,' I said. 'See what you can find.'

'I take it I'm on the payroll.'

'You know I'll see you right.'

He laughed. 'Why not just reduce the rent, man?'

I put down my empty glass and rose to leave. 'Find Susie Jenna and I might just do that.'

I was back at the office by twelve, in time for Jim Burroughs to acquaint me with the latest news.

'Your friend Harriman's out of jail.'

'How did he escape?'

'He didn't. His time was up: full remission. Came out this morning.'

'Strange he never mentioned it when I spoke to him. You can bet he'll be looking for the tape, but at least he's too late to kill Edgar Marshall.'

'That'll be some comfort to Edgar in his coffin, to know he can't die twice,' said Jim sarcastically.

I told him what I'd learnt about Owen Jenna from Badger.

'A bird in the country, eh? That's enough motive to convict him if only we could find the body.'

'You're forgetting, Jim. You're on the other side now; we're trying to prove he's innocent.'

'All the same,' said Jim. 'That's something he conveniently forgot to tell us.'

'Not to mention the money he seems to have come into.'

'He's killed her,' said Jim firmly. 'He's just using us to make himself look innocent.'

'Expensive way to do it.'

'Let's forget about Jenna for a minute. How did you get on with the Skidmore lead?'

'Total waste of time. Bernard was a wonderful, well-loved pillar of society just as everybody says he was. Actually, I nearly thought I had something. He told this George Cox he had to stop off in Ormskirk on the way home so he couldn't give him a lift.'

'An assignation perhaps?'

'That's what I thought except Mrs Skidmore reckons it was an excuse not to travel with Cox because his smoking upset Bernard.'

'Ormskirk, you say?' said Jim thoughtfully. 'Have you still got that list Mrs S. gave you?'

I pulled it out of my wallet and handed it to him.

'I thought so,' he said. 'Look, top of the page: Mr and Mrs Loder, Southport Road, Ormskirk.'

'They're a couple, Jim. He's hardly likely to be calling round for a quick jump at two in the morning with Mrs Loder while Mr Loder snores away upstairs. Unless, of course, he was working the video.'

'Clutching at straws, I'll admit, but we've nothing else to go on. Might be worth a visit.'

'It's not even market day,' I said, 'but you're right.'

I dialled the number and almost immediately a woman answered.

'Mrs Loder?' I enquired.

'Yes?' She sounded young and coquettish on the phone but I figured that, being a friend of the Skidmores, she was likely to be over fifty.

It was a bit like those seventy-year-old women who work the telephone sexlines and tell their panting callers that they're sixteen and wearing gym-slips. Wait till video phones come out; they'll soon be back in their rest homes living on their pensions.

I explained that I was investigating the death of Bernard Skidmore and I'd like to have a word with her. Her reaction was surprising. At first she sounded confused and reluctant but then she started to ask

110

questions about his death as if eager to learn more.

'Could I call round and see you?' I asked.

'Not here,' she said quickly. Too quickly. 'Can we meet in town somewhere?'

'Ormskirk, you mean?' We settled on Taylor's Coffee Shop in Moor Street at three o'clock.

'At last,' I told Jim Burroughs when I'd replaced the receiver, 'I think we may have unearthed something here.'

Chapter Twelve

Mrs Loder may not have been as young as she sounded but neither did she look fifty. I'd have put her at no more than thirty-nine. She had long, flowing dark hair, a wide smile and eyes of such a deep violet hue I thought she must wear coloured contacts. She had on a brightly coloured top with matching skirt and looked vivacious; she reminded me of Nanette Newman.

It was easy to pick her out – she was the only woman sitting alone – so I walked over to her table by the window. 'Mrs Loder?'

'Mr Ace?' She smiled and took my hand. 'Do call me Diana.'

'Johnny,' I said. 'Can I get you another coffee?'

'That would be nice.'

I ordered myself a tea to go with it and watched her as I stood in the self-service queue. She took a mirror out of her handbag and gave her lips a quick refresh.

'One coffee,' I said, returning with the tray.

She opened the handbag again, took out a tube of sweeteners and dropped one in her coffee. 'Better for the figure,' she smiled, leaning back to display it for my approval.

Instead I asked her how long she'd been having an affair with Bernard Skidmore.

To her credit, she never faltered. She took a spoon, stirred her coffee, drank a couple of sips and calmly said, 'Two years.'

So Irene Tidd had been right about 'Skiddy's' inclinations.

'How did you know?' Diana added.

'A wild guess.' She was the type of person I felt it best to be honest with. I guessed, too, she would respond to compliments. 'I had a vague idea before I came out here and now that I've met you, I know he wouldn't have been able to resist you.'

The dark violet eyes shone and she looked away. 'Nobody ever knew.'

I got the full story. The Loders had moved to Ormskirk three years ago and had joined the local golf club where Bernard Skidmore and his wife were also members. Mr Loder, Dougie, was a civil servant like Bernard Skidmore and the couples became friends.

'Elspeth never . . . how shall I put it? . . . satisfied him,' Diana announced with relish. 'One of those lie on your back, think of John Major types, you know what I mean?'

John Major would have been the last person on anybody's mind whilst having sex with Diana Loder, I thought.

'One day, Bernie brought some golf clubs round for Dougie when Dougie was away and that was that.'

'And you think nobody knew?'

'I'm sure they didn't. We carried on going out as a foursome, not all that often, maybe two or three times a year. Bernard kept Elspeth happy enough, a new car every couple of years, expensive clothes. As for Dougie, he's not too interested in the physical side of things any more. As long as he can get a round of golf in, he's happy as Larry.'

Much the same as George Cox said about Bernard Skidmore. How self-deluding people could be. Elspeth had said she was fulfilled – but that could mean anything. There were women in the nineteenth century who would carry a lifetime memory from a stolen glance across a dinner table.

Or perhaps Dougie and Elspeth were having it away on the side.

'He was coming to you the night he was killed, I take it?'

Her voice took on a sad note. 'Yes, Dougie was out of town with work. How do you know?'

'He told a friend he couldn't give him a lift that night as he had a call to make in Ormskirk.'

She looked alarmed. 'Elspeth never knew that, did she?'

'Yes, but it's all right. She thought Bernard was making an excuse not to ride in this man's car because he smoked.'

She smiled. 'Sounds like Bernie. He hated smoking.'

'The thing is, Diana, Mrs Skidmore thinks her husband was murdered.'

'What!' She almost knocked her coffee over.

'She believes somebody tampered with his car.'

'But why? Who'd want to kill Bernie? He wouldn't harm a fly.'

'Your husband, for starters. If he'd found out about your affair.'

'No, not Dougie. Like I said, he wasn't bothered about all that. He'd probably have thanked Bernie for standing in for him.'

I doubted it but didn't say so.

'What about Elspeth?' she suggested. 'I bet she'd be a vindictive sod if she had any inkling we were at it.'

'She's the one who hired me, so it won't be her.' I smiled. 'Have you any other lovers, Diana, who might have been jealous of the attention you were giving to Bernie?'

'Not at the time,' she whispered. 'And not since . . . so far.'

I didn't take up the invitation, although I was certain it was offered. It wouldn't take too long, I felt, before Diana found a replacement for Skidmore. 'I might need to talk to Dougie,' I warned her then, 'but don't worry, I won't drop you in it.'

'What will you say?'

'Just ask him if he knows if Bernie had any enemies. Maybe someone at the golf club.'

'Don't say you've talked to me.' I promised her I wouldn't. 'Poor Bernie,' she said. 'I waited all night for him. I thought he'd got drunk or something and had been taken home. Then Elspeth rang the next day and told me he'd had an accident. It could still have been an accident, couldn't it?'

'It could,' I admitted, but I was starting to get the feeling that it wasn't. The dam had been breached. How many more secrets about Bernard Skidmore were yet to come out?

I made it back to the office before Jim left to pick up Roly.

'I was right,' I told him. 'Skidmore's armour plate of virtue has been pierced. He's been getting a leg over Mrs Loder for the past two years, which means we've got a motive for Mr Loder – assuming he knew about it, of course.'

'Do you want me to go and see him if you're busy with the Jenna thing?'

'No, you're OK, I'll go tomorrow when I get back from Chester. You can see if there's anything on file on Loder though.'

'Will do.'

'I'm going down to Stanley's Casino tonight,' I said, 'to see if Owen Jenna shows up again.'

'You think he could be there?'

'A fair chance. Anyway, it'll be a night out for Hil if he's not.'

Hilary was pleased at the prospect of a night's gambling. Personally, I prefer to chance my money only when the odds are in my favour rather than the bank's. That's why I never buy lottery tickets.

We ate first at the Rat and Parrot pub in Bold Street, then walked round the corner to the casino.

Business was brisk. The lure of easy money was as strong as ever. I noticed that most of the players were either pensioners or Chinese. Old ladies in fur stoles and dripping with jewellery sat at the tables, their hard eyes glinting like Steve McQueen's in *The Cincinnati Kid*.

Owen Jenna was on the American roulette wheel, a blonde bimbo beside him with a thrusting cleavage.

'If her tits go any higher she'll be able to wear them as shoulder pads,' commented Hilary bitchily.

I smiled. 'You're only jealous.'

She pressed against me suggestively. 'You've never complained. Anyway, mine are as big as hers any day.'

I couldn't disagree. 'She's probably got one of those new bras with gel in them – you know, "the implant in the cup instead of in you".'

Hilary shuddered. 'Don't even talk about silicone. Makes me feel ill.'

I collected twenty pounds' worth of chips at the table from the croupier, split them with Hilary, and we moved across to the 'Merry Widower'.

'Surprise,' I said, taking the seat next to him which was vacant. Hilary stood behind me.

'Mr Ace. Is this just a coincidence or have you brought me news?'

'Pure coincidence. May I introduce Hilary Taylor, Owen Jenna.'

He turned to acknowledge Hilary and I looked hard at his companion until he was obliged to return the convention. 'Pleased to meet you, Miss Taylor. Er, this is my niece Chloë.' She gave a knowing grin that belied the title he gave her.

'Lucky tonight?' I asked, noting the substantial piles of chips beside him.

'So so.' He stood up. 'I think we ought to have a private word, Mr Ace.'

'Sure.'

I let Hilary take my place and followed him to the bar. 'It isn't what you think,' he said.

'It never is,' I replied. 'But I wasn't thinking anything, Mr Jenna.'

'She's not my real niece, Mr Ace. That is, she's not . . . let me explain.'

The explanation wasn't a simple one but I took it to be that Chloë was the daughter of his cousin who had gone across to Ireland on business and Jenna had promised to keep an eye on her. All entirely platonic, of course.

'Not a blood relation, as such, but not, as you might have first thought, a . . .' He searched for an appropriate word.

'Casual shag?' I suggested.

He looked livid but managed to blurt out the word, 'Quite.'

'Have you come into money, Mr Jenna?'

'Why do you ask that?'

'I don't know.' I tried to make it casual. 'Coming here, I suppose.' I vaguely gestured to the well-dressed crowd earnestly throwing chips onto the green baize.

'I like the ambience here, the air of anticipation, everyone thinking they could win a fortune on the throw of a dice. I'm not a big gambler:

117

I like a little flutter but no more than that. But let me ask *you* a question: have you made any progress yet in the search for my dear wife?' The word dear was heavy with sarcastic overtones. 'After all, finding her is what is important.'

Only, I thought, to prove his innocence. I was sure that Susie Jenna wouldn't be welcomed back to the connubial home with open arms if she eventually took up the role of The Prodigal Wife.

'I've spoken to a few people and I'm following up a couple of leads.'

'Make sure you keep me up to date on your progress.'

He made it clear the conversation was over and we returned to the table, where Hilary was looking quite elated.

'I put it all on number ten, my birthday,' she cried, 'and it came up.' She pointed to a large pile of chips at her side. 'Isn't that lucky?'

'It's because today's Friday the thirteenth,' I said, 'lucky for some.' We hung around for another hour, time enough for her to lose everything she'd made. Owen Jenna never spoke directly to me again although I heard his companion address him as 'Uncle' a couple of times, followed by a suppressed giggle.

Hilary came back to the flat and Roly moved dutifully to his basket when he saw her.

I was on edge and realised I was waiting for her to make some crack about Maria but she didn't. Instead, she took off her top and bra and sat on the bed swinging her boobs from side to side. 'Look,' she said. 'No implants.'

I thought of Bernard Skidmore, driving excitedly through the night, anxious to get to Diana Loder. Had she been waiting for him, naked and inviting like this?

And what about Chloë, Owen Jenna's 'niece', or 'bunny' as Badger had caller her? Presuming, of course, it was the same girl. Jenna could be running a string of dubious 'relatives'. It was not too difficult to imagine her in Jenna's bed. Except his mother was staying with him to look after the children. Where else would they go?

Both these cases seemed to revolve round sex. I'd decided when I set up the agency that I wouldn't take cases involving matrimonial disputes yet here I was, seemingly stuck with two of them.

'Well?' said Hilary, interrupting my reverie. 'Do you want me or not?' She reached out and pulled me onto the bed.

As it happened, I needn't have worried about the direction my work was taking. By tomorrow night, I'd be involved in another murder.

Chapter Thirteen

The phone call came before nine o'clock. He must have rung immediately he received my letter. Hilary was still asleep.

'You the bloke what wrote to me about the Beatles tape?' It was a young man's voice.

'The John Lennon tape, yes.'

'What do you want for it?'

'I don't know. What's it worth to you?'

'How do I know it's kosher? What's it look like?'

'It's an open-reel tape, recorded before 1963. You'll know it's genuine when you hear it.'

'I'd have to see it.'

'No problem. Where and when?'

'Give me your address and I'll come round.'

I remembered what had happened to Edgar Marshall. I didn't intend ending up the same way.

'It's rather inconvenient for you to come here. My wife doesn't know I'm selling it. Can I bring it to you?'

He hesitated. 'I'll meet you somewhere.'

'You're in Chester, aren't you?'

'Er, yes, that's right.' He didn't sound too sure.

I wanted to make it somewhere public where I was less likely to be ambushed. 'Then how about on the city walls under the Eastgate clock at noon?'

Again he hesitated before replying. 'Yeah. That'll do.'

It looked more likely by the minute that he could be my man. He didn't appear to have any premises and he was obviously reluctant to invite me to his house.

I made breakfast and took Hilary hers in bed. 'I've got to go out to Chester,' I said, 'but you have a lie-in. What time are you on duty?'

'Not until twelve, but don't worry, I'll let myself out like I usually do.'

I remembered I'd left the tapes at Maria's so I went into the lounge to ring her, being careful to close the bedroom door. I didn't want any more comments from Hilary. I still hadn't mentioned the holiday with Maria to her.

'Can you bring the tapes to the library and I'll pick them up?' I asked. Maria said she would.

I dropped Roly off at the office and told Jim about Owen Jenna's bit of stuff.

'You reckon he's giving her one?' he asked.

'Without a doubt, but that doesn't automatically mean he killed his wife. He's had affairs before, remember.'

'She's brown bread, Johnny,' declared Jim. 'I can feel it in my bones.' Another one. Him and Accordion Billy both.

'Anyway, at least there's news on the tape front, Jim.' I recounted my conversation with the caller from Chester.

'Do you think he'll turn up?'

'Bound to. He wants to get his hands on the tape.'

'What did he sound like?'

'Young and uneducated.'

'Hah! Probably an undergraduate at one of the new universities they've created to keep the dole figures down. Just you take care.'

My next stop was the Picton Library and Maria. I was lucky to grab a meter nearby.

'Was Hilary with you when you rang me?' were Maria's opening words when she came to the library counter.

'Why do you ask that?'

'Just the way you were speaking, that's all. Furtively, as if you were afraid she'd hear.'

'You're observant,' I said.

'Have you left her at your flat?'

For a wild moment, I had visions of Maria going round there and a raging battle ensuing, but I quickly dismissed the thought. The illicit liaisons in the Skidmore and Jenna cases were obviously affecting my thinking.

'I'm meeting this man in Chester who wants to buy the John Lennon tape,' I said, changing the subject.

'Oh, Johnny, be careful. What if it's the same man that Edgar Marshall got in touch with?'

'I'm hoping it is, although then I'll have to prove he killed Marshall.'

'Ring me when you've left him,' she said, 'or I'll be worried about you all day. Here are the tapes. I left the tape recorder at home – was that all right?'

I told her it was. 'I think I'll just take the one tape,' I said and put it inside a briefcase I'd brought along. 'You hang on to the other for me. I'll call as soon as I can, I promise.' And I set off to meet Edgar Marshall's possible murderer.

I took the Birkenhead Tunnel and the A41 to Chester, making sure I was giving myself plenty of time to find an empty parking spot. Chester is a nightmare city for motorists but then, aren't they all nowadays? Until the government develops a light rail-tram system linking every town in a kind of reverse-Beeching operation, people will have no alternative but to use their cars, however much they're penalised, and gridlock will set in everywhere.

I managed to find a place on the edge of town and walked to the city walls alongside the river which, in the August sunshine, was almost as full of boats as the roads were crammed with vehicles. I climbed the stone steps up to the old Roman path on top of the walls, passing several tourists with cameras and guidebooks.

It was a minute to twelve when I reached the clock, Chester's most famous monument. Below me, Eastgate was thronged with Saturday shoppers. I looked around to see if I could spot my man. Two teenage girls in mini-skirts and halter tops were stood giggling, probably waiting for boyfriends, and an old lady with a shopping trolley was taking a breather.

I felt a tap on my shoulder and wheeled round. He was in his early twenties, over six foot tall and dressed street style in a Levi cord blouson, T-shirt, combats and Cat boots. There was an air of aggression about him.

'Beatles tape?' was all he said. I nodded. 'Let's have a look then.'

I wondered if this was to be his new modus operandi. Mug the punter and make off with the goods. 'Not here,' I said. 'There's a pub on the next block, we'll go there.'

Reluctantly, he accompanied me back along the walls, down some steps and onto a street leading back towards the river.

'A beer all right?' I asked him when we got inside the pub.

'Bitter.'

I bought halves of bitter and cider and took them to the table where he was waiting uncertainly. I made sure I sat between him and the door.

'Where is it then?' he said after he'd taken a few sips.

'First of all, who are you? I like to know who I'm dealing with.'

'Joey's the name.'

I didn't want him to know my real identity. 'Albert,' I said. 'Albert Cronkshaw.'

'Let's see the tape then.'

I took it out of the briefcase and handed it to him. He examined it carefully. 'It says on the label *Bobby and the Voxtones at the Iron Door*.'

'That's Lennon's sense of humour,' I explained. 'Bobby and the Voxtones used to play with The Beatles on the Liverpool circuit. If you listen to the tape, you'll know it's Lennon.'

Now he looked annoyed. 'How can I listen to it? I've nothing to play this on. It could be anybody.'

'I've got a Grundig reel-to-reel recorder,' I said. 'Tell me where you live and I'll bring it round with the tape.'

'Friggin' hell. All right, I'll accept it's genuine. I'll give you a ton for it.' He pulled out a wad of ten-pound notes.

'You must be joking. You're looking at five grands' worth there.
At least.'

'Come off it,' was all he managed to say.

'Up to you.' I took the tape from him and put it back in the case.
'Tell me, did you get many replies to your advert?'

'What?'

'In the *Record Collector*.'

'A few. Why?'

'I just wondered. Did any of the other people offer you a John
Lennon tape like this?'

His answer was too aggressive. 'What do you mean? No, no one.
Why, who else has one?'

'Nobody I know of. Look, if you want to hear this tape, I'll come
back and bring a recorder over with me. Give me your phone number
and I'll ring you to fix a day.'

'I'm not on the phone.'

I took out a business card containing just the address and phone
number of the Dale Street office. 'I see. Well, if you want to come
over to Liverpool, this is my office and I keep all the equipment
there. I'll be able to play the tape to you, that is if you're seriously
interested.'

He took the card and put it in the side pocket of his combats.

'When are you there?'

'Ten to five most days, but ring first to make sure.'

At this point I stood up and walked out of the pub. I anticipated
one of two things might happen. He might make a grab for the case
or he might have an accomplice nearby to try the same thing.

In the event, neither happened. I walked round the corner from
the pub and waited in a doorway. It was five minutes before he
appeared, heading for the city centre. He didn't see me.

I gave him a good start then set off after him, keeping him in sight
until he turned a corner. I ran briskly forward but, by the time I
reached the adjacent road, he had disappeared in the crowds.

So much for my prowess at trailing a suspect. Maybe I should
have trained Roly. However, I'd done what I wanted to do which

was set a bait. Now I'd see if the lad followed it up like he, or somebody, had done with Edgar Marshall.

Chester was even more crowded than I remembered it from the old days with The Cruzads, when we used to play at Quaintways on a Monday night, supporting bands like Roxy Music and Thin Lizzy.

I called at The Mill Hotel beside the canal for a bar snack lunch and rang Maria to assure her I was safe.

'Do you want to come round tonight?' she asked.

'Love to, but it wouldn't be until after seven. I'm probably going over to Ormskirk when I get back from here.'

'After seven's fine. I'll cook a meal and you can watch your *Match of the Day*. Unless you'd rather go out somewhere?'

'A meal would be nice.' So would *Match of the Day* as Everton would probably be on. They were playing at Tottenham, a crucial game after the Villa defeat midweek.

I realised that I was seeing much more of Maria these days, but it seemed to suit me that way.

'Any good?' asked Jim, when I got back to the office. Jim had taken to coming in on Saturdays to avoid having to go round George Henry Lee's with his wife and his credit card.

'Dunno. He looked a right toe-rag. I reckon he's fronting for someone, he looks too thick to have thought of it himself.'

'Did he offer to buy it?'

'Handed me a fistful of tenners. I told him I wanted five grand.'

'And?'

'Nothing. I gave him this address so we wait and see what happens. The bait is set.'

'Let's hope your security pal's done a good job then.'

As part of the deal with Eddie Smeddles, we'd had the office fitted with a state-of-the-art CCTV system which included the facility of automatically locking the doors after any intruders had broken in.

'You can fill the room with tear gas if you want,' he said, 'and choke the buggers to death,' but, much as we appreciated the idea, we decided against that.

126

'I checked for form on Douglas Loder,' said Jim, 'but he's clean.'

'Never mind – it was worth a try. I'm on my way to see him now, all being well.' I picked up the phone and rang Diana Loder's number. A man answered and I asked to speak to Douglas Loder.

'That's me,' he replied pleasantly.

I explained that I was acting for Mrs Elspeth Skidmore and wanted a few minutes of his time to discuss her husband's accident. He seemed to think it was something to do with insurance and I didn't disillusion him.

'Do you want to come round now?' he suggested. 'We're not going out at all.'

'I'll be there within the hour,' I told him. I gathered Roly and hurried down to the car. I was on double yellows in Temple Street.

I switched on *Five Live* on the car radio to keep up to date with the football scores. By the time I reached Ormskirk, Everton were leading Spurs at Tottenham by two goals to one, two penalties converted by Unsworth. Things were looking up.

The Loders lived on the main road to Southport, on the edge of town. The house was only a three-bedroomed semi but it was expensively and tastefully furnished. Whatever her indiscretions, Diana made her husband a comfortable home.

'My wife, Diana,' said Dougie Loder as he led me into the front room after we'd introduced ourselves. He was a couple of inches shorter than her and a good few years older.

Diana didn't bat an eyelid. 'Pleased to meet you.' She took my hand and quietly squeezed it.

'Mr Ace has come about poor Bernard, dear.'

'Really? A very sad business. Bernie was a lovely man. We were very upset, weren't we, Dougie?' Before he could answer, she added, 'I'll put the kettle on and let you men talk.'

As soon as she left the room I turned to Dougie and came straight to the point. 'Mrs Skidmore believes her husband was murdered, Mr Loder. Is there anything at all you can tell me that might substantiate this claim?'

'Good Lord. Whatever makes her think that?'

'Had you heard any rumours about him at all?'

'Such as what?'

'Shady business deals, women on the side, the usual sort of thing.'

He looked shocked. 'No, not Bernie. The man was a paragon. Besides, civil servants don't get involved in business.' He explained to me how he and his late friend were mere pen-pushers for the State.

'What about the ladies?'

'Elspeth kept him on too tight a leash for that, although I wouldn't have said she needed to. Bernie would have preferred . . .' don't say it, I thought, '. . . a good round of golf any day.'

Diana walked in at that moment with a tray of tea things. She must have heard her husband's last remark because she made an 'I told you so' gesture with her mouth.

We talked about Skidmore over the tea. I asked the couple if his work as a magistrate had brought him any problems that they knew of.

'Like what?' asked Dougie.

'Threats, maybe.' But they knew of none.

'He did have a bit of a squabble with one of the fellows in his singing group,' ventured Dougie. I raised my eyebrows. 'He was in this barbershop quartet. Bernard was the leader and he replaced one of the long-serving members with this younger bloke for this show they were giving. The old 'un was none too pleased.'

'Do you know his name?'

Bernard thought for a minute. 'Somebody Barker. I met him once. A miserable old sod he was. I didn't blame Bernard at all. Crawford Barker, that was it. Lived in Maghull.'

I wrote the name down in my notebook. 'Not a common name,' I said. 'I should be able to find him.'

'I should think so.'

'He packed a lot in, Bernard, didn't he? Singing, golf, his work on the bench and I believe he was in a quiz team?'

'That's right. Monday or Tuesday nights were his quiz nights.

They played at a pub in Southport, I forget which one.'

'I don't suppose it's important.' Unless he'd thrown somebody out of the quiz team too and then there'd be somebody else with a grudge.

'Might have been the Hesketh, I'm not sure.'

'Like I say, it probably doesn't matter.'

I thanked them for their time. 'Call round anytime,' whispered Diana as she saw me to the door.

I wasn't tempted. Maybe at twenty I'd have taken her up on it. In fact at twenty, I'd have driven fifty miles for the merest possibility of some horizontal jogging, but not any more. I was reminded of the line in Roger McGough's poem, 'Today's Not a Day for Adultery', about venturing out in wet weather: '*At your age, a fuck's not worth the chance of catching flu.*'

I used to see McGough perform with The Scaffold at Hope Hall before he became one of the so-called Mersey Poets. I always felt he'd have made a better Poet Laureate than Pam Ayres. In the end, neither of them got the job.

I trudged wearily back to the RAV4, where a patient Roly was waiting. I'd told him we were going to Maria's and he seemed pleased.

I, however, wasn't quite so happy. The Skidmore case had come to yet another dead end and I was less than hopeful that the relegated singer would make the suspects list, though I'd probably visit Mr Barker just to make sure.

No, Bernard Skidmore was so squeaky clean and efficient he'd even managed to conduct a two-year affair without upsetting anyone. Who would want to kill such a saint?

I caught the last reading of the football results on the car radio and it didn't help my mood. The Blues had lost 3-2 to Spurs, two goals in the last ten minutes condemning them to their second defeat in a week.

I was relieved to get to Maria's.

'I'm a bit early,' I apologised.

She kissed me fondly. 'That's all right. Sit down and I'll bring you a glass of wine. I'm doing us a fish pie with Mediterranean vegetables.'

'Sounds fabulous.'

It probably was, but I never got the chance to find out.

My pager bleeped a message, *Ring Jim. Urgent.* It gave a number I didn't recognise.

'It's Albert Cronkshaw,' he said when I got through. 'He's been murdered.'

Chapter Fourteen

Jim had received a frantic message from the ex-drummer of Bobby and the Voxtones just after five o'clock. Albert had arrived home from an afternoon in the pub and thought he heard movements upstairs.

'Lucky I'd given him my home number,' said Jim.

Jim had told him to stay where he was and he drove straight round there but, by the time he arrived, he was too late. The front door was open, and when Jim went in, he found Cronkshaw lying on the lounge floor with the side of his head caved in.

'Just like Marshall,' I commented.

'No. Marshall had his throat cut. This fellow used some blunt instrument, maybe an axe. Cronkshaw had put up a fight but either there'd been more than one of them or the other fellow had had the measure of him.'

'Or he had a weapon and Albert didn't.' I felt guilty about not returning Cronkshaw's gun.

'The place has been trashed, of course, drawers turned inside out. They were obviously looking for the tape.'

'Where are you now? What is this number?'

'I'm at Cronkshaw's, waiting for the squad car to come. I think you should get down here right away. They're going to have to tie this in with Marshall's death.'

I groaned. So much for my quiet dinner. I'd be lucky to see a bed before breakfast. I told him I'd be right over.

'What's happened?' asked Maria, knowing from the look on my face it was something terrible. I told her and she put her arms round

131

me. 'All along I've said that tape was dangerous. Do you think it's the person you saw in Chester who's done it?'

'No.'

I didn't see how it could be, not so soon. I'd given Albert's name, purely out of whimsy, but I knew there was no way I could be responsible for his murder. I hadn't given his address and, as far as I knew, Joey had no knowledge of the real Albert Cronkshaw.

No, the person who'd killed Albert must have known about him already and been keeping tabs on him right from the moment he'd killed Marshall. I didn't doubt it was the same person who'd committed both murders. But who was he?

'Save my meal,' I said ruefully. 'I'll have it for breakfast. Where's Roly?'

'In bed already, I think. Leave him. He'll keep your place warm for you.'

The police had arrived when I reached Cronkshaw's house, which was near the old Green Lane tram depot, not far from Edgar Marshall's garage.

A forensic team was setting up their impressive array of equipment and Jim Burroughs was talking to one of his ex-colleagues in the hall.

'This is Detective Inspector Bennett, Johnny, Mike to his friends.' Bennett was a tall, bronzed man with square shoulders and a cherubic face. 'Mike was the station tennis champion,' Jim added, presumably hoping to introduce a note of informality into the proceedings. Mike and I shook hands.

'Jim tells me you were working for the deceased.'

'He hired us to find out who murdered his friend, Edgar Marshall,' I said quickly. No reason to tell Bennett that we were actually supposed to be protecting Albert Cronkshaw from harm. Why advertise your failures?

'Is that so?' He sounded sceptical. 'Let's go upstairs into one of the bedrooms where we won't be disturbed. We need to sit down and sort all this out.'

The sorting took two hours. Needless to say, Mike Bennett was none too pleased that the John Lennon tape had not been mentioned originally in connection with Edgar Marshall's death, especially when I had obviously known it was the main reason for the break-in. Nevertheless, I still saw no grounds for mentioning my visit to Chester and I noticed Jim kept quiet about that too.

'So, Mr Ace, the story you told the officers at the scene of the crime, namely that you'd called to see Marshall about repairs to your car, was inaccurate.'

I admitted it was. 'But, at the time, I didn't see a connection between him once owning this tape and his murder.'

'But you do now?'

'Now that Cronkshaw's been murdered, I agree it's possible.'

'What do you know about Marshall other than he once owned the tape?'

'Only that he mended cars for a living and, in his earlier days, he was Bobby of The Voxtones. Remember, I never met the man when he was alive.'

'You don't know anything about his financial situation, for example?'

'No. Why, is it relevant?'

'It may be. He paid a thousand pounds in cash into his account a few days before his death.'

'Perhaps he had another John Lennon tape and he sold it.'

'That's what I thought. But you don't know of one?'

'No.'

'How did you find out it was Marshall who put the tape into the auction?'

'From the auctioneer. It wasn't a secret.'

'So why go round to see him? You'd already bought the tape legitimately.'

'I was curious to know where it had come from and if there were any more like it.'

'And you say there weren't?'

'According to Albert Cronkshaw there was only the one. Marshall had been mending The Beatles' van, found the tape lying inside and kept it.'

'Did you know Marshall's house had been broken into on previous occasions, presumably by somebody looking for the tape?'

'I met a burglar called Frank Harriman in Altcourse prison, oddly enough concerning another case. He told me he'd broken into a flat in Old Swan looking for a Beatles tape, and I realised it was the same one that I had.'

'But you didn't tell Harriman that?'

'Certainly not. But that's when I went to see Marshall again.'

Bennett jumped in quickly before I had time to cover up my slip. 'Again?'

'Yes. I'd been to the house the day before I saw Harriman, but Marshall was out.'

'What made you break into the house on the second occasion?'

'I just had this feeling something was wrong. I'd rung the bell and there was no answer, then I remembered Harriman saying he'd entered through the back window. I went round the back and, sure enough, it hadn't been fixed so I climbed in. And that's when I found Marshall's body.'

'If you'd never met him, how did you know it was Marshall?'

'It was his house, his bed. A fair assumption, I would have thought.' Now it was my turn to be sarcastic.

'Where did Cronkshaw come into it?'

I explained how Cronkshaw had subsequently called at the office looking for the tape, and how I'd had to break the news to him of his friend Edgar Marshall's death. I didn't mention the gun, not least because I still had it and I thought it might come in useful on some future occasion.

''He wanted protection as much as anything,' I admitted. 'He was frightened that whoever killed Marshall would come after him.'

'He was right too,' said Bennett bitterly. 'But why do you think they killed him? After all, he didn't have the tape.'

'Neither did Marshall, come to that, and it didn't save him either.'

'Who knows you've got the tape now? Where is it, by the way?'

'At my girlfriend's. As for who knows, search me. Anyone could find out my address from the auction rooms if they've traced the tape that far. I mean, how else would they have found Cronkshaw?' I didn't need Bennett to tell me that I must be next on the murderer's guest list.

'And you've no idea who the killer might be?'

'Only that Harriman can't have killed Edgar Marshall because he was inside at the time.'

'He may have had an accomplice.'

'You'd better ask him. It's not my job any more. My client's dead.'

Detective Inspector Bennett looked stern. 'As long as you have that tape, I think you'll find you *are* involved, Mr Ace, whether you like it or not. I'm pretty sure these people, whoever they are, won't give up that easily. However, this time I should appreciate it if you'd contact us as soon as you have any information.'

Suitably admonished, Jim and I were allowed to leave.

'I wonder who else does know about this tape?' Jim asked as we walked to our cars.

'Harriman's the only one who we can say definitely.'

'Plus Joey, of course. He could have killed Marshall even if he didn't touch Cronkshaw.'

'That one could still be down to Harriman.'

Jim looked doubtful. 'I can't see there being two different murderers, can you?'

I couldn't. The Chester connection puzzled me. 'We know Harriman did the first break-in at Marshall's. If this Joey character was the second, the one that scrawled *we'll be back* on the wall, he could have come back and killed Marshall like he promised.'

'But Joey wouldn't have known about Cronkshaw.'

'Not so far as we are aware, unless . . .'

'Unless what?'

'Unless Joey was at the auction too.'

'You were there. Do you remember seeing him?'

I hadn't taken too much notice of the people around me and certainly couldn't recall the youth I'd met in Chester as having been

135

present. 'I can't be a hundred per cent certain but I don't think so, no.'

Jim went on. 'Harriman knew about Cronkshaw. Albert said he was there when he first called round to see the tape.'

'But Harriman couldn't have killed Marshall.'

There was a silence as we both considered the dwindling options. We were going round in circles.

'So Bobby and the Voxtones have joined the singing dead,' I remarked at last.

'The what?'

'Something Maria said. All the old rock 'n' rollers that are no longer with us, she called them the singing dead.'

'Sounds like a good name for a band. Who's the lead singer – Buddy Holly?'

'Very funny.'

'You're forgetting, though, Johnny – The Voxtones' bass player emigrated to Australia. He's probably still alive.'

'I wouldn't bank on it. Might have been savaged by koala bears and left for the vultures.'

'I don't think they have vultures in Sydney,' said Jim, icily.

'Possibly not.' I stopped as we reached the cars. 'I don't know about you, Jim,' I said, 'but I've had enough for today. I'll see you in the office on Monday morning.'

'Before you go—' I was putting the key into the RAV4, '—how did you go on with that Loder chap in Ormskirk?'

'Oh, a wasted journey. He'd no idea his wonderful chum Bernie had been slipping his wife one. And now he never will.'

'So we cross him off the suspects?'

''Fraid so. He did mention some old chap who might have a grudge though – somebody our kindly magistrate had booted out of his barbershop group.'

'Hardly grounds for topping him.' Jim sniggered.

'Precisely. I tell you what though, if you're ever looking for a bit on the side – you know, a change from Rosemary – I think Mrs Loder may well be willing to take you on if you'd like to pop along and interview her.'

Jim shuddered as he opened his car door and quickly slid into the driving seat. 'Not with my angina, Johnny. I'm thinking of putting bromide in Rosemary's cocoa as it is. I'll see you on Monday.'

I reached Maria's in time for the start of *Match of the Day*. Maria was lying on the settee with Roly beside her.

'I suppose you'll want your dinner now.'

'I certainly will, I'm starving. I've had nothing since a soup and sandwich in Chester at lunchtime and that seems like days ago.'

'What is it they say? "Your dinner's in the dog".'

'What!'

She laughed. 'Not all of it, though I must say he seemed quite partial to fish pie.' Roly drooled at the mention. 'I'll pop it in the microwave. There's still some wine left in the bottle.'

I watched the goals on TV as I ate. Everton were unlucky. They'd played well enough at Tottenham to earn a draw.

Maria waited until I'd finished my meal and the programme was over before asking me about the murder. There was nothing much more I could tell her.

'He was a big man but he wouldn't have stood a chance against someone young and fit who had a weapon in his hands.'

'I'm just relieved it wasn't you, Johnny,' and she put her arms round me and kissed me. 'I played the tape again whilst you were out,' she said in a brighter voice. 'It's quite good, isn't it? What'll happen to it when you sell it?'

'Probably it will come out on a CD released by one of the majors. That is, unless Paul McCartney buys it for his private collection.'

'You could make a fortune from this, Johnny.'

I supposed Edgar Marshall had thought the same.

I stayed over at Maria's all day Sunday. We took Roly for a walk on the beach and had lunch at the BS, as the Blundelsands Hotel is known locally. I finally went back to my flat in the early evening, after we'd watched *Heartbeat*. I wanted to see if I had any messages, but there were none. Out of curiosity, I checked the office ansaphone on the remote and the sound of Owen Jenna's voice came on. He sounded angry but scared. The message was short and to the point.

'Can you get down here? Somebody's tried to kill me.'

I didn't go round but I rang him. He'd calmed down quite a bit but was still a trifle incoherent with rage.

Slowly I prised the story from him. He'd been in town, crossing Mount Pleasant, making for the multi-storey where he'd parked his car, when this vehicle, which had been parked by the side of the road, started up, accelerated and drove straight at him. Luckily, he'd seen it just in time and leapt out of the way.

'I don't suppose you got the number, but did you notice the make of car?' I asked.

'No, but I think it was a taxi.'

'A taxi?' Not the usual vehicle to use in a deliberate hit and run.

'I'm sure it was. Not a black cab, a private hire one. There was a plate on the back. I think he'd been waiting for me.'

It seemed silly asking Owen Jenna if he had any enemies. After the never-ending newspaper updates about his missing wife, most of them containing scarcely veiled suggestions that he'd killed her, it was a wonder that a lynching party had not already strung him up on a gibbet outside St George's Hall.

'Any idea who it might have been?'

'Most people in this city want me dead and it's all that friggin' woman's fault.' He sounded so genuinely annoyed, I could have almost believed that he hadn't done away with Susie after all.

He grumbled on about his missing spouse for a few minutes until I eventually said, 'Come in to the office in the morning and we'll work out some plan of action.'

I arranged to meet him at eleven, intending to make sure I was there an hour earlier to have time to discuss the case with Jim.

In the event, I was at Dale Street for ten past nine, just the length of time it took me to drive there after Jim's phone call to say we'd been burgled.

They'd turned the place over good style. Every drawer was flung on the floor, papers scattered everywhere, cupboards had been ransacked and chairs and tables overturned.

'Bastards,' hissed Jim through clenched dentures.

'Look on the bright side,' I replied. 'At least they didn't shit on the photocopier.'

'Never mind that, look at the wall.'

The message had been sprayed on with black paint. *We'll be back* it read.

'Exactly the same inscription that was left at Edgar Marshall's when his flat got turned over.'

'Must be the same people.'

'Which lets out Harriman because we know he couldn't have done that one.'

Roly sniffed his way carefully round the room. 'Thinks he's a bleeding bloodhound,' snarled Jim. 'He should have been here to stop them.'

'What went wrong with the security system?' Eddie Smeddles was going to have some questions to answer.

'Well, they smashed the camera lens in for a start so we've no video record of them. As for the alarm, it was still going off when I came in but nobody took a blind bit of notice.'

'At least we know why they came. They were after the John Lennon tape.'

'We knew that anyway. We were expecting them,' Jim snorted. 'Your pal Eddie's got a lot to answer for.'

'I can't understand it,' I said. 'Why didn't the security door trap them after they got in?'

'Simple. They blocked it open with the wastepaper basket.'

So much for modern technology.

'Have you rung your lot?' I asked.

'I wish you wouldn't keep saying my lot. I left the Force months ago. They're not my lot any more.' He seemed excessively touchy and I wondered if he was missing the involvement of police work. Either that or his piles were playing up.

'Sorry.' When he didn't reply, I ventured, 'So they're on their way, are they?'

He managed a 'yes' and I went into the kitchen to brew up and fetch Roly his bone.

Two constables arrived an hour later and took a few details before promising that someone from CID would call back to carry out a scene of crime investigation. By this time, Jim had calmed down, we'd restored the desk and chairs to a semblance of order and I was able to recount the phone call from Owen Jenna.

'He's on very dodgy ground,' he said, 'claiming somebody tried to run him down. It's an easy enough thing to say, but bloody difficult to ever prove. Didn't Skidmore's missus say the same thing about her old man?'

'Yes, in London Road. She said he'd jumped into a doorway to save himself.'

Jim looked sceptical. 'No, I can't buy it. I mean, even if it were true, you'd never convince a jury. Too much doubt.'

'Jenna did say the car only started moving when the driver recognised him.'

'Even so, in a court of law, you'd never get a result on an attempted murder charge. The best you could hope for would be dangerous driving.'

'Maybe,' I mused. 'Unless, of course, the driver had a motive for killing that particular person.'

'Possibly,' conceded Jim. 'But half Merseyside would feel they had a motive for running down Owen Jenna.'

'That's what he said, too.'

'What's the score with the floosie? Did he mention her?'

'No, but his mother's there looking after little Wayne and Kylie so he can hardly have her shacked up there. Besides, the tabloids would soon latch on to it if he had.'

'So he was nipping over to hers for his mattress-dancing sessions then?'

'I suppose.' I didn't feel Owen Jenna's extra-marital activities were a vital part of the case. After all, it was a known fact that he'd always had his 'floosies' as Jim called them, even when Susie was with him.

'We're going to have to look at this from a different angle,' I said. 'I think we'll have to make the assumption that Susie Jenna is alive and take it from there.'

'What difference will that make?'

'We've always gone along with the popular view that she's really dead, so we've been concentrating on Owen Jenna and what *he's* doing – possibly because we're hoping to catch him out, just like the police seem to be. I think we ought to turn all our attention to Susie. Who were her friends? What did she do with her time? We don't really know much about her.'

'We know she was a housewife and mother.'

'And her parents were dead, yes, but what about work? Most women have at least a part-time job these days. What did she do before she was married? Had she been married before? Jenna said she went out clubbing at weekends, so who was she with? We don't know about any of her mates.'

'I see what you mean.'

'Owen should be able to give us some of the answers. He'll be here any minute.'

'Before he comes,' said Jim, 'this Joey character you mentioned, from Chester. It might not have been him who trashed the office, you know. Thinking about it, it's more likely to have been Harriman. He'd remember you from your visit to Altcourse.'

'He wouldn't connect me to the tape though. Remember, I told him I was there to talk about Bernard Skidmore's death.'

'Yes, but what if it was Harriman who killed Cronkshaw? Cronkshaw would almost certainly have told him you'd got the tape, if only to try to save his own skin.'

'Didn't work, did it?' I tried to sound flippant but Jim's hypothesis had the ring of truth. In which case, Harriman must have thought I was taking the piss out of him in prison. I'd allowed him to tell me how badly he wanted this tape and said nothing about being the person who actually had it.

'It's not only the tape he'll be after,' warned Jim. 'He'll feel he has a score to settle with you and you said yourself he was dangerous.'

I'd no time to worry about this last statement because just then Owen Jenna arrived. He wore a white polo shirt with a navy stripe which showed off his suntan but he seemed to have more lines on his face than when I'd last seen him in the Casino.

'We had burglars,' I explained as he looked around the office at the chaos. 'Nothing was taken and everything's under control. Have a seat and tell us again about last night.'

I allowed him to repeat his story of the attempt on his life. There was nothing more he could add to what he'd told me on the phone.

'Have you been in touch with the police?' I asked.

'No, I haven't. Even if they believed me, I don't feel they'd bother to do much about it. They never have before.' He laughed bitterly. 'Maybe it wasn't a taxi, maybe it was an unmarked police car.'

'Whatever it was, we must assume it was a genuine attempt to kill you,' I said, 'in which case you need to be extra vigilant in case they try again.' I was glad he didn't ask for round-the-clock protection. Our record in that department was not good. 'However, the chances are it was just some nutter. A professional wouldn't miss.'

Before he could dwell too closely on my last remark, I fed him some questions of my own about his wife.

'It's all been in the papers,' he said wearily. 'Everything you need to know.'

'She's described as a housewife, Mr Jenna, but what did she do before you were married?'

'Worked in an office.'

'Where was that?'

'She had a few jobs. Never stuck at anything long.'

'Did she have a part-time job at all after she had the children?'

He seemed reluctant to answer. Perhaps the thought of a working wife offended his sense of masculinity. 'She helped a friend out a few times,' he admitted at last.

'Where was that?'

'This firm she worked for, when they needed an extra typist.'

'Perhaps you'd be good enough, Mr Jenna,' broke in Jim, 'to

make us a list of companies for whom your wife worked. That is, if you are serious about us finding her.'

He couldn't say much to that except to agree.

'What about her social life?' I asked. 'Where did she go at nights and who with?'

'I told you, she went clubbing in town.'

'Who with?'

'I don't know who they were.'

'You mean, she could have been with other men?'

'No, I don't,' he thundered. 'She just said she was going out with the girls.'

'And you don't know who they were?'

'I wasn't her keeper.'

'What about her family?'

'She had no family. Her parents were killed abroad and she was the only child.'

'Aunts, uncles?' mused Jim, speculatively.

'No one,' repeated Jenna.

'Had she been married before?'

'Certainly not.' He made it sound as if he regarded women who remarried as second-hand goods.

'It must have been like a feudal kingdom in that house,' I said to Jim Burroughs after he'd gone. 'Woman as chattel, man as king of the lair.'

'About time they brought the system back,' grumbled Jim who had regular battles with Rosemary over his consumption of Newcastle Brown.

'What do you think, then, about Jenna?' I asked him.

'He seemed very reluctant to part with any information about his wife's comings and goings.'

'He'll tell us in the end,' I said confidently. 'Has to, if he wants to retain any credibility – and he's already spent a grand trying to convince us he means it.'

'So why try to hide everything?'

'I believe he genuinely doesn't know who she went out with. As long as it wasn't another man, he probably didn't give a shit.'

'I notice you didn't ask him about the floosie,' Jim snorted.

'No point. And her name is Chloë. It would only antagonise him.'

Jim leaned back in his chair and took a sip from his mug. 'Ugh, cold.' He put it down. 'What's next on the agenda?'

'I'll contact Joey in Chester and invite him round to hear the tape.'

'Do you think he'll bite? After all, he's already had the address from when you saw him.'

'True, but if it was him that broke in here, he's gone away empty-handed so he needs to get in touch with me again to find out where the tape really is.'

'I suppose so. And if it wasn't him that broke in?'

'Makes no difference. He still wants the tape.'

'Right. And what about Skidmore?'

'I'm going to see this barbershop fellow, Barker. You know, for a minute this weekend, I thought we'd hit onto something with Skidmore but it's all gone pear-shaped again.'

'Accidental death then?'

'Guess so, but I'll give it this one last crack. In fact, I'll go there now while I think about it. Leave you to deal with the CID.' I just managed not to say 'your lot'.

Barker actually lived in Lydiate, just past Maghull, in Hall Lane, out in open farming country. When he opened the front door and invited me into his lounge, a record of the D'oyly Carte version of *The Mikado* was booming out of the hi-fi.

He turned down the volume and indicated I should sit on one of the chintz-covered chairs circling a mahogany coffee-table. Crawford Barker was a small man with a ring of silvery hair and a similarly coloured tuft under his nose that could have passed for a moustache in a poor light. He wore a woollen cable-knit cardigan in beige.

'Bernard Skidmore,' he repeated, when I explained the reason for my visit and we'd exchanged regrets about the magistrate's demise, 'had every right to replace me in the quartet. His voice had

144

the beginnings of that wavering high-pitched whine which often occurs in men of advancing age. 'Even if I didn't agree with his decision.'

'And you didn't?'

'I may be getting on,' he grumbled, 'but my pitch is better than the young bounder who took my place.'

'You were replaced with a younger singer then?'

'And someone new to the group.'

'So you feel rather aggrieved at Mr Skidmore?'

Surprisingly, Crawford Barker chortled. 'On the contrary, he did me a favour. The very day afterwards, I was offered a part in the Maghull Operatic Society's next production which I was delighted to accept. They're an excellent company, you've probably seen them.'

'A few times.' I changed tack. 'Was Bernie a well-liked man, generally speaking?'

'Oh yes. A bit self-righteous but not a man to make real enemies. I'd say his wife is probably feeling guilty that she didn't pick him up from his outing, so she feels she has to pass on the blame.'

It was a thought that hadn't occurred to me but I didn't give it much credence. Men didn't have their wives ferrying them from Gentleman's Evenings, especially if, as in Skidmore's case, they had a secret liaison planned for later. More likely, he was in such a hurry to get to Mrs Loder that he overshot the corner, with fatal consequences.

I left Mr Barker to his Gilbert & Sullivan and decided to drive across to Parbold and take a look at the corner myself.

Traffic on the road in question was pretty constant. It was the main drag up to the M6 from Burscough, and also the route to Standish and Wigan. On the night in question, however, there would have been few cars about.

The road came down steeply from 300 feet. I drove to the top of the hill and stopped at a pub called the Wiggin Tree at the summit.

'Time for lunch,' I informed Roly. I went in and ordered a chicken sandwich which I took, along with my cider, to a table outside, collecting the dog from the car on the way.

The view looking down over the West Lancashire plain was pretty spectacular. I could see the twin spire and steeple of Ormskirk Church, Liverpool's cathedrals and Southport's gasholders below me and, in the distance, right out to the Irish Sea with Blackpool Tower to my right and the Welsh hills to the left.

Roly seemed more interested in scraps being fed to him by two children at the next table.

When we'd finished eating, I took the Toyota slowly down the hill, to the annoyance of the vehicles building up behind me, until I came to the spot where Bernard Skidmore had come off the road.

It was a tight right-hand bend and I could quite easily see how somebody not familiar with the road might overshoot it. Especially at night. Especially with a couple of drinks inside them.

The lamp-post he'd hit was still awry and the fence was still unmended where his car had smashed through before overturning and catching fire spectacularly in the field behind.

I turned off on the Upholland Road and stopped at Ashurst Beacon to give Roly a run on the heath before making for the M58 back to Liverpool.

'Any joy?' asked Jim, when I got back to the office.

'No. Barker's harmless and it turned out Skidmore did him a good turn kicking him out of his band.' I explained about his higher aspirations with the Maghull Operatic. 'I don't reckon we can do much more with Skidmore, Jim. Nobody hated him and I've been to inspect the road. It's a very dodgy bend. Mika Hakinnen could have trouble with it on a bad night.'

'So do we tell Mrs S. she was mistaken, as we thought all along anyway, and wrap it up?'

I hesitated. 'Leave it for a day or two.'

'Got to justify the fee, you mean?'

'No. Just a hunch I have.'

'But you just said . . .'

'I know I did, but it occurs to me that if anybody *had* wanted to do away with our Bernard, they had the perfect opportunity that night. Him safely in the hotel, his car unattended outside.'

'But the motive, Johnny? You said it yourself, everybody loved the bleeder. I say we ditch the Skidmore enquiry and start worrying about who trashed this office. You know, looking at this mess, it seems to me it was a good job we weren't here at the time of the break-in or we could be singing along with Skidmore now in the clouds.'

I thought so myself and I knew that whoever our visitor was, he'd be out there waiting for me, ready to strike again. I didn't find this knowledge comforting.

I had a date with Hilary at eight. We were going out for a meal then back to her cottage in Heswall. I'd arranged for Roly to stay overnight with Geoffrey. He hadn't been too keen until I promised him a bonus in his wages. 'Danger money, is it?' he grunted. I dropped off the dog at the Aigburth Road office on the way to the hospital to pick up Hilary.

'Where do you fancy eating?' she asked.

'I thought we'd go to the Village Hotel in Bromborough. It's on the Hi-Life card so we might as well take advantage.'

Last Christmas, Hilary bought me a year's subscription to a dining club which entitled the holder and guest to up to fifty per cent discount on meals in over two hundred pubs and restaurants in the area. We'd easily got our money's worth from it over the months.

'Fine.'

The hotel was busy, there was a buzz in the restaurant and the meal was good. I had the chicken, Hilary chose the salmon and we shared a bottle of Muscadet.

Between the dessert and the coffee, she leaned across the table and said, 'Your birthday's on a Sunday this year, isn't it?'

'I'll take your word for it.'

'It is. Well, on the Saturday night, can we go and see *Phantom of the Opera* at the Empire? It's the last night and I really want to see it. Then we can go back to yours and I can give you your present . . .' her shoeless foot stroked my thigh under the table as she was speaking '. . . and we can spend your birthday together.'

Her words struck me with the force of a blow to the stomach. My holiday with Maria was starting that same weekend. I'd not yet worked out what I was going to tell Hilary. Now I wouldn't have time. I felt sick.

'Can't we go one day in the week?' I suggested hopefully. 'It'll be packed out on the last night.'

'It's packed out every night but I've been promised a couple of tickets. Part of your present,' she added.

There was no way out for me. 'There's a bit of a snag with that, Hil, I'm afraid,' I began. She looked at me sharply. 'I've promised Maria I'll go to the Norfolk Broads with her for a week and we leave on that Saturday.' Hilary never spoke but her lips tightened.

'It's with her sister and her husband,' I explained. I figured if she knew it wasn't a cosy twosome she might feel better about it.

I was wrong.

'Oh, you're really getting your feet under the table there, aren't you?' she cried. The couple at the next table looked across as she raised her voice.

'It's not like that.'

'I knew that Maria would be trouble one day. She's like a rash, creeps up on you and before you know where you are, she's smothered you.' Hilary stood up and threw her napkin on the table. 'Don't bother to take me home, I can find my own way.' And she stormed out.

Hilary had never reacted like this before. But then, I'd never taken anyone else on holiday before. I didn't follow her. Instead, I reached out and poured myself another glass of wine.

It hadn't been a good week. Of my first three real cases, two had reached unsatisfactory impasses whilst I seemed to be under real danger of imminent death from the third. I still hadn't got my radio show back and now, my girlfriend of twenty years had walked out on me.

What more could go wrong?

The answer was, plenty.

Chapter Fifteen

Roly hadn't been best behaved at Geoffrey's. He'd eaten the remains of the Sunday roast lamb, gorged himself on a box of Roses and was sick in the night all over the lounge Axminster. Most of the vomit consisted of silver paper.

Luckily, Geoffrey's mother loved dogs and especially Roly who always saved his best smile for her. The creep.

I arrived late at the Ace Estates office for my Tuesday morning visit. On my lonely return to the flat at midnight, I'd got through another bottle of inferior hock and fallen asleep on the lounge floor to the accompaniment of a Chess compilation blues album on repeat play on my juke-box. Now, after eight hours of subliminal Elmore James, Buddy Guy, and a selection of Chicago blues wailers, I had the mother of headaches to show for it.

'A hard night, boss?' enquired Geoffrey unnecessarily. I just glared at him.

I hadn't made up my mind whether or not I should ring Hilary, but I remembered reading once in a magazine a piece of advice from Errol Flynn. 'When in doubt, leave it out'. He had actually been talking about steps to avoid catching syphilis at the time but I felt it held up in my situation.

'I've got a tenant for Kirkdale,' said Geoffrey brightly. 'An Indian girl – works at the Royal Infirmary. Hilary will probably know her.'

'I wouldn't know about that.' Geoffrey glanced quickly across at the tone of my voice but wisely said nothing.

I attended to the week's paperwork, which took me twice as long as normal. I also wrote the letter to Joey in Chester, inviting him to come to Dale Street on Friday to hear the John Lennon tape.

At lunchtime, Jim Burroughs rang. 'I thought you might still be there. Owen Jenna's been in with that list of his wife's jobs.'

'That was quick.'

'I think he's realised he has to make a show of co-operating.'

'I'll be in later.'

I couldn't face lunch. Instead I risked a glass of Andrews.

Geoffrey watched the bubbles bursting in the glass. 'I should have given some to that dog last night,' he declared. Roly looked pained.

I got across to Ace Investigations in the late afternoon, and found Jim poring over some papers at his desk.

'Where's Jenna's list then?' I said impatiently.

He gave me a shrewd glance. 'A night on the tiles, was it?'

'I was at a Marathon Beetle Drive at the Grassendale Women's Institute, OK? Now give me the frigging list.'

'All right, keep your shirt on.' He handed over a typewritten sheet of paper. 'Jenna was right about one thing, his wife's had a few jobs in her time.'

I studied the list. 'This is interesting. She once worked at the Smedley Hydro in Birkdale. That's where Bernard Skidmore worked. Coincidence, do you think?'

'I wouldn't read too much into it. It was before she met Jenna and most people have worked at Smedley at one time or another. It's the National Registrar's office. They get through more part-time workers there than cabinet ministers have call girls.'

'Who are European Carriages? She's done three stints with them, the first one seven years ago.'

'That's the outfit Jenna himself works for. That's probably when she met him.'

'Sound a bit grand, doesn't it? I thought he was in car rentals.'

Jim checked the dates. 'She doesn't seem to have worked there since they were married.'

'It's obvious why, isn't it? He was having an affair with this other woman who worked there. He wouldn't have wanted Wifey around to witness their knee-tremblers in the stationery cupboard. Do we have her name, by the way, the harlot?'

'Hang on, I've got the *Sun* cutting somewhere.' Jim shuffled papers in his file. 'Here we are: *attractive 26-year-old Mrs Lisa Charnock*. Quite a looker, judging by the photo.'

'I thought the police weren't MCPs any more?' I studied the picture. '*Mrs*, eh? I wonder what her husband thought of it all? I might go and have a word with this Mrs Charnock.'

'If she's still working there.'

'I'll find her if she isn't. Where's the friend that Susie Jenna's supposed to have done the typing for? She doesn't seem to be on here.'

Jim peered at the list. 'Hasn't he put her down? Must be because it wasn't a proper job.'

'Remember to ask him next time he's in, it could be important. You know what's odd, Jim? We still don't know the names of any of her chums.'

'Perhaps she had none.'

'Then who was she with all these nights she was supposed to be out on the town? No, she must have had some. She'd meet other mums at playschool, for instance.'

'I've been through the newspaper reports. Lots of people have been interviewed but they've mostly been neighbours. No friends.'

'I've read them. All the neighbours said the Jennas were a nice family that kept themselves to themselves. What they really meant was, "He used to beat the shit out of her but I don't want to get involved".'

'You're probably right.'

'I'll ring Mrs Charnock,' I said. 'Throw me the phone book. I presume she's still working there.' I dialled the number.

'Good afternoon, European Carriages, Sandra speaking, how may I help you?' The usual receptionist-speak. It's hard to tell the people from the robots these days.

'Mrs Charnock, please.'

'I'm afraid Mrs Charnock no longer works here, sir.'

'Do you have a forwarding address or phone number?'

'I'm sorry, but we aren't allowed to give those out.'

'Oh.'

'Are you a friend of hers, by any chance?'

'Yes.'

Her voice brightened and lost some of its robotic overtones. 'Because if you are, I can tell you she's working at GPT in Edge Lane.'

I thanked her and broke the call.

'She's moved,' I said to Jim, and looked up the GPT number. Getting through to her wasn't as difficult as I'd feared, bearing in mind the hundreds of employees there. Three minutes later I was talking to the lady who had been one of Owen Jenna's lovers and she agreed to see me after work.

We met in the Queens Drive pub, somewhere easy to park. I recognised her without any trouble from the tabloid photos. She had spiky red hair and prominent cheekbones highlighted by the extravagant use of blusher. As mistresses go, she looked the part.

'Mrs Charnock?'

'Call me Lisa,' she said, and flashed me a beaming smile, exposing large white teeth. 'So you're Johnny Ace, then? What's happened to your radio show? I never used to miss it of a night.'

'It's a long story,' I said. 'Let me get you a drink.'

She went for a gin and tonic. I stuck to my usual half of cider although I didn't know how well it would mix with the Andrews.

'As well as the radio show,' I began, 'I run a detective agency and I'm currently investigating the disappearance of Susie Jenna, Owen's wife.'

'Really?' She sounded interested but in an oddly detached way.

'Yes,' I said, 'and obviously, I've read all about you and Mr Jenna in the papers.'

'Hasn't everybody?' It didn't seem to bother her.

'How long were you doing it with him, Lisa?'

Again, no embarrassment and no hesitation. 'A few months, that's all, and it was well before Susie went missing.'

'Did you know her?'

'Never met her but Owen used to talk about her. Married men do that, don't they? Everything about the wife that annoys them, it all gets dragged out.'

I got the impression that Owen Jenna wasn't Lisa Charnock's first married lover. 'What annoyed Mr Jenna about Susie?'

'Oh, just the usual things. Spending too much money, giving all her attention to the children instead of him. She hadn't cottoned on to the fact that men are like children and have to be treated as such.'

'And you have, eh Lisa?'

She smiled knowingly. 'It doesn't take much learning.'

'Have you any kids?' I asked her.

'No.'

'What does your husband do?'

'I haven't got a husband. He went long ago.'

I felt he'd done well to escape but didn't say so.

'I live on my own now.' She didn't elaborate.

'Did you ever think of shacking up with Owen Jenna?'

'You're joking – not that he asked me. He just wanted a bit of fun and that suited me. No ties. I was the antidote to his wife.'

I wondered if she'd proved as expensive an antidote to Owen Jenna as the wife he was seeking solace from. Either way, he could probably afford it. After all, Lisa Charnock hadn't been his only 'floosie'.

'Susie Jenna worked at European Carriages at one time, didn't she?'

'I believe so, but it was long before my time. I wasn't there all that long and, like I say, I never met her yet I probably know more about her personal idiosyncrasies than her best friend does.' The smile lit up her face again for a second, like a neon light being switched on and off. It was a cruel smile.

'Who was her best friend?'

'I've no idea.'

'Was there anybody at European Carriages she was friendly with?'

Lisa thought. 'A woman called Doreen used to talk about her sometimes.'

'Doreen who?'

'I don't remember her second name. Her husband used to do some driving for us.'

'Does she still work there?'

'Don't ask me, I've been gone nearly a year.'

'What sort of company is European Carriages exactly?'

She laughed. 'A glorified bloody taxi service, that's all.'

'And Owen Jenna's the what? Office manager?'

'Don't kid yourself,' said Lisa. 'He may tell people that but I know better. Owen Jenna owns the company. He *is* European Carriages.'

'Really? Why would he keep that quiet?'

'There's an awful lot of scams that go on in the taxi world, Johnny, and Owen Jenna's into most of them. If the balloon went up tomorrow, he'd want to make sure his name never came up on any records.'

'Like what?'

'Apart from the usual meter fiddles, you mean? Well, I did hear stories of cigarettes and liquor being brought over from the Continent on mini-buses taking pensioners on trips to Disneyworld.'

So much for the old image of the smuggler with his eye-patch and cutlass, carrying his loot from sailing ships into secret caves by moonlight. Instead, this contraband seemed to be hidden amongst the zimmer frames and jars of Complan belonging to travelling geriatrics. I wondered what bearing these revelations might have on the case but none sprang immediately to mind.

'One last question, Lisa. What do *you* think has happened to Susie Jenna?'

She shrugged. 'Dunno.'

'Do you think Owen might have killed her?'

'If he did, he hasn't told me.' She didn't appear to be unduly concerned either way and I was relieved to terminate the interview. I don't like unfeeling women and this was one cold bitch. She was quite prepared to grass on Owen Jenna regarding his alleged smuggling activities and she'd obviously taken pleasure in humiliating Susie Jenna by sleeping with her husband.

Yet who was I to judge, with the Hilary and Maria situation in my own life?

After leaving Mrs Charnock, I drove back to the flat, catching the last part of Shady Spencer's show on the car radio. He was playing Tina Turner's 'The Best' yet again. 'At least play Bonnie Tyler's version for a change,' I screamed at the dashboard.

My head ached worse than ever and, some hours after the event, the enormity of Hilary's actions was beginning to sink in. Hilary and I didn't finish with one another. It wasn't like that. We just WERE.

I'd gone some months without seeing Maria, when she thought I was being unfaithful with a client, but strangely, she'd never bothered about me seeing Hilary. She never saw Hilary as a threat.

Yet Hilary obviously regarded Maria as one.

I could have told them that neither was a threat to the other. I had always needed them both and nothing was about to change on my part.

But what if it was on Hilary's?

I didn't have too long to ponder about it. As I drove through the gates of the Waterloo Dock and pulled to a halt in my parking space, a man stepped from behind the adjacent car and swung open the driver's door of the RAV4.

'Mr Ace, just the person I wanted to see,' smiled Frank Harriman.

Chapter Sixteen

'We meet again.' His smile was not reflected in the cold eyes that I well remembered from Altcourse prison. 'I think we have some business to discuss.' He wore a T-shirt, denims and a thin zipped jacket.

'What's that?' I looked around. Roger the security guard was nowhere to be seen. It was seven o'clock and the car park was devoid of people.

Roly was asleep on the back seat.

'Come on, Mr Ace.' His voice took on an impatient edge. 'The John Lennon tape. You're not going to tell me you haven't got it when I know you have?'

'I certainly am.'

'Cut the crap, Ace. You're going to get me that tape now.'

His mistake was to pull out the knife too soon. I hadn't stopped the engine. Before he could use the weapon, I pushed hard against his chest. He lost his balance and fell backwards against the other car, dropping the knife. Then I put the car into reverse and sped backwards out of the lot.

Harriman scrambled to his feet and started to run after me. I slammed on the brakes, pushed the automatic lever into drive in time to meet him head on. There was a sickening thud as the impact threw him into the air.

I jumped out of the car to check the damage. The bumper seemed to be unmarked. Harriman lay on the ground a couple of feet to the side. He didn't move. I suppose I shouldn't have knocked him down but I don't like people pulling knives on me. Admittedly, I'd hit him harder than I meant to, but at least I'd stopped short of running him over and it could have been worse. The RAV4 could have been fitted with bull bars.

Roger came running up from the other end of the car park, alerted by the bang.

'Mr Ace. What happened?' He was panting badly.

'Ran straight out in front of me. Couldn't avoid him.'

The security guard leaned over the victim. Harriman was still breathing and a groan escaped his lips. 'I think he's coming round. Do you know who he is?'

'He's an ex-con, Roger, although he'd tell you he wasn't really a criminal. Look in his eyes and you'll know you wouldn't want to meet him on a dark night.'

On cue, Harriman opened his eyes and stared from one of us to the other. At that moment, a Mercedes drove up behind the RAV4 and the driver sounded his horn to get past.

'Watch him while I move the car,' I told Roger.

I climbed into the driver's seat and manoeuvred the car into a nearby empty space, allowing the Merc to pass, then I drove back to my own parking space.

'Sorry to wake you,' I said to Roly, still reclining on the back seat, 'but I've just been attacked. Come on.'

He yawned and reluctantly dragged himself out of the car. I locked the door with the remote and considered replacing him with a Rottweiler.

The whole episode couldn't have taken more than two minutes but it was two minutes too long. When I reached the spot where I'd left Harriman, Roger was lying there instead. Of Harriman there was no sign.

I bent over the security guard. He was out cold but, as far as I could tell, not seriously hurt.

'What happened?' I asked him as he started to stir.

He sat up and rubbed his head. 'The guy jumped me. He must have only been winded. I wasn't expecting it. Hit me on the temple with the side of his hand like in one of those martial arts films.' He got to his feet shakily. 'Trying to rob you was he, Mr Ace?'

'Something like that, yes. Come on, I'll help you back to your hut. Do you need a doctor?'

'No, no. I'll be fine. Just a bit sore, that's all. I'd better ring the police.'

'No need, Roger. It's all over now.'

'Are you sure?'

'Yes, really.' I gave him a ten-pound note. 'For your trouble. I'd appreciate it if you could forget it.' The last thing I wanted was another grilling by Inspector Mike Bennett.

'Very kind, Mr Ace.'

Once I was safely back inside the flat, I rang Jim and told him that Harriman had attacked me. 'I ran him down,' I said.

'It was only yesterday you told me that people don't get run down deliberately,' he said.

'I was wrong. There's an epidemic of it.'

'Where is he now?'

'Vanished but he'll be back. He wants that tape, Jim, and he'll stop at nothing.'

'Is it still at Maria's?'

'Yes, and I think I'll leave it there for the time being.'

'Very wise. Are you all right?'

'I'm glad you finally asked. I'm sound.'

'Changing the subject, how did you get on with Owen Jenna's ladyfriend?'

'Pretty good. It appears that European Carriages is a front for an illegal import business, would you believe? They bring in cigarettes and liquor from the Continent over and above the personal allowance.'

'So that's where Owen Jenna's getting all his cash?'

'Lisa Charnock reckons so.'

'Don't you?'

'Probably, but it could be the drivers doing it without his knowledge.'

'I prefer the first option,' said Jim. 'And what about Mrs Jenna?

159

Did you find out if she had any chums there?'

'One, a girl called Doreen. She was there when Susie was and she only left the firm a short while ago. Her husband's one of the drivers.'

'Do we know where she is now?'

'No, but it should be easy enough to find out from the company.'

'Why not ask Jenna? He should know.'

For some reason, I didn't want to involve Owen Jenna at the moment. Call it another hunch. 'He's not too co-operative. I'd rather do it my way.'

My way was to call round in person at European Carriages next morning. Their office was in the new Brunswick Business Park, formerly the old Brunswick Dock. It was a brand new building surrounded by several car parking spaces and newly planted shrubs.

The receptionist was a friendly girl with a heavy Scouse accent.

'You're Sandra, are you?' I asked. 'I spoke to you on the phone the other day, about Lisa Charnock.'

'I remember.'

I gave her my business card. It transpired she listened to my radio show and was only too willing to give me any information.

'Do you have a personnel manager?' I asked her.

'Only me, luv. I keep all the staff records. Who did you want?'

I explained I needed to trace a woman called Doreen who had worked there some time ago.

'Oh, I know Doreen,' she said. 'Her husband was one of our drivers.'

'That'll be her,' I said.

'She only left a few weeks ago. After her husband died.'

'Oh, sorry about that.'

'Yes, she took it bad. We was all very upset. She was a good laugh, was Doreen.'

'She was a friend of Mrs Jenna, I believe.'

Sandra looked at me blankly. 'I've never seen Mr Jenna's wife. She was before my time, I'm afraid, and I'm not likely to meet her now, am I?'

'That depends if she's dead or not. What's the general opinion in the firm about her disappearance?'

She glanced about her nervously then lowered her voice. 'He's done her in, that's what I think and most of the girls here think the same, but don't say I said so, will you?'

'Not a word. Is he not popular with the staff?'

'He's OK, I suppose. Leaves us to get on with things but he's got a nasty temper if you upset him.'

'He's the office manager, isn't he? But who actually owns the company?'

'It's supposed to be a Mr Jacques and a Mr Quigley but we've never seen them.'

'How many of you work here?'

'Three girls on the admin side. They do the leases, arrange the private hire side as well as the taxis and book the coach parties.'

'Quite a big operation then?'

'We've got four coaches on the road, eight mini-buses and any number of cars.'

Not just a tinpot taxi firm then as Lisa Charnock had suggested. 'Do the company own all the hire cars or do some belong to the drivers?'

'Both. We have some owner-drivers and others on contract. Part-time and full-time.'

'What department was Doreen in?'

'Admin like the other girls.'

'Where's she working now, do you know?'

'No idea.'

'Have you got her address?'

'I'll find it for you.' She went across to the shelves on the back wall and pulled down a blue ledger. 'Here we are, have you got a pen?'

'Yes.' I pulled out my notebook and waited.

'Doreen Harward,' she said. 'Seven—'

I interrupted her. 'What name did you say?'

'Harward.'

'You said her husband died recently. How did he die?'

'He was knocked down outside a pub last February. You must have read about it in the *Echo*. The fellow what ran him over got six months. Should have got six years if you ask me.'

'I think I read about it. Was his first name . . . ?'

'Des,' she replied. 'Des Harward.'

Chapter Seventeen

I tried to work out the implications of this startling new revelation but I couldn't immediately see anything to tie it to Susie Jenna's disappearance.

The receptionist gave me the Harwards' address and I wrote it down. They lived in Knotty Ash, Ken Dodd country, on the other side of the ring road from Old Swan.

'Had Des been with the company long?'

'A few years. He was one of the regulars.'

'I seem to remember the papers describing Des as a part-time taxi driver.'

'He was part-time in the sense that he owned his own vehicle and worked when he wanted to, but he'd been with us a fair time.'

'Did he do the continental runs?'

'Quite often, yes.' She looked a little suspicious now and her tone was chilly. 'I thought it was Doreen you wanted to see.'

'It is and you've been most helpful. I'll send her your regards when I see her, shall I?'

This brought her smile back. 'Tell her to call in and see us. We miss her.'

I drove straight over to Knotty Ash and knocked on the door of the Harward house. It was opened by a lad in his late teens holding a screaming baby under his arm. A wet nappy was hanging down the leg of its Babygro.

'Yes, mate?' He was smoking a cigarette and spoke out of the side of his mouth.

'I'm looking for Doreen Harward.'

'She's left, pal. We live here now.' Smoke curled from his cigarette into the baby's face.

'Do you know where she's gone?'

'Dunno, mate. Never met her. We bought the house through an agent.' He shut the door in my face before I had a chance to ask any further questions.

On impulse, I knocked on the door of the adjoining semi. An old lady answered. 'You're not double glazing, are you?'

'No, I'm looking for Doreen Harward, actually. I thought, you being her neighbour, you might have some idea where she'd gone.'

'Come in, will you?' She led me to the living room at the back of the house. A plate, cup and saucer from breakfast were still on the table, next to a copy of the *Daily Mail*, and Ken Bruce regaled us from a radio-CD unit on a bookshelf.

'Radio Two,' she said unnecessarily. 'It keeps me company in the mornings. Would you care for a cup of tea?'

'Not just now, thanks. Has Doreen been gone long?'

'Only a few days. The young couple next door have just moved in. She works, you know, behind the bar at the pub up the road. Out all hours, she is. He hasn't got a job – just looks after that baby. Poor thing, it cries all the time . . .'

'Doreen,' I broke in. 'Can you tell me how I can find her?'

She inspected me carefully. I put her age at late sixties. I could see George Cox's wife in her, ten years down the line, but judging by the single cup on the table, this lady's husband hadn't lasted the course.

'She's gone to live in France.'

'France!' I couldn't keep the surprise out of my voice. 'Did she leave an address with you, by any chance?'

'Yes, but only to forward any mail. I call next door every morning just in case anything comes for her but she said not to give her address to anyone.'

'I'm investigating a murder,' I announced. 'Doreen's friend. Doreen herself may be in grave danger. I need to get hold of her right away.'

'Oh dear.' She looked confused. 'A murder, you say? It's not that Susie Jenna, is it? Have they found her body?'

'You knew Susie?'

'Oh yes. She was a friend of Doreen's. She used to come and see her from time to time.'

'What did Doreen think happened to her?'

'The husband had done it. It's obvious. That's why the police are searching everywhere.'

'Have they questioned you?'

'No, but I know Doreen spoke to them. She told them she thought he'd killed her. Who are you from, anyway?'

I gave her my business card. 'You can ring my office to confirm who I am. But I do need to speak with Doreen.'

'I haven't got a telephone number, just her address. I suppose it will be all right, in the circumstances.' She went over to a drawer in an old dresser and took out an envelope. 'Here you are – she's in a place called Beaulieu sur Mer.'

I had heard of it. It was a resort, a few miles from Nice on the shores of the Mediterranean. Playground of the rich.

I noted the address and thanked the lady. 'Don't worry about giving it to me,' I assured her. 'You've done the right thing. Doreen will thank you for it.'

'Are you going to see her?'

'Yes. Any message you'd like to send her?'

'No, not really. Just send her our love, me and Otto.' She nodded to a white Persian cat asleep in front of the gas fire.

'Your name is?'

'Mrs Latham. Don't let anything happen to her, will you?'

I promised I wouldn't and left her to Ken and Otto. I was anxious to get back to the office and acquaint Jim Burroughs with the startling news about Doreen Harward.

'Pure coincidence,' he announced. 'Got to be.'

'There must be some connection,' I insisted. 'I visit two people in prison about Bernard Skidmore's death – Harriman and Nigel

Abram – and they both crop up in our other two cases.'

'There's a simple explanation,' said Jim. 'A common denominator. Skidmore was a magistrate. Harriman committed a crime and Harward was the victim of one, so they both passed through his hands. The natural course of the law.'

'I wonder.'

'Nothing to wonder about. Nigel Abram didn't know Harward from Adam. It was an accident pure and simple when he ran him over. Random chance, the insurance companies call it. As for Harriman, he had nothing whatsoever to do with the Jennas and neither of them killed Skidmore so, end of story.'

I didn't argue.

'What did you find out about Doreen's relationship with Susie Jenna?'

'They were friends all right. Susie used to go round to Doreen's.'

'Presumably Mrs Jenna was friendly with Des as well?'

'I don't know. It doesn't necessarily follow.' I made a mental note to check on Des Harward's activities before his unexpected death. 'According to the lady next door, Doreen thought Owen had killed Susie.'

'Doesn't everyone? What about the people who own European Carriages, Johnny? Who are they?'

'Jacques and Quigley are their names but the receptionist said she's never seen them and Lisa Charnock reckoned that Jenna really runs the show.'

'Which means he's set up the rackets. Do you think either of the Harwards were involved in the smuggling?'

'I've no idea yet but I find it odd that Doreen's sold up and gone to live in France. What's she running away from?'

'Her husband's dead, her best friend's murdered, perhaps she'd just had enough and wanted a complete break.'

'The South of France isn't the cheapest place in the world. I wonder where she's got the money from.'

There seems to be a lot of money floating about in that firm, one way and another. Owen Jenna's gambling, for a start.'

'One interesting thing, Jim. Owen Jenna said a taxi had tried to run him down. What if it was one of his own?'

'Mutiny in the ranks, eh?'

'Could be.'

'What's your next move then?'

'I'm seeing Maria tonight. I'm going to leave Roly at hers and take a plane to Nice tomorrow. I need to have words with Doreen Harward. She's a vital part of this jigsaw, I'm sure of it.'

Jim looked shocked. 'That's going to push up the expenses, Johnny.'

'You're behind the times,' I told him. 'It's cheaper to fly from Liverpool to Nice nowadays than it is to go by train from Lime Street to London *and* it takes half the time.' No wonder the railways were in a mess.

'When will you be back?'

'I don't know. As soon as I've found out what's going on with Doreen Harward. She's our only lead so far.'

'What about this fellow from Chester – Joey, isn't it? You've asked him to come on Friday to talk about the tape.'

'If he phones, put him off till Monday.'

I went back to the flat to pack a flight bag for the journey; socks, underwear, toothbrush and a change of T-shirt. I didn't intend staying more than one night if I could help it. I also threw in my camera, useful to have for substantiating evidence.

I brought up the Easyjet site on the Internet and booked my plane ticket, then I set off for Blundelsands and Maria's at seven. I hadn't seen her since the disagreement with Hilary. Come to that, I hadn't heard from Hilary either but I hadn't yet given in to the temptation to ring her.

I parked outside Maria's flat and Roly followed me to the front door. As I waited for her to answer my ring, I noticed a white van pulling up a few doors down on the other side of the road. Nobody got out. And then Maria opened the door and I thought no more about it.

We drove out to the Bay Horse at Formby for the Carvery. The locals had staged a protest when the old pub was turned into a modern restaurant but the place was full so I supposed that good food at reasonable prices served by pleasant staff had silenced the critics.

I brought Maria up to date with my progress on the three cases.

'This Harriman character seems very determined to get hold of the tape,' she observed.

'He's a fanatic,' I warned her, 'and dangerous with it.'

I told her about my planned trip to Nice and she said she'd be delighted to have Roly.

'What are you hoping to get from Mrs Harward?'

'I don't know, but in some strange way she appears to be connected to all three cases. I need to find out if she really is involved and, if so, is it just chance.'

'You know the man who ran her husband down, the one you saw at Kirkham prison?'

'Nigel Abram? Yes?'

'Didn't you say he'd met the Harward family?'

'That's right. He wanted to apologise but he said they didn't want to know, would have happily seen him hanged.'

'Sound like a nice bunch.'

'Mmmm. I suppose if you were mown down in the street, I'd not be inclined to share a pint with the driver.'

'Except it wasn't the driver's fault.'

'Even so.'

We went on to chat about other things, including the forthcoming holiday with Kaye and Alex. I found I was quite looking forward to our week on a boat.

We finished off the meal with tea and coffee and I wrapped up a doggy bag of beef and turkey for Roly, a consolation for him not being allowed on the premises.

'It's the Health and Safety Act,' a very young waitress with *Karen* on her badge explained to me. 'Dogs aren't allowed by law anywhere where food is served.'

There's so many new laws under New Labour, we'll soon all be a nation of criminals.

'He probably wouldn't have liked it here anyway,' I said. 'You don't allow smoking.'

'What did you want to say that to the poor child for?' chided Maria, when Karen disappeared, red-faced. 'She must think you're stupid.' I knew that Hilary, with her off-the-wall sense of humour, would have appreciated my remark more than Maria did.

Suitably chastened, I said, 'I'm sorry. It's just the petty rules that annoy me.' I often found myself apologising to Maria. Perhaps the rebel in me resented her civilising influence.

We drove back in a strained silence. I hadn't meant the evening to turn out this way but I had a lot on my mind.

When I pulled up outside her flat, I noticed the white van had gone. It was only when we went inside and another tenant, one of Maria's neighbours, came out that I had cause to think about it.

Mrs Comfort was a widow of eighty-five who lived alone in the adjoining flat. She was so thin, her clothes hung on her bony frame like sheets flapping on a clothes maiden, but she had all her wits about her and was not lacking in spirit. In the Roaring Twenties she'd probably have been one of the Bright Young Things.

Now she was shaking.

'Maria, my dear, thank goodness you're home. Somebody has been trying to break into your flat.'

'What!'

'It was just after you'd gone out. I heard your new dog barking and came into the hall. This man was outside your door with a chisel in his hand.'

'What did he look like?' I asked.

'Only a youth, nineteen maybe, slim. I asked him what he thought he was doing. I didn't like the look of him. He had mad eyes.'

Harriman, I thought immediately. 'What did he say?' I asked her.

'Nothing. He stopped what he was doing and glared at me. I think the dog put him off. It was howling by this time and scratching at the other side of the door. In the end, he ran off.'

'If you see him again, Mrs Comfort,' I said, 'you must ring the police straight away.'

169

Maria opened her front door and we went inside. Roly greeted us enthusiastically, standing on his hind legs to lick our faces. I gave him his Bay Horse beef and turkey which he wolfed down.

'You reckon it was Harriman?' said Maria.

'He must have followed me here. I saw a white van behind me when I arrived earlier but I didn't think anything about it at the time.'

'Do you think he knows I've got the tape?'

'I don't know. He'd searched the office and it wasn't there so my flat had to be favourite.'

'Which is why he ambushed you.'

'But he must have suspected that I'd move it to a safer place.'

'So he followed you . . .'

'To where the tape was all the time. Hell! Sorry, Maria. What am I going to do with it now?' I didn't want to put her in any more danger. Harriman was a man obsessed who would go to any lengths to get his hands on the tape.

'Is there anywhere at the Picton library that you could hide it?' I asked her.

'Yes. My personal locker in the staff room. He'd never get past security there.'

'Right.'

She clung to me. 'I'm frightened, Johnny. Do you think he'll come back?'

'No, I'm sure he won't.' But I didn't feel too confident. 'Anyway, you'll have Roly. Just watch yourself going in and out of the flat.'

Neither of us felt like making love. Although our earlier contretemps had been forgotten, the fear of a possible return visit by Harriman had put us both in a subdued mood. My mind, too, was on my forthcoming trip and what I might find out from Doreen Harward. All of which added up to a night devoid of wild passion.

We left for the library after breakfast next morning, Roly remaining on guard in the flat. Maria gave Mrs Comfort her key to enable her to let him out into the garden during the day.

'And I'll let you have the spare, Johnny, just in case you need to get in for anything.'

I could see no sign of the white van as we drove away, but I made sure I escorted Maria right up to the door of the library.

'Don't forget to ring me when you get to France,' she said, 'and take care.'

I next called in at the office to inform Jim Burroughs of Harriman's visit to Maria's. 'He's determined to get that tape. I'm worried he might come back here, thinking he missed it first time round.'

'More likely he'll try your flat.'

'He'll find nothing there and security's pretty tight since the other night.'

'So where is the tape now?'

'At Maria's library.'

Jim approved. 'It'll be as safe there as anywhere.'

Half an hour later, I was at Liverpool Airport on my way to Nice. I left the RAV4 in the car park, less than a hundred yards from the terminal building, and checked in at the desk.

I had well over an hour before the plane was due to board so I went up to the new restaurant for an early lunch. I chose the Trinidad Chicken and it was better than I'd had in many five-star restaurants. Who'd want to fly from Heathrow?

Once through Passport Control, I bought a *Daily Post* from the bookstall. A small paragraph on an inside page reported that no trace had been found of the missing wife, Susie Jenna, after an area of wasteground had been dug up in Altcar. The usual waif-like photograph of her, looking like Audrey Hepburn on hunger strike, was printed alongside. Police said they remained baffled as to her whereabouts.

I wondered if I would find the answer hundreds of miles away on the shores of the French Riviera.

The Easyjet 737 landed five minutes early at Nice. The sun was shining along the Promenade des Anglais and I was very tempted to hop on a bus to St Tropez and forget about Doreen Harward. Instead, I hailed a taxi to the city centre and booked in for the night at the Hotel Excelsior, a large and ornate Victorian building just a few hundred yards down the road from the station.

171

Beaulieu sur Mer was on the Monaco line, which then headed out to Italy, to San Remo, Genoa, Rome and Naples. I wasn't going that far. My journey took six minutes and cost just £1.14p. Rail travel in France is cheap, which makes up for the exorbitant fares charged by French taxi drivers.

The train stopped first at Villefranche where, from the station, I could see a huge white cruise liner anchored in the quaint harbour below. Tina Turner has a house in the hills overlooking Villefranche. I wondered if she was up there looking out on this same view.

Beaulieu was like something out of the twenties. There was an air of rich indolence about the small town, as if the spirit of Noël Coward was all around. Palm trees lined the Promenade, a beautiful Baroque building stood next to the Casino, the harbour was full of private yachts, and a Greek temple set in its own gardens jutted out into the bright blue waters of the Mediterranean. Close your eyes and you could imagine Somerset Maugham drinking pink gins on the terrace against the background hills of the Col d'Èze.

The address I had for Doreen Harward turned out to be a modern block of flats near the centre of town.

A pair of decorated glass doors led into a large vestibule which boasted a polished darkwood floor, large tropical plants in giant stainless-steel tubs and a row of bells on a board on the wall.

I pressed the bell for Flat Three. Doreen Harward was in Flat Seven but I wanted to get closer than the hallway. I'd have to pretend to be delivering a parcel.

'*Oui*?' enquired a voice.

'*Poste,*' I replied, hoping it meant the right thing, and a buzzer sounded, allowing me to open a further door which led to the elevator and stairs.

I chose the thickly carpeted stairs. Flat Seven turned out to be on the third floor. I rang the bell at the side of the door. There was the sound of a television being turned down and footsteps coming towards me. The door was pulled open to reveal a woman with short black hair and a pale complexion.

I caught my breath in astonishment. So this was how it felt to meet a ghost.

'*Bonjour*. Can I help you?' asked Susie Jenna.

Chapter Eighteen

Five minutes later, I was sitting in the small lounge of the flat opposite a person who had been, indeed still was, the subject of a nationwide search. 'I don't know how the hell you found me, Johnny Ace,' she said angrily.

'Pure coincidence. I was looking for your friend, Doreen Harward.'

'This is Doreen's flat. She's out at the moment. Why did you want her?'

I explained about being hired by Owen Jenna to find his missing wife. 'Everyone, including the police, believes Owen has murdered you.'

'Good. That's what I want them to think.'

'So the only way he can prove his innocence is by producing you alive and well. Unfortunately, he thought the police weren't doing their best for him. They seemed more interested in finding your body than tracing you.' She smiled at this. 'So he hired me to look for you. Doreen was one step along the trail.'

Susie took out a cigarette and lit it. 'They wouldn't have found out much from her. She'd already told the cops she thought I was dead.'

'How did you get out of the country without a passport?'

'Simple. I *had* a passport. Did you say you'd met Doreen?'

'No.'

'Doe is a real blonde bombshell with all that goes with it, the red lips and big boobs. Wait here.'

She rose and went into another room. She was gone for five

175

minutes and when she returned, she was wearing a tight scarlet dress, which accentuated curves she hadn't had before, a blonde wig and bright scarlet lipstick. *Stars in Your Eyes* presents Susie Jenna as Marilyn Monroe.

'I just wanna make lurve to you,' she purred in a husky voice and laughed. 'Like it? Meet Doreen Harward.'

I understood. 'You booked a ticket in her name and used her passport?'

'That's right. It was *so* easy. Then I posted it back to her. I was across the Channel before Owen realised his bloody tea wasn't on the table.'

'Why did you go?'

'I left my husband for one simple reason,' she said. 'I'd had enough.'

'Of his brutality, you mean, or his affairs?'

'Both – and everything else. Owen isn't a nice man. He's cruel – mentally cruel, I mean. He has to dominate anyone he has a relationship with.'

'What about the children?' I could understand her leaving Owen but it was difficult to justify a mother abandoning her own offspring, especially at so young an age.

'I'd have been no good to them dead and that's how it would have ended up if I'd have stayed.'

'You don't really think he'd have killed you?'

'Or I'd have killed myself, taken an overdose. I'd done it before.'

Obviously not very wholeheartedly, I thought cynically. Then: 'Have you no intention of getting in touch with them again?'

'Best they think I'm dead. Owen won't take long to find a replacement for me.'

'Why didn't you just leave him, get a divorce?'

She blew a ring of smoke into the air. 'I don't know. Couldn't be doing with the aggro, I suppose. He'd have fought it, there would have been a lot of unpleasantness. This way, it was over in a day and, besides, it was a way of getting back at the bastard. I knew everyone would think he'd done away with me.'

'Aren't you frightened someone will recognise you?'

'Out here? Not really. I wear the wig when I go out.' She giggled. 'People think we're twins when Doe and I are together.'

'How long has Doreen had the flat?'

'Years. She and her husband bought it as a holiday home.'

'Was Doreen's husband in on your scheme?'

'No, poor Des knew nothing about it. This was a woman thing. You knew he'd been killed, I presume?'

'Yes.'

'That was what made Doe decide to come out here to live with me.'

'Were she and Des close?'

'Inseparable. She was devastated by his death.'

'Des worked for Owen, didn't he?'

Susie paused. Perhaps she was not sure how much I knew about the running of European Carriages. 'He was one of the drivers,' she said briefly.

'What about the postcard you sent to Owen saying you were going to Greece? I presume you sent it – it was in your writing.'

She laughed. 'Oh, that? That was Doe's idea. I wrote it and she posted it in Liverpool. It was just to get Owen in more lumber because it was so obviously a fake.'

She was right. The papers had said police regarded it with suspicion.

She stubbed out her cigarette. 'What do you intend doing now? Are you going to race triumphantly back to England and say you've found me and claim the booty? Is there some booty? There should be.'

I half expected her to take a gun out of her bag and tell me she didn't want to shoot me but it was the only way to preserve her secret. Instead, she offered me a drink. 'I've got beer or whisky.'

'Cider?' I didn't really expect it but she surprised me.

'How about some *cidre*? That's French cider, very appley and not as gassy as the English stuff.'

'Perfect.'

She was right. It wasn't as strong as Scrumpy Jack but very pleasant to drink. Susie had a glass of Glenfiddich on the rocks.

'So?' she said, leaning back in her chair, still wearing the wig and red dress and rasping in her assumed Hollywood accent. 'What's your next move then, Mr Detective?'

'I'd like to talk to Doreen.'

Her eyebrows shot up. 'Doe – why? I'm here and it's me you've come to find, isn't it?'

I didn't answer her. Instead I asked, 'What was the work you were doing for Doreen?'

'How do you mean, work?'

'Your husband said you were doing some freelance typing work for a friend. I guessed it might be Doreen.'

'Well done, Mr Marlowe.' Back came the Marilyn voice again, heavily laced with sarcasm. 'Go to the top of the class.' She carried on in her normal tones. 'There was no work. It was just an excuse to go round to Doe's. Owen didn't like me having a life of my own.'

'But you managed to get out at night. According to Owen, you spent the weekends out on the town.'

'That was in the later days. Anything to get out of that house.'

'Who looked after the children?'

'Owen's parents, if Owen was going out, which wasn't often.'

'He said he did the housework and took the kids to school.'

'It was on his way, why shouldn't he?'

'And the housework?'

'What housework? It doesn't take much to shove a few clothes in a washing machine or dishes in a dishwasher.'

I got the picture and was starting to see things from Owen Jenna's side. But which came first, his philandering or her attitude? I didn't excuse wife-beating but I could see the basis of a motive. Now he was branded a murderer. But was he a smuggler as well, as Lisa Charnock had suggested, and was somebody really trying to kill him as he obviously believed?

Susie had gone across to the dresser for more whisky. I declined the offer of another *cidre*. I still hadn't finished the first bottle. Susie sat down again with her replenished glass.

'Cheers,' she said, then took off the blonde wig and threw it across to an easy chair in the corner. Her short black hair somehow looked incongruous against the slinky red dress. 'I hope you're not expecting to take me back with you like some conquering hero with his captive.'

'No, but I'm bound to report that you are alive and well.'

'If you can prove it, you mean? It's your word.'

'I hardly think there'll be a problem. For instance, a couple of pictures of you coming out of this apartment might do the trick.'

'They can't make me go back. I've done nothing wrong.'

'At least it'll save the taxpayers' money wasting police time searching for you.'

'You'll be letting that bastard off the hook.'

'Enough is enough, and he is my client, Mrs Jenna.'

'I'm Susie Wishart here, my maiden name.'

'Whatever.'

'Pat on the back then,' she said. 'You go on home. You've solved the case, brownie points from Owen.'

'Maybe,' I said. But there was more for me to do. 'What time do you expect Doreen back?'

'You still want to speak to Doe?'

'Yes. And don't tell me she'll be late because I'm not in any hurry. I can wait.' I didn't know what she could tell me but I suspected that Doreen Harward could well be the glue holding the pieces of the jigsaw together. That is, if she was prepared to talk.

'Sorry to disappoint you, Johnny,' said Susie, 'but Doe won't be back until tomorrow. She's gone to visit some friends in Cannes.'

I didn't know whether to believe her or not. Was this a ploy to prevent me from meeting Doreen Harward until they'd had time to get their stories straight?

One thing, Susie Jenna was quite laid back, not noticeably worried that her friend might return at any minute. I realised that when she'd left the room to change her dress, she'd had time to ring Doreen on a mobile, wherever she was, and warn her of my arrival.

There was no point in my hanging around. 'In that case, I'll call again in the morning,' I told her.

'If she's back.'

'I shan't be returning to England until I've seen her,' I warned. My flight was actually booked for the following afternoon but it would be no problem to change it if necessary.

'Ring me first,' she said, and wrote her number on a scrap of paper. As she did so, I took out my camera and quickly snapped a couple of shots. She wheeled round quickly but I gave her a reassuring smile.

'Just to confirm you exist.'

I had half an hour before my train back to Nice was due so I took a walk along the seafront to get a closer look at the Greek Temple. It was called Villa Kerylos and was open to the public. I bought a ticket and followed the tourists round, ending up on the terrace where I was served with Darjeeling tea and apple tart at a table overlooking St Jean Cap Ferrat, otherwise known as Millionaires' Paradise.

Edgar Marshall's garage in Old Swan seemed a lifetime away, which reminded me I needed to ring Jim Burroughs to see if he'd heard from Joey in Chester about the John Lennon tape or if there had been any sign of Frank Harriman. But most of all, I wanted to tell him how I'd accomplished what the Merseyside Police and the might of the British press had failed to do. I'd found Susie Jenna.

I stopped at a *tabac* on the way to the station and bought a couple of phone cards. The next train was due in five minutes so I caught that and as soon as we arrived at Nice station, I went to find a phone booth.

'You're sure it really is Susie Jenna?' exclaimed Jim when I told him.

'Jim, she's been on more posters than Lord Kitchener. Besides, I spent the afternoon with her and I took a couple of photos.' I gave him the address but told him not to ring the police until the following afternoon. I wanted a chance to talk to Doreen Harward without the world's press joining in.

'You realise this is exactly what Gypsy Gloria predicted, Jim, when I saw her in the Atlantic?' I could imagine the old girl sitting there, skeletal hands clutching her crystal ball. 'You were rather rude about her, as I recall.'

He was no more impressed now. 'Load of bollocks, all that psychic rubbish. Did Mrs Jenna say why she'd run away?'

'Couldn't stand her old man and thought doing it this way would give her a quick getaway *and* put him in the dock.'

'She was right on both counts, but what about the kids?'

'Doesn't seem to give a shit. She's one hard lady and I suspect Doreen Harward might be much the same.'

'So when are you bringing her back?'

I told him I didn't think that was on the agenda. 'All we can do is break the good news to Owen Jenna and to the police.'

'This puts Jenna in the clear.'

'So we've earned our fee with another grand to come.'

'The police aren't going to be happy,' sighed Jim, 'all the money they've spent searching for her. It'll have knocked holes in their annual budget.'

I agreed. 'Plus they're made to look fools and they can't even do her for wasting police time.'

'What was it you were saying about Doreen Harward?'

'A tough cookie, I reckon. She and Susie Jenna go together like Thelma and Louise.'

'Who?'

'It's a film, Jim, forget it.'

'What's your plan now?'

'I'm seeing Doreen Harward in the morning. I'm curious about this smuggling angle.'

'Hang on, nobody's paying us to look into that. You've found Mrs Jenna – end of job.'

I wasn't sure. 'There's the matter of Des Harward's death. If Lisa Charnock's right, it's likely he was involved with the illegal imports scam at European Carriages. We've had Owen Jenna claiming someone tried to run him down and kill him so I'm suddenly suspicious. They could both have been on someone's hit list.'

'You're not suggesting Nigel Abram's a contract killer, for Christ's sake. The man's a chartered bloody accountant.'

'Everybody moonlights these days, Jim. I'm sure I saw my GP behind the bar at Shorrocks Hill the other week.'

All the same, recalling my meeting with him at Kirkham prison, I didn't have Nigel Abram down as a budding mafioso. He gave every impression of being a respectable citizen who'd never heard of Des Harward before Harward stumbled in front of his car.

But what if Abram HAD been waiting for him, intent on running him over? Why would he do that? Who might have hired him?

'You might as well say Bernard Skidmore could be another potential victim,' Jim said.

'Skidmore?'

'That story his missus told us about him nearly getting run over in London Road.'

'I'd forgotten about that.' Although I didn't see how it tied in. There was no connection between Skidmore and European Carriages.

Jim's voice interrupted my musing. 'When are you coming back?'

'I'm hanging on to speak to the grieving widow, but I should be home tomorrow night. Anyway, quickly, before my phone card runs out, has there been any action on the John Lennon front?'

'Nothing at all, Johnny, no word from Joey.'

'What about the break-in at the office?'

'Forensic drew a blank, no identifiable prints.'

'Which means there were prints but none they could match, is that it?'

'I suppose so,' admitted Jim.

'Which means it couldn't have been Harriman because they'd have his prints on file.'

'Unless it was Harriman and he wore gloves.'

'Then whose were the prints they found?'

'Anybody's and everybody's. The cleaners maybe, Eddie Smeddles, you name it.'

'All right.' I felt deflated. We were back to dead ends again.

'Oh, and Mrs Skidmore rang,' said Jim.

'I'd forgotten about her. What did you tell her?'

He sounded sheepish. 'I didn't tell her to forget it, but I did say it was looking unlikely her husband's death was anything but an accident.' His tone became defiant. 'I know you said hang on a couple of days, Johnny, but . . .'

'It's OK, Jim. You're probably right. It was just a hunch I had.' The pips rang out in my ear. 'Must go. The money's running out. I'll be in touch.'

It seemed ages since my airport lunch, and the apple tart at Villa Kerylos. I walked down to the Rue Masséna. Most of the tables outside the pavement cafés were full but I managed to find a vacant one at Le Quebec restaurant where I had half a chicken with chips and three more bottles of *cidre*.

It was a warm night, the giftshops were open and African market traders were selling a variety of craft goods like carved wooden figures and knitted clothes.

A young couple at the next table were having a row in French. He had a bushy black moustache and seemed to be denying something, shaking his head from side to side. She shouted histrionically at him between mouthfuls, waving her fork in front of his face until she suddenly stopped, clattered down her cutlery, picked up what looked like a grilled sardine from her plate and threw it in his face.

The young man slowly wiped his nose with the side of his hand then suddenly reached forward and slapped his girlfriend sharply across the cheek. She yelped, jumped up, grabbed her handbag and flounced off, to be lost among the milling crowds.

The man glanced round at the captivated faces of his fellow diners,

183

and shrugged his shoulders after his departing companion. A cheer went up. He raised his arms in appreciation and continued with his meal.

Feminism didn't seem to have reached this part of the Riviera yet.

'*L'addition*,' I called to the *garçon*, handed over the francs and made my way down to the sea-front. The dome of the Negresco Hotel was silhouetted against the night sky and I could see the lights of planes leaving the airport at the other end of the bay.

I used my second phone card to call Maria. She'd had no prowlers, Roly was fine and the John Lennon tape was safely locked up at work. I told her I'd be back the following night.

'Be careful,' she said. Then: 'I miss you.'

I left the phone card in the slot and toyed with the idea of ringing Hilary but, in the end, decided against it. I didn't want an inter-continental argument. Better to see her face to face and sort things out.

The rooms at the Excelsior were large with high ceilings and I slept well in a king-size bed with an ornate wooden headboard. Next morning, after breakfast, I rang Susie Jenna's number and a different voice answered.

'Is that Johnny Ace? This is Doreen Harward. I believe you want to see me?'

My guess was that Susie had rung Doreen a second time, as soon as I'd left the flat last night, to say the coast was clear. Ample opportunity to work out their strategy.

'That's right.'

'Why don't you come on over then? Are you in Beaulieu now?'

'I'm in Nice, but give me an hour.'

I checked out of the hotel and hurried to the station. I was lucky, a train was just leaving for Menton and I made the flat in thirty-five minutes.

Susie Jenna was right: Doreen Harward was a dead ringer for her film star alter ego, albeit a slightly older version. She had the blonde hair, the Mick Jagger pout, even the tight dress finishing above the knee to reveal shapely tanned legs.

'So you're Johnny Ace?' She smiled sardonically. 'And are you an "Ace" investigator?' Her voice had a hard edge to it and, unlike Susie with her overtones of the Wirral, Doreen's accent was pure Dingle. The overall effect was more Lily Savage than Marilyn Monroe.

'Yep, sure am,' I replied in Humphrey Bogart vernacular, thinking I should have brought the trilby from the *Daily Post* photo.

We sat down and Susie Jenna brought in tea. She was back to her own identity, without the blonde wig. I wasn't fooled by the cordiality. They'd have their story off pat.

Doreen did the honours with the tea then asked, 'What do you want to know?' She sounded confident.

'I did come here to find Susie but I'm also intrigued about what's going on at her husband's company.' I turned to Mrs Jenna. 'I take it you know he owns European Carriages?'

She neither confirmed nor denied it. 'Go on.'

'I want to know about the wine and tobacco racket that's going on there.'

'I don't know what you're talking about.'

'I was speaking to Lisa Charnock this week. She told me all about it. One of your husband's mistresses,' I added.

'Really?' interposed Doreen coolly and turned to her friend. 'She's the woman who told the papers she was having an affair with your husband, Susie. You can't believe a word someone like that says.'

'She said she knew your husband too.'

At this last bit, Doreen snapped, 'Des? How did she know Des?'

'I believe he drove for Owen Jenna occasionally.'

'So what? It wasn't a secret.'

'Who are Quigley and Jacques?'

'Never heard of them.'

'They're supposed to own the company.'

'How would I know? I was just a paid employee.'

'Like Lisa Charnock, eh? And she seemed to know quite a bit

about your affairs. Maybe Des told her some of the family secrets in their more intimate moments.'

'Des never looked at another woman, you bastard.' She jumped up ready to strike me but I pushed her back on the seat and carried on.

'There's talk of a smuggling operation going on and Owen appears to have come into a lot of money suddenly.' I didn't bother to mention his 'niece'. 'I wondered how much you and Des might have been involved.'

'Did you?' Still non-committal. I remembered something I'd read in a book by Edward de Bono, the man who invented lateral thinking. He called it the 'po' theory. Introduce a wild card, an outrageous statement into a conversation and wait and see what it draws out. It seemed worth a try.

'Des Harward was run over, right? Well, Owen said somebody in a taxi tried to run him down the other day. Perhaps Des's death wasn't an accident after all.'

This stirred Mrs Harward into a reaction. 'Come on, get real. You don't really believe that?'

'Why not?'

'The guy who hit him didn't know him from Adam.'

'So he says. Nobody challenged the fact.'

'No, I don't believe it,' said Doreen.

Susie looked at me intently. 'You say someone tried to kill Owen?'

'Owen says they did.'

'If he says so, then they probably did. He's not easily frightened, my husband.'

'Who do you think would want him dead?'

She laughed. 'Me for a start.' She saw my face. 'And lots of other people, I imagine. He's a man who makes enemies.'

'Like who?'

'How should I know?'

'What do you know about the business, Mrs Jenna? You worked there once, didn't you?'

'Only for a short time. I was the archetypal young secretary who married the boss, wasn't I?' She said it with a noticeable irony.

'Was anything funny going on then?'

'I wouldn't have known if there was, but Doreen's the one you want to ask about that.'

'Your husband gave me a list of places you'd worked. You were at Smedley at one time?'

'Not for long. Doe gave me a job there.'

I turned to Doreen. 'So you worked there as well?' Was this a coincidence? I thought for a moment. 'You didn't by any chance know a man called Bernard Skidmore?'

Doreen paled. 'Why do you ask that?'

'No special reason. His name came up in another case and he worked at Smedley too.'

Susie answered. 'It's a big place,' she said. 'You can't know everybody.' Again that trick of answering without saying yes or no.

I didn't pursue it but I felt sure that, whatever she said, they had both known Bernard Skidmore. Why would they refuse to acknowledge the fact?

I returned to the subject of Des Harward. It seemed to be Doreen's Achilles heel. She became agitated when I said anything against him.

'I'll tell you what I think,' I said. 'I believe Des tried to steal Lisa Charnock from Owen. Owen got to hear about it and put a contract out on him.'

'Don't talk bloody ridiculous,' stormed Doreen. 'Des's death was an accident.'

I persevered. 'I don't think so. I think he was murdered. Maybe it wasn't Owen. Maybe you found out he was playing around and you arranged the accident.'

That did it. Doreen leapt to her feet and started screaming. 'All right, you bastard, all right. I'll tell you what you want to know. It doesn't matter now with Des dead, and who cares about that shitbag Jenna.'

She paused for breath. I waited.

'Des didn't work *for* Owen Bloody Jenna, he worked *with* him –

and, yes, Owen and Des were Quigley and Jacques.'

'Ah.'

'Satisfied, are you?'

'If you both dislike Owen so much, I'm surprised you've come out here whilst he stays behind and rakes in all the money. I take it Owen never let you get your hands on Des's share when he died?'

Susie spoke up. 'No, but we're going to get it, aren't we, Doe?'

'How?' I asked.

'One of the drivers is a personal friend of mine. He's arranging it for us.'

I remembered that Owen Jenna had said it was a taxi that tried to run him down. 'You mean, you're going to have him killed?'

'I'm the third partner in the business,' said Susie Jenna quietly, 'a silent partner. It was the insurance money from my parents' accident that Owen used originally to set up the company. With Des gone, when Owen dies, the company's mine.'

I stopped for a moment to formulate my reaction to this latest bombshell. Not content to abandon her two small children, she had allowed her husband to be suspected, and possibly convicted, for murder, and was now cold-bloodedly discussing hiring a hit-man to kill him. And this was the wronged missing wife that the Great British Public were agonising over.

Owen and Susie Jenna deserved one another, and Doreen Harward, in aiding and abetting them, was not much better.

'Who would run the operation with Owen dead?' I enquired.

'We would.' Susie Jenna, who had remained calm throughout, put down her cup. 'Doe and I. I shall reappear as the grieving widow who emerges from hiding, ready to assume control of our business after my cruel husband has been tragically killed in an accident.'

'But Owen isn't dead and I've just blown your hiding place, so where does that leave you?'

'Neither of us are wanted for anything,' said Doreen. She had regained her composure, happy to have let her friend take over the tale. 'We just go back to England a little earlier than we planned.'

'With Owen still in charge and news of your smuggling operation relayed to the Customs and Excise people? I don't think so.'

'There is no evidence of any criminal misdemeanours, I can assure you,' declared Doreen Harward confidently. 'We covered our tracks well. As for Owen Jenna, I take it you haven't heard this morning's sad news?'

'What news?' As she spoke, a sinking feeling struck me.

Susie Jenna beamed. 'I'm a widow, Mr Ace. Mr Jenna was killed in a tragic accident in Liverpool last night.'

Chapter Nineteen

'It's true,' said Jim Burroughs. 'He was knocked down by a hit and run on the Dock Road about eleven o'clock last night. He'd been working late at the office and apparently he'd stopped off at the Atlantic for a drink on the way home.'

I was phoning Jim from Doreen Harward's flat. She seemed anxious that I should confirm Susie Jenna's announcement there and then.

'Bang goes that other grand he owes us then,' I groaned. 'I take it they haven't found the driver?'

'Not a sign.'

'Seems a bit odd that, Jim, Owen Jenna drinking in the Atlantic. It's hardly his sort of place – unless, of course . . .'

'What?'

'Unless he was meeting someone.'

'Could be, although if he was, they didn't turn up. Witnesses in the pub say he had one drink, looked at his watch and left.'

'Who found him?'

'A couple of guys who left five minutes after him. He was lying dead in the gutter. They ran back in the pub and called the police.'

'So he was decoyed to the pub and the car was waiting for him when he came out.' Pretty well as Jenna had described to us the earlier attempt on his life.

I looked across at the two recently widowed women. 'Mr Jenna and Mrs Harward are with me now, Jim. They'll probably be returning home shortly to take control of the family business of which Mrs Jenna is now the sole owner.'

'Is that so now?' Jim whistled softly. 'Very interesting.'

'Precisely.'

'So I can tell the officer in charge of the case to expect them?'

'You have all the details,' I said carefully. I wanted to make sure the police in England knew where to find the two women in case they changed their mind about returning.

'Understood,' replied Jim, who was an expert at coded telephone calls, as I well knew from a previous occasion when I was held prisoner by a nutter in a Kirkby tower block.

'I bet you wish you'd come here wired up – eh, Mr Ace?' said Susie demurely after I put down the phone. 'As it is, nothing you've heard in this room counts for anything.'

I made a mental note to speak to Eddie Smeddles on the subject of surveillance equipment.

'When do you leave?' I asked. 'I presume you've booked your ticket? Wait a minute though.' I spoke to Susie. 'You haven't got a passport, so you can't go anywhere.'

Susie grinned. 'Wrong again. Doreen went over to my house when Owen was out and collected it.' Probably whilst he was at his 'niece's', I thought. 'Owen's mum and dad always got on with Doe.'

Doreen stood up. 'Nice of you to pop in, Johnny. May I call you that? Perhaps we'll run across one another again in Liverpool.'

'I'm sure we will, although you'll probably regret it when we do.'

Susie laughed. 'You've no proof of any wrongdoing on our part, you know. Look, you did what you came out for, you found me, why not leave it at that?'

'I suppose you could call it a sense of justice.' One of the reasons I'd gone into this business.

'Justice?' screeched Doreen. 'If there was any justice, Des wouldn't be dead now.'

'You still say Des's death was an accident?'

'Of course it bloody was, and the bastard who did it will pay for it, I can promise you that.'

'He's already paying for it,' I said. 'He got six months in prison.'

'And you think that's enough, do you, for taking an innocent man's life?'

I didn't challenge the description of her late husband, although innocent was not a word I would have used to describe Des Harward.

'Abram didn't mean to kill him. As far as I understand it, your husband was drunk and fell under his wheels.'

She said nothing but, for a moment, I could see real evil in her eyes and I remembered what Nigel Abram had told me about the Harward family's reaction when he called on them to apologise.

'I think enough has been said.' Susie Jenna stood up. 'Goodbye, Mr Ace, and I'm sorry about your thousand pounds.' She smiled as she added, 'Trust Owen to welch on his deals.'

'Until the next time,' I said, making my way to the door.

'There won't be a next time,' said Doreen Harward angrily.

'I wouldn't count on it.'

I left the flat and walked down to the sea-front where I stopped off at a little bar for a beer. I had four hours to kill before my plane took off. I took the drink to an outside table where I watched the rows of luxury yachts moored in the harbour. There was serious money out there and just a few miles down the coast was Monte Carlo.

I'd no idea what my next move should be. The problem was, as far as the cases went, we'd run out of clients. Jenna and Cronkshaw were dead. We'd had a grand from the Jenna case, and weren't likely to get any more, and Cronkshaw was killed before he'd had a chance to cough up a penny. Why waste any more of my time on Susie Jenna and her dodgy company? As for the John Lennon mystery, I'd got the tape so why bother about Edgar Marshall and Albert Cronkshaw?

The simple answer was, I wanted to know the truth.

The Skidmore case, too, was on its last legs. I couldn't see any justification for taking any more money from Elspeth Skidmore. I'd given it my best shot but, in the end, there was just no evidence of any wrongdoing.

And yet, I still felt Doreen Harward was concealing something when I mentioned Skidmore's name – although I couldn't for the life of me see what it could be.

Tomorrow was Saturday but there was no Premiership football because of international matches. I wondered if Hilary had been trying to get in touch with me. We were supposed to be going to the Everyman Theatre on Thursday to see *An Audience with Gerry Marsden*. I'd bought the tickets ages ago. Would she still be coming? I couldn't believe after twenty years it was all over.

I took a bus back into Nice. With the temperature in the high eighties, topless sunbathers and swimmers filled the beach alongside the Promenade des Anglais. It was never like that in New Brighton.

I didn't have long to linger round the airport as Easyjet worked on just a one-hour check-in time. I bought two bottles of perfume, one each for Hilary and Maria. Perhaps I was being optimistic.

The flight back was quicker; barely an hour and a half had passed before I saw the Liver Buildings below me beside the silver ribbon of the River Mersey as the plane circled to line up to the runway approach.

I was at Maria's an hour later. Roly was delighted to see me, standing on his hind legs and licking my face enthusiastically.

'He's been well-behaved,' smiled Maria, 'and Mrs Comfort has taken quite a shine to him. She bought him a ball and spent the afternoon playing with him in the garden. Is mushroom risotto all right for dinner?'

'Wonderful.' Over the meal I told her about the extraordinary outcome of my trip to France.

'Are you going to tell the police that Owen Jenna was murdered?'

'I don't know. It's my word against the two women and they both seemed pretty confident they'd left no incriminating evidence so I don't see the point. As far as the police are concerned, I've no involvement with Susie Jenna.'

'So you're going to investigate it yourself?' Maria knew me pretty well.

'Guess so.'

'Has Susie Jenna got a boyfriend?' she asked.

'Not as I know of, why?'

'She sounds the sort of woman who would always have a man in the picture, and there's got to be another man somewhere who killed her husband.'

'And you think it could be a boyfriend?'

'What could be easier? I've never been happy about all these hit-men theories. We're not talking *The Godfather* here. More likely she hired somebody she knew and trusted.'

'I could check out the names of all the drivers and see what I come up with.' Owen Jenna had said he thought it was a taxi that had tried to run him down.

I gave her the perfume as we were going to bed. 'Ralph Lauren,' she said, 'my favourite.' She opened the bottle and slowly rubbed small drops of the perfume over the upper slopes of her breasts. 'Gorgeous.' She arched her back, lifting her nipples to my face. 'Like it?' I ran my chin over her soft skin. 'Oooh, that hurts,' she cried, jumping up and almost knocking Roly off his side of the bed. 'You need a shave.'

'Sorry,' I apologised. 'It's been a long day.'

Tomorrow was going to seem even longer.

I left Maria's after breakfast and walked over to the office with Roly. Jim Burroughs was already there.

'Have you seen this?' He waved the *Daily Post* at me. The headline screamed I'M COMING HOME with a big photograph of Susie Jenna alongside and the by-line, *Lost Wife returns a Tragic Widow*.

'If only I'd been a day earlier,' I grumbled, 'we'd have had all the kudos for finding her. The publicity would have been worth a fortune.'

As it was, my name wasn't mentioned at all. Susie Jenna had jumped ahead of me and rung the Merseyside Police as soon as I had left, saying she had heard of her husband's tragic death and was getting on the next plane to Liverpool.

The tone of the article and the accompanying editorial was sympathetic towards the 'ill-used loyal wife', although there were reservations about the way she'd left her children, not to mention the waste of police time spent searching for her.

Owen Jenna's death was treated as a total accident. A police spokesman put forward the theory that joy riders, probably over the drink and drive limit, were the most likely culprits, but admitted that no progress had been made so far in finding them. Garages were asked to report cases of cars brought in for bodywork repairs that looked suspicious.

'It's all gone arse about face,' said Jim bitterly. 'We do all the work and end up out of pocket. At least we got that first grand up front.'

'And Mrs Jenna's come out of it smelling sweet as roses when we both know the whole affair stinks.'

'None of our business now. We need more paying clients.'

'We've had the five hundred from Mrs Skidmore,' I reminded Jim.

'And that's all we'll get from her too,' he sighed heavily. 'Another one bites the dust.'

I sang a couple of lines of the song. 'Queen,' I said automatically. 'Top Ten in 1980.'

'Hey, that would be a good number for us to do in the act,' Jim said brightly.

At the mention of The Chocolate Lavatory, I quickly changed the subject. 'Maria reckons the man who ran Owen Jenna down could be one of the drivers at European Carriages – maybe Susie Jenna's boyfriend.'

'I didn't know she had one.'

'Neither do I, but it's a possibility, isn't it?'

'So what are you going to do about it? I take it you're carrying on with this unpaid investigation.' He emphasised the word 'unpaid'.

'Nothing else to do at the moment, Jim, so I might as well. I thought I'd go up there Monday morning and check it out.'

'Like you say, we've nothing else on.'

'What about the break in? No more news on that? Have we not heard anything from Joey?'

'Not a whisper.'

'It's days since I wrote.' I was puzzled. 'He must have got the letter by now.'

'We'll just have to wait for his next move.'

Before we could speculate what that might be, the phone rang. It was Badger. 'You wanted to know about the late Merry Widower as was, man. Come over to my place. I've got an interesting story about Mr Owen Jenna that you might like to hear.'

Chapter Twenty

I walked back to Maria's flat to pick up the RAV4 and, with Roly in the back, drove over to my house in Livingstone Drive where Badger lives in one of the top-floor flats.

I left Roly on the floor below with Pat Lake and her invalid mother. Pat is a middle-aged spinster who incongruously goes to heavy metal concerts and mixes with bikers. For some reason, she's taken a shine to Roly.

'I'm glad you're here,' she said, 'because I've bought that dog a proper collar.' She produced a thick black leather affair dotted with fearsome metal studs. 'This'll look better than that poncy tartan thing he wears.'

Roly didn't look too keen but I left him to his fate and carried on upstairs.

Badger's flat looked more than ever like a Victorian conservatory, with the foliage of dozens of plants obscuring the shelves of books, DVDs and CDs. One of them looked suspiciously like cannabis. The sound of a Puff Daddy album was pounding out of a pair of giant speakers attached to a 300-watt silver hi-fi, half hidden behind a huge potted palm.

Badger was dressed as flamboyantly as ever in a grey shirt, black jacket and silver tie, all of which toned perfectly with his long black dreadlocks.

'You still interested in the sadly departed Mr Jenna?'

'More than ever, Badger. What can you tell me?'

'Coffee first.' I followed him into the kitchen where he set up an expensive-looking Gaggia machine that wouldn't have looked out of place in the Ritz.

'Does it do cappuccino?' I asked, as he turned various dials and fed in milk and ground coffee. I wouldn't have been surprised if it had produced a five-course meal.

'No problem.'

We returned to the lounge, carrying our drinks in large coloured mugs.

'Right,' he said, lowering himself into a big wickerwork chair. 'Where should I start?'

I sat in the matching chair. 'How about with who killed him?'

'Can't tell you that, but I've been doing some digging into his business affairs. He ran a nice little coaching operation, bought, they say, with his wife's money.'

'Tell me something I don't know.'

'It's a front, man.'

'I know. Illegal imports.'

'And exports,' added Badger. 'Small-arms to the continent which find their way back to Ireland.'

Surprise, surprise.

'How do you know all this?'

Badger looked cagey. 'I have a friend who drives for them occasionally.'

I didn't probe. Badger had always mixed with nefarious characters and he didn't get his Porsche out of a Christmas cracker. 'Go on.'

'There's been mutiny in the camp. The Merry Widower had a partner who wanted more of the action.'

'Des Harward,' I nodded.

'And his dear lady wife.'

'But Harward's dead.'

'And so now is our Mr Jenna, which leaves his Very Merry Widow in the driving seat.'

'I know all this, Badger. What I need to know is, who helped them dispose of Owen Jenna? And what was the story behind his sudden fortune?'

'Insurance policy on his late partner, A few hundred grand payable on accidental death to the remaining partners, namely the Jennas.'

An acceptable motive for killing Des Harward.

'And now a second partner meets with an accident. The insurance company are going to wonder about this one.' I knew, though, that that would depend very much on the coroner's verdict. As Jim Burroughs had pointed out, the Crown Prosecution Service have a hard job proving murder by motor accidents.

'And they say lightnin' never strikes twice, man. It sho' did for Mrs Jenna.'

I thought about this. Susie Jenna had virtually admitted to me that she'd got rid of her husband. Had she got rid of Des Harward too? And how far was Doreen Harward involved? Maybe the two women had planned it this way from the start. Doreen had made a big thing of being distraught when her husband was killed but that could have been a blind.

I decided I needed to have another chat with Nigel Abram.

'Shame her old man had such a short time to enjoy his little bunny and them two widow ladies is going to clean up,' Badger said, shaking his head.

'They know the police and the Customs are on to them now. I don't think they'll be able to carry on the business.'

'Who said anything about carrying on? European Carriages is about to be taken over. They're bailing out. Don't you see,' he said exasperatedly, 'they cop for the insurance, sell the company and jolly off to the South of France. You knew Owen Jenna had a yacht out there?'

I didn't, but I saw now why Doreen had bought her flat in Beaulieu.

I persisted. 'Who killed Owen Jenna, Badger?'

He coughed. 'I am on the payroll for this, aren't I, man? My expenses is high. This is dangerous undercover work.'

'I thought you had a friend in there doing all the digging.' But I didn't argue. 'How much?' I sighed.

'Two hundred.'

The profit margin on the job was being erased by the minute. First the trip to Nice, now Badger's cut. I took out four fifties and handed them to him. He folded them carefully into a black calfskin wallet and continued.

'The name I've heard is Graham Bowlands. He's one of the part-time drivers.'

'That figures.'

'They do say,' Badger lowered his voice to a whisper for theatrical effect, 'they do say that Mr B. may have been doing a line with the Merry Widow.'

That struck a chord. Maria had asked me if Susie Jenna had a boyfriend, someone to do the dirty work.

'Thanks, Badger,' I said, standing up and making for the door. 'Keep in touch and let me know as soon as you hear any more.'

On the way down, I knocked at Pat Lake's door. Roly was waiting for me, resplendent in his new bondage collar.

'You should get him an earring,' suggested Pat. 'Make him look striking.'

I was stopped at the front door by Giles, the young accountant who lived on the ground-floor flat. 'The sink drain seems to be blocked in the bathroom,' he complained.

That's the trouble with visiting the houses. Once the tenants see the landlord, they seem to feel the necessity to complain about something.

'Have you rung Geoffrey?' I asked.

'It's the ansaphone.' Even Geoff was allowed the weekend off.

'He picks up the messages every evening,' I answered confidently. 'He'll sort it. At least the toilet's working.'

I drove back into town, found a parking spot in Victoria Street and took Roly into Cavern Walks and the Lucy in the Sky café.

I saw the anxious look on Margie's face when she spotted the dog. 'You needn't worry, we're eating at the outside tables,' I assured her, and ordered a curried-chicken jacket potato.

'On your own?' queried Margie.

I told her about the row with Hilary.

'She'll come round, Johnny, You've had Maria for three years now and it hasn't bothered her before. Besides, hasn't Hilary got that doctor fellow up at the Infirmary?'

'He's more of a friend,' I said, although I'd always suspected they slept together. As long as she'd stayed with me I hadn't let myself think about it.

'The situation obviously suits you both or you'd have got married long ago. Now what about Everton on Wednesday? We're at home to Wimbledon.'

'We should beat them.'

'Beat them? exclaimed Maggie. 'We'll hammer them with Franny up front with Kevin Campbell.'

She went off to fetch my meal and, when it came, there was a saucer of chicken for Roly. Margie looked at him closely. 'That collar looks painful. You'll be getting the poor beggar tattooed next.'

I had the afternoon free. I went back to the flat and rang Jim Burroughs at his home. 'I need to go to Kirkham prison to see Nigel Abram again,' I told him.

'A bit late for that, Johnny. I forgot to tell you, I heard while you were away that he came out last Monday.'

So it was possible that Nigel Abram, having killed Des Harward, could have been behind the wheel of the car that mowed down Owen Jenna. Yet I still couldn't see the accountant as a contract killer. 'Have you an address for him?' I asked.

In his usual efficient way, Jim had. The Abrams lived in a semi-detached house in Maghull.

Leaving Roly in the flat, I drove out through Walton and Aintree to Maghull. The house was on the other side of Northway, a few miles from Lydiate where I'd visited Crawford Barker, the deposed elderly barbershop singer. That seemed like a lifetime ago.

Nigel Abram's wife answered the door. She looked like the teacher she was. Her corn-coloured hair was tied back in a pony tail with an elastic band, she wore no make-up and sported a pair of navy knee-length shorts, unmatching blue canvas shoes and an off-white T-shirt with a message condemning fox-hunting.

'Mrs Abram? I'm Johnny Ace. I wanted to speak to your husband.'

She looked at me disapprovingly. 'I've heard your show on the radio and I can't say I agree with many of your ideas.'

'Hunting with hounds is the most humane way of dealing with foxes,' I said, adding, 'urban people should not presume to tell country people how to conduct their affairs.'

'I wasn't referring specifically to that subject,' she said. 'Some of your other views . . .'

'I didn't come here for a debate, Mrs Abram. Why don't you ring my phone-in and we can discuss it on air.' Except I suddenly remembered that I didn't have a show any more.

'You'd better come in.' She led me into the house and through the patio doors in the dining kitchen to the back garden where Nigel Abram was mowing the lawn.

'Glad to see you're back home,' I greeted him.

He stopped pushing and turned off the power. 'Oh, it's Mr Ace. How's the radio programme coming along?' I realised he was referring to my excuse for my visit to Kirkham prison.

'Abandoned, I'm afraid. Other topics came up and it was shelved.'

'I can't say I'm sorry. I just want to forget all that ever happened. But if the programme is cancelled, why are you here?' I showed him my business card. 'I'm investigating the affairs of a company called European Carriages. The man you ran over, Des Harward, was a partner in that company. What I need to know is, had you ever met him before?'

Abram looked at me as if I was slightly mad. 'No, never in my life. I'd never heard of the bloke. What makes you think I had?'

I phrased it carefully. 'I don't, but a suggestion was made that there were people who wanted Des Harward dead – which made his actual passing rather a lucky coincidence for them.'

'You don't seriously think I'm a Mafia hit man?' He laughed at the idea and, here in this suburban garden, I had to admit it was more than unlikely. 'Who were these people who wanted rid of him?'

'Let's just say there are certain people who have benefited from his death.' But, as I said it, I didn't really believe any more that Des's death was anything but a genuine accident. This meant, of course, that my hypothesis that his wife had arranged it had gone out of the window. Her show of grief, however theatrical, had been genuine.

'You told me about meeting his family,' I said instead. 'They weren't very pleasant to you, if I remember.'

'Pleasant isn't the word. I was lucky to escape with my life when I went round there. His wife was screaming at me and his cousin threatened to break my legs when I came out.'

'Hang on, you never mentioned that before,' I said. 'What was this cousin's name?'

'Let me think.' I waited. A magpie landed on a branch of a hawthorn tree at the end of the garden. The distant hum of a plane broke the quiet summer silence, trailing two lines of exhaust cloud.

'Yes, that's it,' he said carefully. 'Mrs Harward shouted to him, "Kill the bastard!" and as I made for the door she screamed, "Get him, Graham!" Yes, that's what she called him – Graham.'

I rang Jim Burroughs when I returned to the flat and filled him in on this latest development.

'So this Graham Bowlands, who is Des Harward's cousin and possibly Susie Jenna's lover, is the man you think killed Owen Jenna? Is that what you're saying?'

'He's favourite at the moment, Jim. Harward's death was an accident, I accept that now, but Mrs Jenna virtually told me she'd arranged for her husband to be killed. Who better to do the job than her own boyfriend who was also tied in with the Harwards?'

'And he's driving for the firm as well, which means it's odds on he's involved in the smuggling.'

'Possibly only as a gash hand.'

'We need to find Bowlands and quickly.'

'First thing Monday morning, I'll be down at the firm's offices. Incidentally, Jim, I've had another idea about the John Lennon tape.'

'Go on.'

'It's the Beatles Convention at the Adelphi next Sunday. Do you remember Albert said Marshall was thinking of taking the tape there?

It seemed like not a bad idea. I thought I might book a stall myself and see the reaction.'

'What the hell for?'

'It might bring Harriman and Joey out of the woodwork. I'll get Marty to put a piece in the *Daily Post*, saying this rare Beatles tape has just been discovered and that I'll have it on display at the Convention.'

'I can't see them falling for that. Besides, surely Harriman's gone to ground? He must know the police are looking for him in connection with Cronkshaw's death.'

'He's so obsessed I think he'd risk it. As for Joey, he's stupid enough. Either way, it's worth a try: it can't do any harm. Can you sort it out, Jim, and I'll see you on Monday.'

I toyed with the idea of ringing Hilary. I had the weekend free, as Maria had gone to stay with a friend in Grasmere for a couple of days. I'd hoped Hilary would have got in touch with me by now; after all, she was the one who'd flounced off. On the other hand, if I wanted to be proud about it I could sit around and wait for ever.

I rang.

'It's me,' I said.

'Oh.'

I'd never felt awkward with Hilary before but I couldn't think of how to start. In the end, 'I'm sorry,' we both said together.

'I thought you might have rung,' she said.

'I've been away.' As if that were a reason. 'To France.'

'Whatever for?'

I explained briefly about Susie Jenna.

'I saw the headlines in the *Post* this morning. Her husband's been killed.'

'I know. Listen, what are you doing tonight?'

She hesitated. 'I'm going to this hospital dance.'

'Oh.' I didn't ask who was taking her.

'I'm not doing anything tomorrow though.'

'Do you want to come round then?'

'About seven?'

'Fine. We're still going to see Gerry Marsden on Thursday, aren't we?'

'Yes, of course.'

I felt much better when I put the phone down but wondered how long I could keep up going out with both women. I'd had a long run but strains were starting to show. The balancing act was getting harder than ever and I knew I could end up losing both.

I cooked myself some pasta with vegetables, opened a bottle of red wine and put the new Paul McCartney CD on the hi-fi. The album was full of the old rock 'n' roll songs he used to sing with The Beatles in the early days at The Cavern.

Probably Bobby and the Voxtones had sung some of the very same tracks on that same stage. They wouldn't be doing so again. Mind you, come to that, what were the chances of Paul McCartney ever setting foot in The Cavern again?

After the frenzied activity of the past week, I was glad of a quiet night. It was only seven days ago that I'd been at Maria's when Jim rang to say Albert Cronkshaw had been murdered. So much had happened since then yet we were still no nearer to finding out who had killed the ex-Voxtones drummer.

I was in bed by midnight and up at eight the next morning, when I went out with Roly to buy a paper. The headlines in The *News of the World* hit me the moment I walked into the shop. EXCLUSIVE – THE SUSIE JENNA STORY – MISSING WIFE TELLS ALL.

She didn't quite tell all. I bought the paper, along with The *Sunday Times*, and took it back home to read.

The photographers had been busy. There was a picture of the flat in Beaulieu, the offices of European Carriages and one of Susie looking sad and forlorn next to a much earlier shot of the not-so-loving couple at their wedding.

In the ghost-written article, Susie declared she'd been a battered wife and had left for reasons of personal safety after her husband had threatened to kill her. Of course, with Owen Jenna dead, none of this could now be contradicted.

A 'friend' – Doreen Harward was not named – had lent her her apartment on the Riviera where she had been in hiding until she heard the dreadful news about her husband's death. She was, the paper said, 'consumed with grief'. She had now come home to be reunited with her children and to pick up the pieces of her life.

I wondered how much Susie had been paid for that pack of lies. It would all help swell the jackpot of the insurance money and the proceeds of the company sale. Not to mention the profits stashed away from the 'import-export' business.

Hilary arrived at seven, looking stunning in a short black skirt and gold mini-top which matched her long blonde hair. 'Hiya, babe,' she said, as if nothing had happened. 'Where are we going?'

We went to the Blue Bar on the Albert Dock. A few Liverpool footballers were in. The Reds, under Gerard Houlier, were hoping for a revival but it hadn't happened yet. I was hoping for a revival myself, but across the park at Everton.

After the meal, I suggested we went over to the Masquerade for a couple of drinks. When we got there, I saw that the club was back to its customary darkness.

'What's happened to the searchlights?' I asked Tommy McKale.

'We only switch those on for the Beach Nights, Johnny. It's mostly just the regulars that come in of a Sunday and they don't particularly want to be seen. They're people of the shadows, you might say. Night people.'

In the gloom, I could see three or four members of the Ince clan drinking at a table.

'Sean not with them?' I asked.

'He's down in London, I believe,' answered Tommy. 'Doing something with computers.'

I was glad he'd managed to get away. The trick would be to stay there. He would be well out of the rackets. Clubland was getting more violent than it had been for decades.

'It's the international gangs,' explained Tommy. 'In the old days, you just had the local villains to contend with, You might get the odd outfit from the Smoke coming up to try and muscle in but we'd soon see them off. Nowadays, though, there's the Russians, the

Triads, the Yardies – Christ, they're coming from all over the fucking world. Look at Manchester, shootings every week and it hardly makes the inside pages.'

'It's the drugs, isn't it? Such big money.'

'Drugs and protection. That's what closed the Hacienda in Manchester, and if they can close the most successful club in the city . . .' He shrugged his shoulders.

'You've not had any trouble yourself?'

'Apart from the odd kids' nights, ours is mostly an older crowd so the dealers leave us alone. We did have a visit once from some people. They sent over a couple of supposed hard men, both tooled up. Came to tell us they were buying the business.'

'What happened?'

'Denis shot them,' said Tommy McKale matter-of-factly, 'and we never heard any more. I think their people got the message when they never returned home.'

'Another drink, Tommy?' I waved across to the barman, a surly little man with rounded shoulders, dressed all in black, his thinning hair cut in an outdated Roy Orbison style. The Big O, another of the singing dead. I gave him the order.

'Vince's night off,' explained Tommy. 'Lurch helps out the odd time.' I didn't need to ask how he got the name.

'No,' Tommy continued, 'the only answer is to legalise drugs because you'll never get rid of them now, they're too entrenched in the culture. The government might as well make the money. It'd get rid of drug-related crime, quality control would improve and it might knock a few pence off income tax.'

'I'm not sure about drugs but brothels certainly,' I said. 'They should legalise those,' and then I saw a frown cross Tommy McKale's face and knew that wasn't a wise thing to say. The McKales were known to have interests in the 'skin' trade.

Hilary broke in. 'You'd end up having Tony Blair as a drug baron and running a prostitution ring,' she laughed.

'Why not? He wants to run everything else.'

The Sunday DJ was playing some quiet soul music, Gladys Knight and the Pips' 'Midnight Train to Georgia'.

'Let's have a dance,' I said to Hilary. We did a few turns round the floor, Hilary pressing herself seductively against me at every turn.

'How's the detective business going?' asked Tommy when we returned to the bar. 'Did anything come of that thing with the magistrates, someone trying to knock them off?'

'No, died on its arse that one.' I told him about the John Lennon tape.

'You touched lucky there, Johnny. Sounds like you could be in for a few bob.'

'I'm taking it to the Beatles Convention at the Adelphi next week. See if there's any interest.'

'I've never been but I believe it gets pretty busy up there.'

'You're not kidding. People come from all over the world. I tell you, Tommy, in a hundred years' time, because of The Beatles, Liverpool will get more tourists than Stratford does with Shakespeare or Haworth and the Brontës.'

'Never mind a hundred years, we could do with them now.'

We finished our drinks and I took Hilary back to the flat. Roly moved to his basket when he realised Hilary wanted the bed to ourselves.

'Is everything all right again now?' I asked her as she took off her knickers and slid between the sheets.

'Never mind all that,' she replied. Her hands reached down and she pushed her tongue into my mouth, exchanging her saliva with mine. I stopped talking.

Afterwards, as we lay there she said, 'What I can't handle is you being emotionally attached to someone else.'

'But I've always had girlfriends like you've always had your doctor friend. What's special about me and Maria?'

'If you don't know, then I can't tell you.' She sighed and stroked my forehead affectionately. 'You don't understand women, do you, Johnny?'

I didn't disagree. I like women, I enjoy their company but their minds seem to run in a parallel universe to men's. What was that book about men from Mars and women from Venus?

'What does that mean exactly, in terms of our relationship?'

'It means,' she said, 'that things will sort themselves out, one way or another.' I didn't find this comforting but it was the best I could get and I again got the feeling that we were moving in new uncharted territory.

Hilary left for her early shift the next morning and I went across to the *Daily Post* office to see Marty about doing the John Lennon tape story.

'Nice one, Johnny. We'll do a couple of photos, it'll make a nice spread. Any joy with the radio show?'

'Not a word. Shady Soddin' Spencer's hanging on in there.'

'He's crap though.'

'Tell me about it.'

I took Roly to the office, where Jim Burroughs was already at his desk. 'I've been on to the people about your stall on Sunday,' he said. 'Bad news. You're too late, they're booked up.'

'Shit.' That was my brilliant plan blown apart. Then I had an idea. Nudger Ainsworth always had a stall at the Convention: I'd ask him to let me use it to exhibit my tape. Nudger was always broke. He'd probably be happy to let me, in exchange for a few quid.

'I'm off to European Carriages,' I told Jim. 'Time to find Graham Bowlands.'

Sandra the receptionist was at her desk as I walked through the stainless steel and glass doors of the European Carriages offices.

'Me again,' I smiled.

She smiled back. 'Hi, Johnny. Fancy you coming in today.'

'Why's that?'

'You know last time you came in, you were asking about Doreen Harward? Well, she's back. She's here today with, would you believe, Mrs Jenna?'

I'd believe it. Susie hadn't wasted much time taking over.

Sandra carried on excitedly. 'You've heard about poor Mr Jenna, I suppose?'

'Hasn't everybody.'

'Such a shame.'

'I thought you didn't like him. Thought he'd killed his wife.'

'It doesn't mean to say I'd wish him dead. Anyway, he didn't, did he? Kill her, I mean.'

No, but she killed him, I thought. To Sandra I said, 'I'm looking for someone else now, a driver called Graham Bowlands.'

'Name rings a bell. I'll check in the book.' Out came the blue ledger. 'Here we are. Oh, he's away at the moment on the continental run.'

'Since when?'

'Since yesterday. He's taken the Paris coach – a day out at Disneyland and two in the capital. He'll be back early Thursday morning.'

I wouldn't have bet on it. Bowlands had every reason for jumping ship in France. Doubtless, too, he'd have taken a last consignment of 'goods' across the Channel with him before the company changed hands. Give Susie Jenna credit, she moved fast.

'I'll call back then,' I told Sandra.

'Hey, before you go, what's happened to your show? You've not been on lately.'

'On holiday,' I replied briefly. It was the only answer I could think of, although the 'holiday' was becoming more like a sabbatical with every passing day.

'Well well, fancy seeing you here.' I turned round to find Susie Jenna emerging from the back office. 'You've tracked me down once, Mr Ace, do you need an encore?'

'No.'

'Then what are you doing here?' Her tone was not friendly.

'Your late husband was a client of mine.'

'*Was* being the operative word. But as he's dead, he can be a client no longer, surely?'

'Naturally, I'm concerned about the manner of his death.'

'Naturally.'

'A rather convenient accident, some might say.'

'They might.'

'I'd be interested to know who was driving the car that ran him down.'

'Wouldn't we all? It was probably the same fellow who killed poor Des Harward except, I forgot, he's in prison, isn't he? What was his name? Allbaum? Alford?'

'Abram. And, for your information, he's out of prison now. But Nigel Abram didn't run down your husband, Mrs Jenna. I believe it was a man called Graham Bowlands, your friend Doreen's cousin.'

'What?' she said absently. Something else had taken her attention. 'Bowlands, you say? Sorry, never heard of him. Look, you must excuse me, I've got work to do.' Suddenly she seemed anxious to get away and I wondered why.

'I believe you're selling the company.'

'That's right.' She saw Sandra the receptionist's face at this news and quickly reassured her. 'Don't worry, luv, your job's safe. The new people are carrying on the business.' She opened the door to the office. 'Goodbye, Mr Ace,' she called. 'I hope you find your lost driver.'

I walked back to the car, puzzled. Why had the mention of Nigel Abram had such an effect on Susie Jenna?

Chapter Twenty-One

On the way back to the office, I stopped off at Mount Street and luckily found Nudger Ainsworth still in bed.

'What time is it?' he asked blearily. He'd shuffled to the front door in an open dressing gown worn over a pair of faded Y-fronts. His feet were bare and grubby.

'Nearly one o'clock.'

'Heavy night,' he explained and led me through to his bedroom. The mattress was laid on the floor and the rest of the space was taken up with more piles of magazines that had overflowed from the living room. 'Sorry about the mess. What can I do for you, Johnny?'

I told him the story of the John Lennon tape.

'Wow, heavy stuff,' he said. 'So you want to put it on my stall? What if any of these geezers tries to rob it?'

'My minders will be with you, don't worry. And I'll be there, of course.'

'Right.'

'What do you sell on this stall?'

'Any memorabilia of The Beatles. I spend fifty-one weeks of the year going round the car boots, jumbles and charity shops for gear. Old Mersey Beats, photos, Beatles wigs, they all sell. The Americans and Japanese can't get enough of the stuff. Old copies of *Mersey Beat* change hands for over £70. Then there's the bootleg records, there's a fortune in them. Almost pay for my year's rent in one go.'

I wished I'd kept all my old copies of *Mersey Beat*, not to mention all my old 45s like Chuck Berry's 'Schoolday' on Columbia, now worth £80 in good nick. Easy to say now.

A thought struck me. 'You move about in record circles, Nudger. Have you ever come across a lad called Frank Harriman in your travels?'

'Is he a big Beatles fanatic?'

'That's the one.'

'Yeah, I've seen him at the record fairs at odd times.' He laughed. 'He's a bit of a weirdo, I'd say.'

That was what they said about Mark Chapman – *after* he'd gunned down John Lennon. I was beginning to worry about Harriman.

'I'd say so too. How about a bloke called Joey, late twenties, comes from Chester?'

'What's he look like?'

I gave him a fair description of the man I'd met under the Eastgate clock.

'Doesn't ring a bell, why?'

'He advertised for Beatles gear in the July *Record Collector* you gave me.'

'No address?'

'Just a Chester PO Box number.'

'Mmmm. He could be a trawler.'

'A what?'

'They're people who go round all the fairs, jumble sales and that, like me, only instead of selling on the gear themselves, like I do, they pass it on to a dealer who gives them a cut.'

'Don't the dealers buy in direct?'

'Not always. For a start, they don't have the manpower to go trawling round the country hoping to find the odd gem amongst a load of dross. And, second, a lot of punters don't like selling to dealers; they think they're going to get ripped off.'

'As they probably are.'

'Quite. Just like the antique game really.'

'So this way, the punters get ripped off by amateurs instead and the dealers get the gear in the end anyway?'

'That's about it.'

'Are there many dealers?'

'Quite a few who specialise in Beatles and Merseybeat items. Like I said, there's big money to be made. Mind you, any showbiz shite sells these days if you know the right people to sell to.'

'I've got Howling Wolf's autograph at home, Nudger. Want to make me an offer?'

'I know someone who would.'

'I'll think about it.' I thanked him for his help. 'I'll see you on Sunday then. Go back to bed, I'll let myself out.'

I stopped off in town for some lunch at Coopers in Bold Street, parking the RAV4 round the corner in Seel Street, just down the road from The Blue Angel, Allan Williams' old club and another of The Beatles' haunts in the sixties, now just another night club.

Jim Burroughs had no news when I returned to the office. 'No word from Joey, nothing new on Harriman. We need some new cases, Johnny, to get some income in.'

'We don't do this just for income, Jim. Besides, you've got your police pension and the money from your gigs. You won't starve.'

'I know that, but we need to cover our overheads all the same.'

'Chill out, for Christ's sake. You've not asked me how I got on at European Carriages.'

'Well?'

'Bowlands has scarpered, taken a coachload of crumblies to Disneyland.'

'Great.' Jim can sound more sarcastic than anyone I know when he tries.

'He's supposed to be returning on Thursday – that's if he doesn't do a runner on the continent, so I'm going back then. And guess what, Susie Jenna was there.'

'Didn't take her long.'

'Tidying up the loose ends, I guess. Something odd though, she sounded strangely interested to hear Nigel Abram was out. Why do you think that could be?'

'We've ruled Abram out, haven't we?'

'Oh yes. Running down Des Harward was an accident, no doubt about it.'

217

'What's your next move then?'

'Nothing much I can do till Thursday.'

I went back to the flat early and ran a bath. There's something decadent about having a bath in the afternoon but lying under the bubbles, I had time to reflect. Everything seemed to have gone quiet on all fronts but I wasn't deceived. This was the phoney peace. There was much still to be sorted and it wouldn't be long before something gave and the shit hit the fan.

I towelled myself down, thought of doing a few exercises but decided against it, and threw on a clean T-shirt and pair of jeans.

As a concession to healthy living, I microwaved a Marks & Spencer's chestnut roast and ate it with a Scrumpy Jack whilst listening to Shady Spencer's show.

Shady had a guest, a pensioner who'd played the bagpipes in World War One. Unfortunately, they'd obviously made him deaf as he couldn't carry on a normal conversation and eventually Shady gave up shouting at him and played a Rolf Harris record instead. Riveting stuff. I wondered what the listening figures were and opened another can of cider, switching off the radio in favour of a Shane McGowan CD. I needed to listen to something more aggressive to counteract the blandness.

Later, I rang Maria to make sure the tape was still OK in her library locker and arranged to take her out the following night.

When it got dark, another two cans and a punk compilation CD later, with the Undertones' 'Jimmy Jimmy' programmed in six times, I allowed Roly to take me for a walk along the dock road.

We stopped off at the Atlantic for a quick glass of cider and found Gloria sitting in a corner, half cut but still breathing. I took her a glass of Guinness over.

'I drink brandies in the evenings, Johnny Ponny,' she said, nonetheless grabbing the glass from me. 'Big ones. Do they call it a treble when it reaches the top of the glass?'

'No, they call it a bloody miracle, Gloria.'

'That's a nice dog, that,' she said, patting Roly's head with her bony fingers. 'Is it psychic?'

Ever since this author called John Sutton wrote a book about pets' star signs, everybody thinks their dog or cat is the next Russell Grant.

'No, Gloria, it's YOU that's psychic and I came to tell you that you were right the other day when you said that the missing woman was out of the country with a friend.'

'I did too. The cards never lie.'

'The cards, my arse. You'd heard something, you old scoundrel.'

She grinned, displaying a row of crooked teeth reminiscent of the targets at a fairground shooting booth. 'Maybe I had, Johnny, and maybe I hadn't, but I'll tell you something now.'

She waited and looked meaningfully towards my back pocket. I drew out a bluey and laid it on the table. She thrust it up her skirt into her usual hiding place and leaned forward. 'More deaths,' she breathed hoarsely.

'Who's going to die?'

'More deaths,' she repeated.

'Are we talking about Susie Jenna?'

'That's all.' She picked up her glass and downed the half of Guinness in one go. 'No more.'

I knew it was a waste of time to press her. 'See you, Gloria,' I said, and made for the door before she had a chance to demand the treble brandy.

As I walked Roly back to the flat, I pondered Gloria's latest prophecy. I wasn't sure what to make of it. Had her 'prediction' about Susie Jenna been pure guesswork – or could she really tell the future? Or, more likely, had she heard some tittle-tattle during her dealings with the local criminal fraternity? Either way, she'd been correct on that occasion. Could she be right now about the deaths yet to come – and whose would they be?

Next morning, I walked down to the Royal Liver Buildings for breakfast in The Diner. I stopped off at the shop to pick up a *Daily Post* on the way in. Marty had done me proud again. Not only had he run the piece about the tape at the Beatles Convention, accompanied by a picture of John Lennon and one of me holding the Bobby and the Voxtones tape, masquerading again as the John

Lennon one, but he also announced a campaign to have my programme reinstated in response to 'a deluge of requests' from readers.

Tuesday was my morning for sorting out the flats so I went round to the Aigburth Road office to see how Geoffrey was coping with everything. He looked suspiciously at Roly, probably remembering the previous week's sick.

'Did Giles from Livingstone Drive ring about his blocked drain?' I asked.

'All fixed, boss.'

'The usual, was it? Hair down the sink?'

Geoffrey grinned. 'Yes. I told him to buy himself a plunger if he couldn't be bothered to put the loose hairs down the toilet. That nurse took the Kirkdale flat,' he added, 'Miss Patel. Moves in tomorrow. Oh, and your chum Shirley rang . . .' Was it my imagination or did Geoffrey smirk as he mentioned her name? 'Wants to talk to you about decorating her bedroom.'

'Not *more* decorating?' What does she want – a Michelangelo ceiling?'

I signed a few letters, wrote some cheques then went into town. I grabbed a bowl of soup in the Bluecoat, spent half an hour looking round the bookshop there and eventually dropped in at the Dale Street office around three.

'Where've you been?' Jim Burroughs demanded. 'I've been trying to reach you.'

'Sorry, Jim, I left my pager at home.'

'You'll have to get a mobile phone like everybody else. For God's sake, even schoolchildren have them now. In this job, contact is vital.'

I knew he was right. What's a fried brain when twenty-four-hour contact is at stake? 'What's it all about then?'

'I've had Mike Bennett on the phone. He's coming over – in fact he'll be here any minute.'

'What's happened?'

'Someone tried to kill Nigel Abram last night.'

'What!'

'Outside his garage. He heard a noise, went out to investigate and they were waiting for him.'

'Is he badly hurt?'

'He's in intensive care but he'll live. An inch either way and the knife would have severed the main artery or punctured his heart. As it is, he's got a collapsed lung.'

'Why is Dl Bennett coming here? What's it to do with us?'

Jim Burroughs spoke carefully. 'Because, Johnny, the knife that was used to attack Nigel Abram turns out to be the same one that killed Edgar Marshall!'

Detective Inspector Bennett arrived ten minutes later, accompanied by a Sergeant Edwards.

'Strange how your name keeps cropping up in this investigation, Mr Ace,' said Bennett sternly. 'You were the one to find Edgar Marshall's body and it was you that Albert Cronkshaw hired before he, too, was murdered.'

'None of this can have any connection with Nigel Abram, surely? He'd nothing to do with the John Lennon tape, nor was he ever a member of Bobby and the Voxtones.'

'Maybe not, but the fact remains, he was attacked with the same knife that killed Edgar Marshall. And there is another common factor.'

'What's that?'

'You. You visited Nigel Abram in prison and again at his house last Saturday.'

'Yes, but that was nothing to do with Edgar Marshall.'

'Then why did you go to see him?'

'Initially, when I went to Kirkham, it was in connection with another case.'

'Which was?'

'A magistrate called Bernard Skidmore was killed in a motor accident. His car came off the road. The coroner said it was accidental death but his wife had other ideas. She reckoned he

221

was murdered and hired me to look into it.'

'I see. And why would she think that?'

'Couldn't accept his death, I suppose.'

'Had she anybody in mind who she thought might have wanted him dead?'

'We thought it could be someone he'd sent to prison who wanted to get their revenge. That's how I came to interview Abram. He was one of six people sent down by Mr Skidmore in the past six months.'

'And what conclusion did you reach?'

'There was no way Abram killed him, or any of the others come to that. I spoke to all six of them and none of them showed any particular ill-feeling towards the bench, certainly not enough to commit murder. Skidmore's death was an accident, Inspector, no doubt about it.'

'Then why did you call on Nigel Abram again at the weekend?'

'Ah, well, that was another case.'

'And he was involved in that too?'

'Indirectly, yes. I take it you know about Susie Jenna, the missing wife?'

'Everybody in Britain knows about Susie Jenna, Mr Ace. With all the TV and newspaper publicity, it's become a *cause célèbre*, but Detective Inspector Fletcher is actually the officer in charge of that investigation.'

'I know Andy Fletcher.' I'd met him a year ago at the Stirling Club when a suspect I was following was murdered in the Gents.

Bennett didn't seem interested in my relationships with his colleagues. 'In what way were you involved with Susie Jenna?'

I explained how I'd been hired by Owen Jenna to find his missing wife. 'He didn't seem to think the police were trying very hard to find her because they were convinced he'd killed her.'

Bennett was not prepared to admit that was true. 'Mrs Jenna's turned up now, as you doubtless know.'

'And Owen Jenna's been murdered instead.'

I realised I'd spoken too quickly. The inspector looked startled.

'Mr Jenna's death is being treated as a hit and run. Have you any reason to suppose otherwise?'

'If Inspector Fletcher is handling Mr Jenna's death then I'm sure he must have considered other possibilities.'

'I asked you, have you any reason . . . ?'

'No, no, just my suspicious nature.'

'Where does Nigel Abram fit into the Jenna enquiry?' asked Bennett.

'Abram was in prison for killing a Mr Harward who ran out in front of his car. It was an accident but he got six months for careless driving.'

'I don't see . . .'

'Mr Harward was Mr Jenna's partner in a company called European Carriages. Mr Jenna benefited from his partner's death by virtue of an insurance policy and, of course, Mrs Jenna will get that money plus the insurance on Jenna's death as well. I was testing the possibility that Mr Harward's death was not accidental.'

'You mean, Abram was hired by Jenna to deliberately kill him?'

'Something like that but, in the event, after speaking to Mr Abram on Saturday, I concluded that he wasn't involved. He'd no idea who Harward was and it was a genuine accident. He'd no chance of stopping and Harward was blind drunk at the time.'

'Yet somebody has tried to kill Nigel Abram. Who do you think that might be and what motive would they have?'

'You say it's the same person who killed Edgar Marshall?'

'No. I said it's the same knife. It could have been used by anybody.'

Jim Burroughs, who had been quietly listening to all this, broke in. 'Let's not split hairs, Mike. There's hardly likely to be two killers using the same weapon.'

'Unless they were partners,' returned Bennett. His colleague, Sergeant Edwards, nodded sagely alongside him.

'What if Marshall's death was purely a burglary: he surprised the intruder, who knifed him in panic? Then the same person broke into Abram's house with the intention of stealing but Abram challenged him and got attacked likewise?'

'Very plausible except, if you remember, nothing was stolen from Marshall's house.'

'Perhaps he panicked and ran off empty-handed.'

But Bennett was not convinced. 'Another thing, we still haven't found the source of the thousand pounds in cash paid into Marshall's bank account. Have you any ideas on that?'

'None at all.' Nor did I see any relevance. He could have been paid for a job he'd done. After all, he was running a business.

'Did you ever mention this John Lennon tape of yours to Abram?'

'Never. I'd no reason to.'

'So that couldn't have been a reason for breaking into Abram's house?'

'No.'

'And there's nobody else you can think of who might wish to harm Mr Abram?'

I suddenly remembered the look on Susie Jenna's face when I told her Abram had been released from prison.

'Mr Harward's family were very hostile to Mr Abram. He went to see them after the accident to apologise. He said they became aggressive.'

'Natural enough, but surely if they'd wanted to effect reprisals they'd have done it there and then, while they were still in a fury, not wait till he came out of prison?'

'You'd think so. But they're the only ones I can think of who might have attacked him. Did Abram not get a look at his assailant?'

'According to him, it was too dark to see anything clearly. It all happened so suddenly and was over in seconds. He didn't have time to get a proper look. All he could say was the man wore a balaclava and an overcoat and was of medium height and bulky. Could be one of a thousand people with a description like that. We don't even know whether he's black or white.'

'Or even Chinese.' Mike Bennett looked at me sharply. 'Just a joke,' I said.

Jim Burroughs ventured a question. 'Have you got nothing new on the Cronkshaw murder, Mike?'

'No, Jim. Forensic turned up nothing. We've got a warrant out for Frank Harriman but he's gone to ground.'

Perhaps, I thought, I should have informed him of Harriman's attack on me outside the flat, but it was too late now.

'And nothing new on Marshall's murder?'

'Until this Abram thing, no.'

'Did you know we had a burglary here last week?' Jim asked his ex-colleague.

'No, I didn't. What was that about?'

'We think it was the same people who broke into Marshall's flat the second time. They left an identical message – *we'll be back* – scrawled on the wall, and it can't have been Harriman because he was inside when Marshall got turned over.'

'How come we weren't told about this?'

'You were,' I said. 'Or rather the police came round and I assumed they would liaise with you.'

'Assume nothing in this job,' hissed Inspector Bennett. 'I take it nobody has been arrested for your break-in?'

'Not heard a word since.'

'We didn't really expect it,' added Jim patronisingly. 'Too many thefts for the Force to deal with these days.'

'All the same, it could have a bearing on the murders. Where is this tape now, by the way?'

'In a safe place, but I'm taking it along to the Beatles Convention at the Adelphi this weekend.'

'Is that wise, Mr Ace, in view of all that's happened so far?'

'Don't worry. It'll be closely guarded.'

'I should hope so, but you'd better be careful. I don't want any more murders on my hands.'

I thought of what Gypsy Gloria had told me. '*More deaths.*'

'I can't see me being assassinated in the middle of those crowds,' I said, but wasn't that exactly what I did expect? The Dallas rush-hour hadn't saved President Kennedy.

When the two policemen had goe, I said to Jim, 'This Abram thing has got to be connected with European Carriages somehow, but it couldn't have been Bowlands who attacked Abram because he's still over in France.'

'Or so we're led to believe.'

'That's true but, assuming for the moment he is across the water, who else is there? I can't see it being Susie Jenna. She wasn't that close to Harward that she'd risk it, not at this stage of the game when she's getting ready to jump ship.'

'Besides, she's a woman, Johnny.'

'So?'

'Abram did say a MAN in a balaclava.'

'An easy mistake. Women of today are like Amazons, Jim. Some of them would look like men even if they wore baby-doll nightdresses – and this one was wearing an overcoat. What about Doreen Harward? She goes ballistic when you mention Abram's name.'

'Possible, I suppose. But how can Doreen Harward be tied in with Edgar Marshall? It doesn't make sense.'

'I know.'

'Abram could well have enemies we don't know about, Johnny, maybe connected with his job, cooked books, tax dodges . . .'

'Or how about this,' I interrupted. 'Marshall had something on Abram and was blackmailing him. That would account for the grand deposited in Marshall's bank.'

'But Marshall's dead now, so who attacked Abram?'

'Maybe Marshall had a partner who's carried on putting the black on Abram after Marshall's death. Abram tells him he won't pay up any more, maybe he threatens to go to the police, so the mystery partner thinks he'll silence him for good.'

'And stabs him but misses his heart. Wait a minute though, Johnny, that suggests that Marshall was murdered by his partner because the same knife was used.'

'Maybe they fell out.'

'Could be. So who have you in mind for the partner?'

'God knows. It's all Fantasy Island stuff, isn't it?'

Jim rose from his chair. 'I'm going to make a brew, I'm parched after all this.'

Roly stood up and followed him into the kitchenette, sensing food might be coming his way, but he was disappointed. Jim wasn't one to waste his ginger biscuits on a dog.

'So what's the plan now?' asked Jim as he brought the mugs back into the office.

'I still go round to see Graham Bowlands on Thursday as before. I can't see any new options.'

'Are you going to tackle the two grieving widows about Abram?'

'I'll play it by ear.'

'Who do you think killed Marshall, Johnny?'

'Pass. We thought it must be the same person who killed Cronkshaw, yet both Harriman and Joey could only have done one or the other murder – so that would mean an unknown third party. What I can't see though is how Abram fits in with any of that crowd.'

'Maybe he doesn't. Could there be three different murderers?'

'But the same knife was used for two of the deaths.'

'All right, just one killer and for some reason he didn't use the knife when he killed Cronkshaw.'

We could have gone on all day but we were saved from further useless speculation by the ringing of the telephone.

I answered it and immediately recognised the voice. I held my thumb up to Jim to alert him. It was Joey from Chester.

Chapter Twenty-Two

'Is that the man with the tape?' Joey asked tonelessly.

'Yes. Who is that?'

'We met in Chester.'

'Oh yes. Joey, isn't it? What can I do for you?' Jim had picked up the extension and switched on the record facility on the ansaphone.

'I seen it in the paper about you taking the tape to the Adelphi on Sunday.'

'That's correct.'

'You promised me first option.'

'You never rang.'

'I'm ringing now, ain't I?'

'So what do you want?'

'I wanna come and hear the tape, don't I?'

'I told you what I'm expecting to get for it.'

'That's OK.'

'Then come here tomorrow afternoon at two, at the address I gave you.'

'I can't come in the afternoon. It's gotta be night.'

The next evening Everton were at home to Wimbledon. The match wouldn't finish until nearly ten o'clock. 'Half-past ten. I can't make it any earlier.'

'Half-past ten,' he repeated. 'At that address?'

'Dale Street.'

'Will the tape be there?'

'It will.'

He hung up.

'Well, what do you think?' said Jim as we both replaced our receivers.

'Take your pick. He's either coming mob-handed, or he's crackers and hopes to persuade us to sell it for peanuts, or he's genuine and he'll sign a cheque for five grand. One of the three.'

'I'll go for number one.'

'So will I.'

'In which case this could get dangerous. Joey could be the one who killed Edgar Marshall, which means he would probably be Abram's attacker as well.'

'We'll need muscle. I'll get Geoffrey over.'

'Will he be enough?'

I patted the drawer of the desk. 'I've always got Albert's shooter if things get out of hand.'

'Oh Christ,' said Jim. 'An unlicensed bloody gun, that's all we need. We're supposed to be a legit operation.'

'We can always say we captured it from our attackers in a struggle.'

'You don't care, do you? You ride roughshod over everything without any regard for rules and it won't do. You'll come a-cropper one day with that attitude, Johnny Ace, you mark my words.'

'So my old schoolteachers used to say, and they were all wrong as well.'

'Cocky bastard.'

I realised, of course, that Jim was nervous about the operation as, with his heart condition and at his age, he had every reason to be. This was a young man's fight. I wasn't even sure what I was doing there.

'You're not coming on this one, Jim. You're staying at home tomorrow night.'

'Think I'm not up to it?' His voice was aggressive but I detected relief in its tone.

''Course you're not bleedin' up to it. All we need is for you to have a heart attack and where would that leave The Chocolate Lavatory? Besides, your Rosemary would never forgive me, dragging you out on a caper like that.'

He didn't argue. 'We've got a full day to prepare,' he said. 'Are you getting Eddie Smeddles to run over security?'

'Not sure. I'll sleep on it.' I couldn't see how Eddie's electronic aids would help in a full-scale punch-up.

I picked up my mug, drained the last dregs of tea and leaned back in the chair. 'Jim, I've been thinking about how Joey fits into all this and I've got a theory. Let's just go over what we know about him and see what you think.'

'Fire away.'

'My guess is that Joey is working for Frank Harriman.'

'But . . .'

'Hang on. Examine the facts. The advert appears in the July *Record Collector*, AFTER Harriman has seen the tape at Edgar Marshall's house.'

'Right.'

'Harriman wants that tape badly but he's already about to get sent down for breaking into Marshall's so he needs someone else to get it for him.'

'But why put an advert in a magazine? He already knows where the tape is.'

'To keep his name out of it. So far, Harriman's the only person apart from Albert Cronkshaw who knows Marshall has the tape. If Joey was caught stealing it, without the advert, the police would immediately connect him to Harriman.'

'Go on,' said Jim.

'And the plan works because Marshall answers the ad just as Harriman hoped he would. Joey doesn't waste time going to see the tape, he just breaks in when Marshall's out.'

'And can't find it.'

'No. So he wrecks the place in a fit of pique, leaving the *we'll be back* message to put the frighteners on poor Edgar.'

Jim took up the plot enthusiastically. 'And then he goes back another day, when Edgar's in this time, to try and force him to hand over the tape. When Edgar won't play ball, Joey sticks the knife in and kills him.'

I stopped to consider this. I was the one who had found Edgar Marshall lying dead in his bed and there'd been no signs of a struggle or, indeed, a break-in. Assuming Joey had rung the bell, why had Marshall gone back to bed after letting him in?

'I'm not happy with that,' I said. 'Logically, Joey would be the one to have murdered Edgar but I was in that room, don't forget, and it didn't look like that to me. No signs of a struggle or anything.'

'He must have done it. If he didn't, who did?'

'I'll reserve judgement on that. Maybe the thousand pounds comes into it somewhere – let's not forget that little mystery. As for Cronkshaw's murder, I'm definitely ruling Joey out of that one, wrong time-scale, but Harriman was released from prison the day before so he could easily have done it.'

'But how would Harriman know where to find Cronkshaw?'

'He wouldn't have been too hard to track down, Jim. He wasn't the Invisible Man.'

'But why kill him anyway because he knows that you're the one who has the tape, not Cronkshaw? He's already sent Joey to Chester to meet you with the cash.'

'At this point, he's not a hundred per cent certain I've really got it. All Joey saw was the Voxtones' tape. I didn't risk taking the real one, and he didn't find anything in our office. I think Harriman was hedging his bets. He went round to Cronkshaw's because he was the last person he knows for sure had the tape.'

'But when he finds he hasn't, why kill him?'

'He's a nutter, Jim. Wouldn't need much excuse. Perhaps it was burglar rage.'

'What?'

'A bit like road rage. Or maybe Cronkshaw went for him, thinking Edgar had dealt with him without much trouble.'

'Edgar had an iron bar by his bed.'

'Albert's mistake. Always carry an iron bar.'

'Or a gun,' said Jim pointedly.

I wondered if I'd returned the gun, would Albert now be in the dock for murder?

'So in the meantime,' Jim continued, 'you read the advert and write to Joey saying you've got the tape. A bit of good fortune for them.'

'Quite. I tell Joey where the tape is, he passes the address on to Harriman who checks it out and finds out I'm not Albert Cronkshaw as I told Joey, but the same guy who came to see him in prison. No wonder he was mad.'

'Especially when they break into the office and the tape isn't there. Why do you think Joey's arranged to meet you this time when he didn't reply to your last letter?'

'When he got my letter, he already knew the tape wasn't in the office so breaking in again would have been a waste of time.'

'I wonder he didn't go back to Maria's for a second look there.'

'He'd know we'd have moved it. But when he read in the paper that I'm taking the tape to the Adelphi on Sunday, he'd realise this will be their last chance. They have to arrange to meet me before Sunday or, by this time next week, the tape could be in London or New York, well beyond their reach.'

'But they're not going to turn up with a sackful of money, Johnny. They'll be coming to steal not to buy.'

'And Geoff will be ready for them.'

'You say that, but you don't know how many of them there'll be. If I were you I'd think about hiring some muscle.'

'I'll think about it, Jim,' I promised.

'What about Abram in all this? Do you think Joey tried to kill him?'

'I don't know but maybe the best idea would be to wait till Joey shows up here and then beat the living shit out of him till he tells us.'

Jim Burroughs smirked. 'You've obviously been on the police training courses, Johnny, and not told me.'

We left it at that. I went back to the flat to get ready to meet Maria. There were no messages for me there. I rang Geoffrey to book him for the following night.

'A minder's job, is it, boss?' He sounded excited. I think Geoffrey fancies himself as a vigilante.

'It is.'

'Just you and me?'

I thought about what Jim Burroughs had said. 'I might invite the McKales to come along.'

'Sounds serious.'

'No, no. Merely a question of guarding the fort.' I tried to make it sound casual but already I was bracing myself for an ordeal to come.

I took Roly with me to Maria's and we left him guarding the flat, just in case I was wrong about Joey returning.

We drove out to Southport to see Lewis Collins in *Dangerous Corner* by J.B. Priestley at the Arts Centre. It's always been one of my favourites of Priestley's 'time' plays and they did it well, although I would never have recognised Lewis Collins from *The Professionals* TV series. He'd put on a few stone since those days.

Back at Maria's, all was calm. I didn't see any white vans lurking in the street as we drove up. Roly was fast asleep on the bed. Maria prepared some cheese biscuits topped with smoked salmon and cream cheese and we ate them with a bottle of wine, sitting at the lounge window overlooking the Mersey Estuary.

I told her about Joey and the proposed meeting.

'One thing puzzles me,' she said.

'What's that?'

'Why does Harriman think you'll waste your time meeting them at all when he knows you want five thousand pounds for the tape and he's already told you he's got no money?'

That had crossed my mind too and the only answer I could come up with was that Harriman hadn't realised I connected him to Joey.

'They've got to believe that I think Joey has a mystery backer who's going to come up with the cash.'

Maria frowned. 'A bit iffy, isn't it?'

'Maybe it is, but let's face it, neither of them are Brain of Britain material. Wasn't it Churchill who said, "Never over estimate the intelligence of the enemy"?'

'I think it was Napoleon,' said Maria. 'And look what happened to him.'

'It'll be OK, don't worry.'

'I still don't like the sound of it,. Johnny,' she said. 'You could get hurt. Why don't you leave it to the police?'

'They wouldn't be interested in a potential burglary. They can hardly be bothered to turn up for real ones. Besides, Albert Cronkshaw was my client.'

Owen Jenna had been my client too, which meant that two out of Ace Investigations' first three clients had been murdered. Not a statistic to attract future business, should the news get out. At least Mrs Skidmore was still with us although, strictly speaking, she was really an ex-client now.

'Albert Cronkshaw isn't your client any more,' pointed out Maria.

'Let's say I have a yearning for justice then.' In another age, I'd have worn a mask and been the Lone Ranger.

Next morning, I rang Tommy McKale. He was at his old boxing gym, now refurbished and re-named The Marina Health and Leisure Club to cater for Liverpool's new fitness-conscious big-spenders.

'Half-past ten I'm expecting them,' I told him after I'd outlined the situation. 'Geoff and I should arrive about twenty past, traffic permitting. I thought you and Denis could be in there about ten and wait in the back, ready in case of trouble.'

'How do we get in?'

'I'll drop you the keys off later.'

It was a quiet day: the lull before the storm. I drove over to Sefton Park and let Roly off the lead for a run. It was only a fortnight since I'd been to visit Irene Tidd concerning Bernard Skidmore's accident, but it seemed like a year, that case well and truly forgotten. Roly ran down to the lake but declined to go in. He sniffed at the water's edge and stepped back nervously. Not an aquatic dog.

On the way back into town, I took the spare set of office keys over to Tommy's other club.

The Marina looked pretty busy, with the usual clientèle of cosmetically improved trophy wives, millionaire footballers and Brad

Pitt wannabes. A far cry from the bouncers, gangsters and street urchins who used to spar in the old gym and a far cry, too, from the dubious punters who frequented the Masquerade.

Tommy was out so I left the keys with the receptionist.

At lunchtime, I went over to Pierre Victoire's, round the corner from Mathew Street, only yards from where Bobby of the Voxtones, alias Edgar Marshall, had stolen John Lennon's tape outside the Cavern over thirty years ago.

I wondered what would happen to the tape in the end. The more I thought about it, the more I feared my claim on it was a tenuous one. Effectively, it could still be described as stolen goods despite the theft having taken place way in the past.

It was three o'clock before I finally made it to the office, carrying the box with the Grundig tape recorder and the two tapes.

Jim greeted me at the door. 'Where've you been? I've had half the world's press screaming to get hold of you – Sky TV, Granada, CNN – you name it.'

'Whatever for?' I put down the box and went into the kitchen to fetch Roly his bone.

'The John Lennon tape. The nationals have picked up on the *Daily Post* article. I tell you, it's big news.'

'Shit. I should have realised. What did you tell them?'

'That you were out of the country till Sunday.'

'Thanks, Jim. That was good thinking.'

'You're returning on Sunday from an unknown destination, in time for the Beatles Convention and bringing the tape with you.'

'Perfect.'

'I'd be careful about being seen though, Johnny. You know what some of these paparazzi are like.' He settled back behind his desk. 'Have you sorted the arrangements for tonight?'

'I'm bringing Geoff down with me after the match and I've got Tommy and Denis McKale stashed away in the kitchen, ready to jump out at the first sign of trouble.'

'The McKales, eh?' He didn't sound happy.

'What's wrong with them?'

'They're gangsters, for Christ's sake, Johnny. Maybe it was OK before, but you're supposed to be legit now.'

'Tell that to the victims of crime. It's results I'm after, not the Nobel Peace Prize.'

He didn't argue. Instead he asked, 'Are you sure you don't want me tonight?'

'Positive, Jim. We'll manage, don't worry.'

'You'll ring me as soon as it's over?'

'Yes. Whatever "it" might be. Right now, I'm more worried about how Everton are going to do against Wimbledon. Never an easy fixture.'

I went into the Winslow for a drink before the game, partly to take my mind off the impending meeting but mostly to soak up the atmosphere. Most of the fans were optimistic. The defeat at Tottenham had been unlucky, the team had played well and Walter Smith was still held in high esteem.

And, as it happened, the fans caught the mood. The Blues ran riot with goals from Barnby, Jeffers, Campbell and Unsworth to no reply from The Dons. It was the best performance of the season and lifted The Blues to seventh in the Premiership.

'It's been coming,' said the man in the seat next to mine in the Goodison Road stand. He wore a blue and white bobble hat a size too large that was only kept out of his eyes by the protrusion of his ears. 'This could be where the revival starts, you mark my words.'

I'd heard it all before. It would only take a couple of defeats and the pages of *When Skies Are Grey* would be full of moaners again.

I left as the injury time board was held up. I'd arranged to meet Geoffrey down the road from the office, outside the Town Hall. It was ten-fifteen when I arrived. Geoff was already there.

'Nobody around yet, boss.'

I wondered if I should have brought Roly but the possibility of gunfire decided me against it. He was frightened enough of fireworks.

I looked up Dale Street towards the Mersey Tunnel, half expecting to see a white van parked in the vicinity, but I was disappointed. I couldn't see any loitering pedestrians either.

'Let's go in, Geoff. They can ring the bell.'

I unlocked the front door and we walked up the stairs. I halted outside the glass-fronted door of the office, listening in case intruders had got inside and were waiting for us. All was quiet. I turned the key in the lock and we went in.

'Tommy?' I whispered quietly in the direction of the kitchen. The door was slightly ajar.

His familiar voice came back. 'We're all set back here, Johnny.'

I switched on the light and motioned Geoffrey to sit down. 'I don't know why we're whispering,' I laughed. 'There's nobody here.'

I wondered if Joey had seen us arrive. Had he been watching earlier, when Tommy and Denis came in? Would he be alone? If not, how many of them would there be? I felt for Albert Cronkshaw's gun which was in the inside pocket of my jacket. I knew Geoff was carrying a steel pipe. Tommy McKale probably had a sub-machine gun in the back.

The minutes ticked by. Tomorrow morning, Graham Bowlands was due back from France. Would I be able to prove he had killed Owen Jenna?

The ring of the bell, when it finally came, startled me. I jumped to my feet and pressed the entryphone switch to open the downstairs door. Footsteps pounded on the stairs: it sounded like only one set. Were the others hiding at the bottom?

The footsteps stopped outside the door. The shape of one man showed through the frosted glass. I waved Geoffrey to one side and opened the door.

'Here you are,' said Joey, walking past me into the room. He was dressed as he had been in Chester, in T-shirt, beige cord blouson and combats. 'I've brought you the money you wanted, now where's the tape?'

He threw a large Jiffy bag down on the desk. Geoff looked on in amazement as I opened it and out tumbled a sheaf of fifty-pound notes.

'Count them if you like. Five grand, like you said. It's all there.'

I was lost for words.

Did Joey really have a mystery backer? If so, why the break-ins? And if he didn't do the break-ins, who did?

'The tape,' repeated Joey.

'Hang on,' I said. I was stalling for time, to work out what this meant. Who was Joey fronting for? 'You haven't heard it yet.'

'Then play it me.'

'Geoff, go down and check the outside door's locked, would you?' I said. Just to make sure we weren't suddenly rushed by invaders.

Geoff trotted off whilst I put the money back in the envelope and fetched the Grundig recorder. Joey watched as I threaded the tape round the spool and switched the knob to Play.

The familiar hissing sound was followed by the acoustic guitar and the voice of the former Beatle filled the room.

'John Lennon,' I said. 'Satisfied?'

'OK. That'll do. I'll take it now.'

'Hang on.' This was all going wrong. The last thing I had bargained for was Joey turning up with the money and I certainly wasn't going to part with the tape.

'What for? You've got the money, haven't you?'

'I want to talk to you about the break-ins.'

'What break-ins? I don't know what you're talking about.'

'This office was burgled, as were two houses in Old Swan.'

'I know nothing about that.' But the expression on his face had altered from one of confident defiance to nervous uncertainty.

'And two people have been murdered.'

The uncertainty changed to alarm. 'I never . . .'

'What about Nigel Abram? Did you attack him on Monday night?'

He started to splutter. 'Who's he? I've never heard of him.'

'Someone stuck a knife in him. The same knife that killed Edgar Marshall.'

'I don't know what you're talking about. I've not killed nobody.'

'But you did break into this office, and into Edgar Marshall's house in Old Swan?'

'No.' Beads of sweat had broken out on his forehead and he looked round in panic towards the door. He suddenly appeared younger than the late twenties I had him down for.

'Who sent you here, Joey?'

'No one, I . . .'

I moved forward, gripped his T-shirt and held him against the wall. 'Where did this money come from?'

'All right, let go and I'll tell you.' I released my grip. For a second I thought he was going to strike me but Geoffrey came back into the office and stood purposefully beside me.

'It's a dealer – I don't know his name. He asked me to bid for him because he doesn't want anyone to know it's him what's buying it. I'm just in it for a ton, that's the truth.'

I didn't believe him. Nobody hands over five grand in cash just like that to a stranger.

'Sorry, Joey. Not good enough. What's his name?'

'I tell you, I don't know.'

I took the tape and put it back in the box. 'Then go away and tell your "employer" that I'll only deal with him. And take your money with you.' He caught the envelope that I threw at him. 'Now scarper.'

He stood still for a second then turned, clutching the money, and ran out of the office and down the stairs. I waited till he was in the street before I called to Tommy and Denis to come out of the kitchen.

'You could have kept the five grand,' moaned Tommy. 'Consultancy fee for your professional advice.'

'Who the hell sent him? That's what I want to know.'

'You should have let me and Denis ask him; you might have got an answer.'

Perhaps he was right. Or should I have kept hold of Joey and phoned the police? Either way it was too late.

'I think you might be needing us on Sunday,' said Tommy.

'Sunday?'

'At the Beatles fair. I take it you're still going along with the tape? Because that's when they'll try to snatch it.'

'I guess you're right.' I was tired. I had a feeling that I'd botched the whole operation. What would Jim Burroughs say about it all in the morning?

As it happened, when I related the story of the evening to him the next morning, he was not too scathing.

'No use beating it out of him,' he said philosophically. 'Only gets you into trouble.'

'Spoken like an ex-cop.'

'Spoken like any sensible citizen,' he retorted. 'Sending for Mike Bennett was probably your best option but, even then, if he'd denied everything, there was no evidence to detain him.'

'At least we'd have found out who he really was,' I said.

'I think I might be able to do that,' said Jim, surprisingly.

'You? How?'

'First of all, I take it you still believe Harriman is the one behind all this?'

'Yes, don't you?'

Jim didn't commit himself. 'You said yourself, no person in their right mind would hand over five grand to a stranger and I agree. But they might trust it to a relative. I think Joey is a relative of Harriman's. You said he was in his late twenties? Maybe he's his elder brother.'

'Where would he have got the money?'

'Obviously he stole it. Give me an hour, Johnny. I need to do some checking. Weren't you going over to European Carriages this morning to see that driver?'

'Graham Bowlands. I'm on my way, Jim.'

'All unpaid work, of course.' Why did he have to harp on about that?

'We want to find out who killed our late lamented client, don't we?'

Over at the Brunswick Business Park, Sandra the receptionist was on duty at her desk as usual.

'Hello again,' she smiled. 'Who is it you've come to see this time?'

'Graham Bowlands,' I said. 'He's supposed to be back from France today.'

'Oh, that's right. Just a minute.' She consulted a list in a spiralled diary beside her. 'That's odd.'

Alarm bells rang. 'What is?'

'According to my sheet here, Ray Partington brought the Disneyland coach back.'

'So where's Bowlands?'

'I don't know. Ray was the relief driver.'

'Are you saying Bowlands could still be in France?'

At that moment, lights appeared on the switchboard. Sandra became confused. 'Ray would know. You'd need to ask him, if he's still around. He may have gone home. Just let me take this call.' She picked up the phone.

'It's all right,' I said. 'I'll go and find him.'

I walked out of the office and round the back to the car park. The company occupied a much bigger area than I had realised. A couple of mini-buses and a coach were parked in bays and, in a large garage at the opposite end of the car park, a mechanic was peering at the underside of a car up on a ramp.

A mechanical car wash was in operation at the opposite corner, dousing one of the company taxis with foam. Obviously, European Carriages ran a complete in-house operation, doing their own repairs and valeting.

I approached a uniformed man polishing a black BMW.

'I'm looking for Graham Bowlands. Do you know where I might find him?'

'Sorry, mate. I'm just doing a day's chauffeuring for them. Ask the lad in the workshop over there. He'll probably know.'

I walked over to where the man was working on the ramp. As I came closer, something about him looked familiar and I suddenly realised where I had seen him before. It was the youth who worked in Edgar Marshall's garage!

Suddenly there was a tie-in between Edgar Marshall and the Jennas. But what did it mean?

I tapped the lad on the shoulder and he spun round. 'Remember me?'

He looked me up and down and shook his head.

'Edgar Marshall's garage in Old Swan a couple of weeks ago.'

'Oh – that's right. You came looking for Edgar.' He seemed on edge.

'I was the one who found his body. You identified him for the police.'

'What was it you wanted?'

'How come you're working for European Carriages?'

'We used to do all their repair work that they couldn't handle. When the garage shut down after Edgar died, they offered me a job.'

'Who's they?'

'Mr Jenna.'

'I'm looking for a driver called Graham Bowlands.'

'He ain't here.'

'Do you know where he is?'

'Somewhere on the continent. He's taken one of the tours.'

'The tour's back, but without Graham.'

'I wouldn't know about that.'

'But you do know Graham Bowlands?'

'I seen him around from time to time.'

'Tell me, why do you think Edgar Marshall was murdered?'

The question caught the lad unawares. 'What do you mean? How would I know?'

'Did you get on well with him?'

'Yeah. He was all right, was Edgar. Some people said he was a tight sod, always out for the main chance, like, but so what? He did all right by me. Gave me a job.'

'So who were his enemies?'

He looked round nervously. 'I can't say. Look, keep away, will you? I don't want any trouble.'

'What's your name?'

'Charlie. Charlie Peyton.'

'Charlie, if you know anything about Edgar Marshall's death, you owe it to him to tell me.'

He hesitated then his eye caught something behind me and he quickly turned away towards the car he'd been repairing. 'I can't say no more.'

I glanced round and, in the distance, I saw Susie Jenna coming out of the offices, dressed in a black business suit with a mid-calf-length skirt, a white shirt and dark tie. A far cry from her Marilyn Monroe persona at Beaulieu.

'Look. Here's my card. Ring me as soon as you can and I'll meet you somewhere.' I pushed the card into the pocket of his grease-stained overalls.

I left him and went to intercept Susie Jenna. 'You again. What is it this time?' she snapped.

'I'm still looking for that driver of yours called Graham Bowlands.'

'I thought I told you I'd never heard of him.'

'You did, but your receptionist has assured me he does work for you.'

Her voice didn't waver. 'He must be one of the new part-timers Owen took on after I'd left.'

'Maybe it was Doreen who hired him. After all, he is her cousin.'

'Is he really? Fancy that. Probably she did then.' She sounded very confident. Almost as if she knew he was safely ensconced in the flat in Beaulieu waiting for her to join him. 'What was it you wanted him for again?'

'I believe he killed your husband.'

'Oh, that's right.' She laughed. 'Well, if you find him you'll have to ask him, won't you? And now, if you'll excuse me . . .'

She carried on to the garage where I saw her exchange a few words with Charlie. I walked back to the RAV4 and drove slowly to the office. I hoped Susie Jenna had not found out I was questioning the lad about Edgar Marshall's death. I didn't know why, but I had the strongest feeling that, if she had, Charlie Peyton's life might be in considerable danger.

Chapter Twenty-Three

'Bingo,' cried Jim Burroughs when I returned to the office.

'What?'

'Joey Harriman, aged twenty-seven, brother of Frank Harriman, native of Blacon near Chester.' He waved a piece of paper at me. 'It's all here in this fax.'

'Good work, Jim.'

'That's not all. A petrol station was robbed on Tuesday night on the Chester to Whitchurch road. Two men with tights over their heads and armed with a knife threatened the attendant, who opened the safe for them and handed over the day's takings. They made off with six thousand pounds. Of course, the security cameras weren't working, the film had jammed, but I'm pretty certain it was the Harrimans.'

'It all fits in. I take it there's no sign of Frank anywhere?'

'Not so far.'

'Have neither of them got any form, Jim?'

'Joey's been done for stealing cars, breaking and entering, robbery – all the makings of a career criminal.'

'What about Frank?'

'Only the one thing, oddly enough. Breaking into Marshall's house that time.'

'Which he made a cock-up of. Obviously he's not cut out to be a criminal. He's pretty inept, even though I reckon he's a very nasty piece of work.'

'Assuming they're not picked up first, what do you think their next move will be?'

'The Adelphi on Sunday, Jim. Got to be. Frank Harriman is obsessed with that tape. He'll risk anything to get it.'

'You're still taking it there?'

'Certainly am. And I'll have the McKales with me again for security.'

'If you must.' Jim sighed at the thought. 'I'll be glad when you've unloaded that tape. It's caused nothing but grief.'

'Not to mention claiming a few lives along the way,' I added. 'And I don't think the party's over yet.'

'How did you get on at European Carriages?' said Jim, changing the subject.

'Very weird. Don't ask me what it is, but there *is* a link between Edgar Marshall and the Jennas.'

'You're joking.'

'No, I'm not.' I told him about my unexpected encounter with Charlie Peyton. 'I'm sure the lad knows something about Marshall's death and, furthermore, it's connected in some way to European Carriages.'

'So Marshall's death may have nothing to do with the John Lennon tape at all, is that what you're saying?'

'That's right.'

'But what possible tie-in could there be to Jenna other than the fact that Marshall did some work for him?'

'I haven't the foggiest idea but I'm convinced the lad knows something and he's frightened to tell.'

'All right, let's suppose for a moment that it was Owen Jenna who killed Marshall. What reason could he have, for God's sake?'

I thought for a minute. 'Try this for size. Marshall had found out about the import racket at European Carriages and was blackmailing Jenna. Remember the thousand pounds cash mysteriously paid into Marshall's account? We never found out where that came from, did we? It could well have come from Jenna.'

'That would give Jenna a motive for killing Marshall all right, but I can't see Owen Jenna doing the deed himself. Who would he get to do it?'

'Graham Bowlands, perhaps?'

'But you've already got Bowlands marked down for killing Jenna.'

'True.'

'On the instructions of Mrs Jenna.'

'Or Mrs Harward. Bowlands is her cousin, don't forget.'

'Either way, I can't see him murdering Marshall for Jenna then turning round and killing Jenna a week later.'

'Perhaps you're right. You always did have a sanguine view of human nature, Jim. Wait until we get hold of Peyton, that's when we'll have some answers.'

At that moment, the phone rang and I ran to pick it up. 'Maybe that'll be him now.'

But it wasn't. It was Ricky Creegan at the radio station.

'Johnny, is that you? Eric Creegan here. I wonder if you could pop in and see me this afternoon?'

'What's this about?'

'Just a little chat, old boy. I'll explain when I see you. Shall we say about five?'

'Five it is.' I put the phone down. 'Ricky Creegan,' I said to Jim. 'The radio station manager.'

'I wonder if he's going to offer you your job back.'

'Maybe.' I wasn't banking on it but I did cross my fingers.

Charlie Peyton didn't ring and at four-thirty I went down to the station. Creegan was waiting for me in his office.

'I'm moving Shady Spencer to a late-evening slot,' he said, after offering me a plastic cup of powdered tea which I refused. Tea isn't tea without leaves.

'Why's that?' I wasn't going to make it easy for him.

'Market research tells us he appeals more to the easy listening, late-night audiences. A bit of relaxing music before bedtime.'

Driving them to sleep more likely. 'Really?'

'Yes.' He was silent for a moment, then: 'Which means we've got the six to seven slot to fill.'

'Obviously. Who were you thinking of getting?'

'Well . . .' He hesitated.

'Maybe one of the Spice Girls would do it,' I said. 'They're very popular at the moment. Or perhaps Bob Wooler could be coaxed out of retirement. Revive the old Cavern spirit.'

'I was going to suggest you might like to come back, Johnny.'

Yes, yes, yes! I screamed inwardly, but I kept my face deadpan. 'I might consider it, Ricky,' I said, 'if the terms were acceptable.'

'Terms?' His face fell.

'I play the records *I* want to play, I conduct my own phone-ins on subjects that *I* choose, and I keep Ken as my producer.'

He looked relieved. 'Then you'll do it?'

'And I want a ten pounds a night rise.'

'Done.'

He agreed so readily, I guessed he must have had pressure from above to reinstate me. The *Post* campaign must have worked. Power to the people.

'Can you start on Monday?' he asked and I said I would.

I looked in on Ken in the studio on the way out. He gave me the thumbs-up sign. 'Back to normal,' he grinned.

'I thought you'd like Shady. No aggro, no controversy.'

'Bores me shitless, boyo. Glad to have you back.' I didn't know why he'd suddenly started calling everyone 'boyo' but put it down to his Welsh ancestry.

I took Roly back home and got changed, ready to meet Hilary for our evening at the Everyman to see *An Audience with Gerry Marsden*.

We went first for something to eat at the Everyman Bistro, beneath the theatre. The place was packed with a mixture of theatregoers, students and university staff.

'Here's a tray,' said Hilary, thrusting it into my hand. 'I'll get the drinks and find us a table while you sort out the food. I'll have the halibut provençal and the blackcurrant pie with cream.'

The queue was fast moving and I was at the table when she returned with two bottles of 'K' cider.

'Are The Pacemakers on as well?' she asked

'No, just Gerry with his guitar. Most of it will be chat, I imagine.'

We were just finishing the dessert when my pager went off. I checked the message. *Ring Jim at office. Urgent.*

'Sorry about this – I won't be a minute.' I left Hilary at the table and ran upstairs to the call box in the theatre foyer.

'Johnny.' Jim sounded agitated. 'Can you get down here? Charlie Peyton rang and he's coming over. He sounded scared out of his wits. Seems to think someone's after him.'

'Keep hold of him. I'll be there in twenty minutes at most.'

Hilary was not pleased at my news. 'I've been looking forward to this concert, Johnny.'

'You go along, Hil, and I'll join you there, as soon as I can.' I gave her one of the tickets and a quick kiss. 'I'm really sorry but this is very important. A man's life is at stake.'

I didn't know how true that might be. Once he made it to the office, Charlie would be safe – but where had he been when he rang?

I reached Dale Street in twelve minutes flat but Charlie Peyton hadn't shown up.

'Where was he when he phoned, Jim?'

'He didn't say but the number will be on the screen.'

Thank God for call display, I thought as I went across to look. It was the European Carriages number.

'He's rung from their office,' I said. 'If the wrong person was listening in, he could be in trouble.'

Half an hour went by and there was no sign of the youth.

'I don't like it,' I said. 'I'm going to look for him, Jim. If he arrives in the meantime, keep him here.'

I'd parked the car right outside the office so I jumped in and raced off towards the Pier Head and past the Albert Dock, making for the European Carriages office a mile along the road.

I swung round the corner at the business park. Nobody was around: not a pedestrian in sight. The office at European Carriages was closed and silent. I drove round the back. Apart from a couple of taxis parked close to the main building, the place was deserted.

And then I saw the smoke. It was coming from a small brick shed to the side of the garage. I drove over, jumped out of the car, and tried to open the wooden door. It was locked. I frantically unhooked the wheel brace from under the seat of my car and chiselled into the jamb until I managed to force the door open.

As I pulled at it, flames rushed out to meet me. I put my head down, took a deep breath and ran in.

Amidst the dense smoke I could make out a figure lying in the corner, half under a counter. I didn't know how badly injured he was or, indeed, if he was still alive. I just grabbed hold of him and dragged his body back to the door, all the time fighting to hold my breath, remembering I'd read somewhere that more people in fires die from breathing in smoke than from burning.

Safely outside, I laid my burden on the ground, heaved the door shut, and took in great gulps of air.

The 'body' beside me stirred. Charlie Peyton had been lucky. The shelf he was under had so far prevented the flames from reaching him. I guessed his main injuries were the blow to his head, which had knocked him unconscious and which was now showing as a massive swelling by his temple, and the effects of the smoke he had inhaled.

At least he wasn't dead.

Now perhaps I might learn the truth behind the murder of Bobby of The Voxtones.

I helped him to a sitting position and he coughed and choked for a minute. 'She knew I'd seen her,' he gasped.

'OK. Steady on, just take it easy. How did it happen?'

'I'm not sure. Mrs Jenna asked me to put a parcel in the storage hut and I think somebody was waiting behind the door. They clobbered me and that's all I remember.'

'You didn't see who it was?'

'No.' He looked round at the blazing shed. 'They meant to kill me, didn't they?'

''Fraid so, Charlie, but they didn't succeed. Now it's up to you to make sure they don't get away with it. Come on.' I helped him to his feet and led him slowly to the car.

'Where are you taking me?'

'To my office. You can meet my partner and tell us the whole story and we'll take it from there.'

'What about the fire?'

'Leave it be. With a bit of luck it'll spread and burn the whole lot down. Serve them right.' Actually they'd probably be pleased. More insurance payouts.

Charlie said no more but closed his eyes as we set off back to the office.

Jim Burroughs looked horrified as we walked in. Charlie's clothes were hanging from him in blackened tatters and his face and hair were covered in soot.

'They've slipped up this time,' I said grimly. 'This one lived and, unlike Nigel Abram, he has a story to tell.'

Charlie slumped down onto the settee. 'Any chance of a drink of water?' he croaked. 'My throat hurts.'

'Sure.' Jim fetched him one from the kitchen. While he was gone, I explained to Charlie who we were and what our official interest was in both his current employers and Edgar Marshall.

He took time emptying the glass. It obviously hurt him to swallow.

'Right,' I said, as he handed it back. 'Tell us, what was the connection between Edgar Marshall and the Jennas? Was Edgar blackmailing Owen Jenna?'

He looked surprised. 'No, of course not. What could he have on Owen Jenna?'

'Illegal shipments for a start. Jenna was bringing in liquor and cigarettes from the Continent. If Edgar had found out about them he could have demanded a cut to keep his mouth shut.'

Charlie shook his head. 'I don't know nothing about that.'

'But Edgar was blackmailing *some*body?' How else could the thousand pounds be accounted for?

The youth slowly nodded his head. 'It wasn't like him to do something like that, but he was hard up. The garage hadn't been doing too well. He'd been working on some scheme for making money but that had fallen through.' The John Lennon tape, I thought. 'He had bills outstanding. People were on to him for payment and a couple of them were leaning a bit heavy on him.'

'I accept the reasons,' I said, 'but I need to know who paid him that thousand pounds and what hold did Edgar have on them?'

Charlie Peyton swallowed heavily and looked straight at me. 'It was Doreen Harward. She paid him the money.'

I remembered what Charlie had said when we first pulled him out of the blazing shed. '*She* knew I'd seen her.'

'Doreen Harward! But why?'

He took a deep breath which made him cough again. 'She came to Edgar for some advice on how to sabotage a car. Edgar told me all about it. She said it was for a book she was writing, a detective story. Edgar gave her all the gen. Then he found out later that she'd been lying. She'd actually done everything he'd shown her to this man's car and the man had been killed.'

'He should have gone to the police.'

'I suppose so, but he didn't know whether they'd believe him. He was being threatened by this loan shark he owed money to so he went to Mrs Harward and said he wanted a grand in cash or he'd tell the police what she'd done. He figured she'd be too frightened to refuse and he was right.'

'But it cost him his life,' I pointed out. 'Not his wisest move.' He'd have done better just hanging on to the £150 I paid for his tape at the auction and forgetting about the blackmail.

'When he told her how to fix the car, he never thought she was really going to harm anyone.' Charlie was anxious to defend his former employer. 'He wouldn't have hurt no one, wouldn't Edgar.'

'Tell me, Charlie, who was this man that Doreen Harward murdered?'

'It was in all the papers. Accidental death, they said, and that was another reason why Edgar thought the police might think he was making it all up.'

'What was his name?' I repeated patiently. But I knew the answer already.

'It was an unusual name. Bernard Skidmore he was called. He was a magistrate, and that's why she killed him.'

Chapter Twenty-Four

'Time to bring in the police,' declared Jim Burroughs. 'Mike Bennett should hear all this.'

He left the room to ring on the extension and I continued listening to Charlie's story.

'Mrs Harward's husband had been run over and killed. She thought the bloke what did it should have been put away for life but he only got six months. She was so livid, she vowed she'd kill both the driver, when he came out, and the magistrate who let him off with such a puny sentence.'

'You think she did the killing herself?'

'I'm pretty sure she did. Why else would she have asked Edgar to show her all that with the brakes?' I reckoned she could have been behind the wheel when Skidmore was nearly run down in London Road too.

I thought of Bernard Skidmore, eating his dinner in the hotel, happily enjoying his Gentleman's Evening, looking forward to meeting his mistress later and all the time, in the darkness of the car park, Doreen Harward quietly working under the bonnet of his motor, fixing the brakes, ready to send the poor bastard to his death.

And, having completed one murder, a few weeks later she waits for Nigel Abram to be released from prison and stabs him in cold blood. Only his good fortune and her poor aim had saved his life.

Hang on – the knife used to stab Abram was the same one used to kill Edgar Marshall!

'Was it Doreen Harward who killed Edgar as well?' I asked.

Charlie broke into tears. 'Who else could have done it? She wasn't one to stand for blackmail. She paid up all right, but only to give herself time before she had a chance to kill him.'

'Why didn't you say something?'

'I didn't twig at the time. He'd had two burglaries so I thought it might have been someone breaking in again. I only realised for sure it must have been her later.'

It explained why there had been no struggle and why nothing had been stolen, but how had she let herself in?

'Did Mrs Harward have a key to Edgar's house?'

'Not as far as I know, but he did keep a spare hanging in the garage. Why?'

Doreen would have known it was there and borrowed it to let herself in. She could have put it back at any time later. She would have gone up to Edgar's bedroom. He would have been surprised but not frightened, until he saw the knife – by which time it would have been too late. Then, with Edgar safely despatched to the Supreme Garage in the Sky, she had calmly hopped on a plane to join her friend, the missing wife, in Beaulieu.

Jim Burroughs came back into the room. 'I managed to get hold of Inspector Bennett. He'll be along within the hour. Anyone fancy a drink?'

He produced a bottle of Scrumpy Jack for me and a Newcastle Brown for himself. Feeling a little better now, Charlie accepted the offer of a can of Boddingtons Draught.

'We've got a result at last, Jim. I hope you haven't seen Mrs Skidmore yet because we've got news for her.'

'Christ,' he said, when I'd repeated Charlie's story. 'What a turn-up.'

'What about Owen Jenna?' I asked Charlie. 'Do you know who killed him?'

'I heard it was a hit and run,' he said. 'You're going to tell me she killed him as well, aren't you?'

'Her cousin did it, actually – the one I was looking for this morning. Graham Bowlands.'

'That's why he hasn't come back then, isn't it? He'll have done a runner in France.'

'I daresay he's expecting to meet up with Doreen and Susie very soon, once the business has been sold.'

'Tell me,' queried Jim. 'I'm curious to know why you went to work for European Carriages knowing what you did about Doreen Harward.'

'At the time, I didn't know she had anything to do with them, other than her husband used to drive for them. It was Mr Jenna who offered me the job.'

'But Mrs Harward was working for them at that time,' I said.

'She used to come to the garage to have her husband's car serviced, that's how Edgar got friendly with her, but I never knew she worked for them as well. She wasn't working there when I started.'

'And by the time you went to European Carriages, she'd left for France.' He nodded.

'Why didn't you tell the police about Edgar blackmailing Doreen Harward? Jim asked sternly. 'It would have shown them she had a motive to kill him.'

'What was the point? I could prove nothing and he was dead. All I'd be doing would be branding him a criminal and I know he wouldn't have blackmailed her if she hadn't been a bad person herself.'

'So you think he felt justified in taking her money?'

'I reckon he felt he was helping to punish her.'

'Didn't it worry you that Mrs Harward was getting away with killing Edgar?'

'I tried not to think about it. I never saw her again after Edgar's death until today. She came into the workshop and I saw her face when she caught sight of me. She marched straight out again but her expression was . . .' He shuddered.

'She didn't know you were working there until then?'

'No, I told you – Mr Jenna hired me. She'd been away. Anyhow, the way she looked at me, I felt frightened. I knew for sure then that she'd killed Edgar and I could be next because I'd been in the garage

257

when she'd asked Edgar about the brakes.'

'And you nearly *were* next,' I said. 'Do you think it was Mrs Harward who hit you?'

'Probably. Mrs Jenna walked with me to the shed then let me go in first with the parcel so it could easily have been Mrs Harward who was hiding inside.'

'And then they set fire to the shed hoping you'd burn to a cinder.' A bit like poor Bernard Skidmore. A thought struck me. 'Did Owen Jenna know what was going on with Doreen Harward and Edgar?'

'I don't think so. Not as far as I know, anyway.'

I didn't think so either. But I was quite sure her bosom pal Susie was fully aware of everything her friend had done.

'My guess, Jim, is that the two grieving widows will be halfway across the Channel by now.'

He looked at his watch. 'I doubt it. What time did they lock you in that shed?' he asked Charlie.

'I don't know exactly. About half-past six, I think.'

'Right. And it's eight-thirty now. You might be right, Jim. Depends where they're flying from.'

'Liverpool Airport would be too easy.'

'Mind you, they would think Charlie here is dead. They wouldn't expect us to be looking for them so soon.'

'True, but they'll probably still be on their way. If you think about it, all their other loose ends have been tied up. Abram's in hospital, Charlie's dealt with, or so they think, Bowlands has already gone on ahead. No, I think they'll be well gone by now. We'll leave it to Mike Bennett to deal with that side of things.'

'I don't suppose you've heard of Bobby and the Voxtones?' I asked Charlie.

'What are they – a pop group? I'm not really into music. I prefer fishing and football.'

'Edgar Marshall used to sing with them back in the sixties. He was Bobby.'

The lad smiled wistfully. 'He always used to be singing round the garage and he said he'd been in a band once but I never knew whether he was kidding.'

'Did you never meet his mate, Albert Cronkshaw, looked a bit like Boris Karloff? He was in the group too?'

'He's too young to remember Boris Karloff,' objected Jim.

'Jim, they're always showing old black and white films on the television. Everyone from the age of three knows Boris Karloff.'

'You mean Bert,' said Charlie. 'They used to drink together, him and Edgar.'

'He was the drummer in the Voxtones. I've got a tape they made,' I said. 'I'll let you have it, Charlie – a souvenir to remind you of Edgar. You were quite fond of him, weren't you?'

'My dad died when I was seven and Edgar was like a second dad to me. I first worked for him when I was fourteen. He took me to watch Liverpool sometimes.'

'We shouldn't hold that against him,' I said. 'Everyone makes some mistakes in life.'

We were interrupted by the doorbell. 'That'll be Mike Bennett,' said Jim. 'I'll let him in.'

'What'll happen to me?' asked Charlie, looking scared.

'You've done nothing wrong, so the law's not after you, and there's no reason why the new owners of European Carriages won't keep you on,' I reassured him.

Detective Inspector Mike Bennett entered the room, accompanied by Detective Inspector Andy Fletcher and two sergeants.

'I'm told you've solved both our cases for us,' he said heavily. I couldn't decide whether he was grateful, annoyed, or whether sarcasm ran in his family.

We were there for another two hours as the policemen made Charlie Peyton repeat his story and Jim and I filled in our bits along the way. A call had already gone out to pick up the widows and Interpol had been alerted to apprehend Graham Bowlands on suspicion of murder.

It was gone eleven-thirty when I suddenly remembered Hilary. 'Oh

Christ,' I said. 'I've got to go. I left my girlfriend at the Everyman.'

The show was over and the theatre in darkness by the time I got back to Hope Street. I rang Hilary at home from a phone box round the corner. She'd been in ten minutes and didn't sound happy.

'I'm really sorry, Hil.' I explained what had happened. Then: 'Do you want to come back over?' I asked hopefully.

'Not now, Johnny. I'm undressed ready for bed.'

'Should I come over there?'

'I don't think so.' So much for my planned night of passion.

'How about Saturday night then? We could go for a meal.'

She cut in. 'I'm busy Saturday.'

'Oh. A hospital dance again, is it?'

'Something like that.' Her tone was cold.

'I'll give you a ring next week then.'

'Fine.'

I went back to the car and drove home. Roly was waiting expectantly at the door. 'All right,' I said. 'A walk it is.'

I took him round the Pier Head and back and discussed the case with him along the way. He seemed to understand most of it, wagging his stump at appropriate places.

I felt everything had worked out nicely. We'd done well for our clients in the end although, I had to admit, they themselves hadn't come out of it too cleverly.

Mrs Skidmore's theory that her husband was murdered had been vindicated, but she was still a widow at the end of it all. Tomorrow I'd go and see her and tell her the full story of her husband's murder. Except for the mistress, of course. No need for Bernard's indiscretion ever to come out. I wondered if Diana Loder had found a replacement for him yet.

We'd tracked down Owen Jenna's missing wife for him as he requested, though whether that was any comfort to him in the next life I wasn't sure.

Similarly, we'd done what Albert Cronkshaw had asked us to do – we'd found his friend Edgar's killer. Unfortunately, we hadn't been able to prevent his own death, an option he might have preferred.

Albert Cronkshaw's death remained unsolved but it was almost certainly connected to the John Lennon tape rather than anything to do with the Jennas.

The obvious suspect was Frank Harriman but I had Joey Harriman down for the break-in at Edgar Marshall's, if only because Frank was behind bars at the time. The *we'll be back* message scrawled on the wall was, I thought, significant. Joey obviously expected his brother to be on hand for future visits.

They possibly both burgled our office, I couldn't tell for certain, but one thing I was sure of was that Joey wasn't a killer. He hadn't got Frank's psychopathic streak.

Nailing Frank Harriman was the last piece of the puzzle to tie up and I had a good idea when it would happen. He would not be able to stay away from Sunday's convention at the Adelphi. The difficulty would be in forcing a confession out of him.

Next morning, I drove out to The Evergreens in Formby to see Elspeth Skidmore.

She led me into her lounge, then excused herself while she went into the kitchen, emerging five minutes later carrying a tray. 'Tea, Mr Ace?' She laid out china cups, poured the tea from a matching pot and offered me a selection of shop cakes from a plate with a doily.

Today, Elspeth looked like one of those women on a Conservative selection committee. Her waved hair had acquired a lilac tint, her perfume, Tweed, could have suffocated a small mammal and her patterned frock reminded me of the worst excesses of Barry Humphries.

No wonder Bernard had taken his little trips out to Ormskirk.

'So I was right,' she said when I'd finished the tale. She looked sad, but not in any exaggerated way. 'Brake fluid, brake cable, same difference. It puts my mind at rest, Mr Ace. I didn't want him to go under a cloud, you see, with people saying he was a bad driver or, even worse, that he must have been drinking. He was such an upright man. And, of course, I wanted to know that whoever did it would be punished.'

'You can rest assured she will be, Mrs Skidmore.'

'Let me have your final invoice then, and I'll send you a cheque.'

Jim would be pleased, I thought. Fees hadn't been too forthcoming in this investigation.

As I rose to go, I looked around the room, at the silver framed photographs of the couple on the sideboard. 'It must be lonely for you,' I said, 'now Bernard's gone.'

'Yes, but his friend Mr Loder comes to see me quite often. We go for days out in his car.' She smiled sweetly. 'His wife is very tied up with charity work, you see.'

'I don't believe it,' I said to Jim when I got back to the office. 'Mrs Holier-than-Thou Skidmore and that old buffer in Ormskirk, Dougie Loder, are having it away.'

'I'll add another fifty pounds to the bill then,' said Jim, deadpan. 'Can't have her enjoying herself.'

The rest of the day was an anti-climax, as there was nothing we could do until Sunday. I rang Maria and arranged to take her out the following night.

'Are you going to the football match in the afternoon?' she asked.

'No. They're at Derby.'

'Then why don't you come round in the afternoon and we can have a meal out and maybe go to the pictures?'

We left Roly in the flat and drove out to Churchtown which has hardly changed since the last century; old thatched cottages, the two original coaching hostelries and the old manor house set in its own grounds where they hold garden parties and country fairs.

It was a hot afternoon and we walked round the Botanic Gardens beside the lake.

'I could get used to this life,' said Maria and I had to agree.

We went back into Southport for a meal at New China City, one of our regular places. Jojo came over to take our order and chatted to us while we decided between the crispy duck pancakes and the chicken and cashew nuts.

The ABC Cinema, round the corner, was showing the new version of *The Thomas Crown Affair*. I'd seen the original with Steve

McQueen and Faye Dunaway back in the sixties and put it among my top ten favourite films.

'Let's go then,' said Maria, who hadn't seen either version.

The cinema was full. It was Saturday night and the film had been well hyped by the media. In the event it was pretty good, maybe not quite as good as the Steve McQueen version, but close.

'I thought Pierce Brosnan was excellent,' Maria said afterward, 'although I kept thinking he was James Bond instead of Thomas Crown.'

'I know what you mean. When Roger Moore played James Bond, I kept expecting that halo to appear over his head after years of watching him as The Saint.'

It was gone eleven when we got back to hers. Automatically, as we turned into her road, I kept an eye out for white vans but none were in sight.

The real bombshell came when we were inside her flat.

We'd settled on the couch with a drink and I'd put the television on for the last bit of *Match of the Day*. Maria sat quietly beside me, her arm in mine. Roly lay at our feet. Everton had lost 1-0 at Derby which wasn't the best news I'd heard all day.

But it wasn't the worst.

The late film came on and Maria picked up the remote control and switched off the set. Then she turned to me and said, 'Johnny. I think I might be pregnant.'

My initial reaction was one of horror which I immediately tried to hide from Maria, but I don't think I was entirely successful.

Over the past year, I'd grown a lot closer to Maria. She was interested in my new career whereas Hilary had always hated my 'private eye' life. Maria was more homely and we had many interests in common.

On the other hand, I'd been with Hilary for over twenty years. She was the sexiest woman I'd ever known and she never demanded any commitment. Except lately. Lately she'd started to question my relationship with Maria, there had been the row over the holiday, and she was also spending more time with her doctor friend.

I'd been content to let things drift, though it was more a matter of keeping both balls in the air at once. The arrival of a baby would send one if not both of them crashing to the ground.

Maria had never made any secret of the fact that she wanted to marry again. Her son from her first marriage was now at university and had been for three years. It seemed to me that being a student could last until early retirement these days if you picked the right courses.

For Maria, approaching forty, time was running out. Did I want to settle down and raise a family? Sometimes I liked the idea, but at other times, the restrictions horrified me.

I wasn't too stupid to realise that, when she made her announcement, Maria had been hoping that I would leap in the air with delight, crack open a bottle of Moët and fix a date for the wedding.

Seeing that didn't happen, she quietly added, 'I don't want you to say anything now, Johnny. You must go away and think about it for a few days.'

I was lost for words. We finished our wine and went to bed. We cuddled together but didn't make love.

I had come to a crossroads in my life. Which way was I to turn?

Chapter Twenty-Five

I was up at seven-thirty to prepare for my day at the Adelphi Hotel. The Beatles Convention is run by Cavern City Tours, who own the Cavern Club, which is actually a replica of the bulldozed original that was situated further along Mathew Street. They also run sightseeing tours in the city but the Convention is their big event of the year.

Nudger had warned me to get there early. Although the doors didn't open until noon, the dealers were allowed in from seven o'clock – and between then and the public being admitted, they transacted a lot of business between themselves.

This suited me as I wanted to try and obtain a fair valuation of the John Lennon tape from the 'experts' before facing the expected raid by the Harrimans.

The McKale brothers were arriving with the punters at midday; the plan was for them to hang around the vicinity of Nudger's stall, on hand for when the trouble started.

Maria didn't get up with me. I took her a cup of tea to bed. Neither of us mentioned the pregnancy. I'd had plenty of time to think about it as I'd hardly slept, and now felt much calmer. I didn't find the idea too terrible after all – and so we parted on friendly terms.

Nudger was already setting up his stall when I arrived. I helped him carry boxes of merchandise from the old Volvo estate he was driving.

'Keep your tape under the counter,' he advised me. 'And don't let it out of your sight. You can't be too careful at this place.' Apparently, a few years ago, one stallholder had over £2000 in cash stolen – the whole day's takings – when he turned his back for a moment to deal with a customer.

I spent the next two hours wandering round the exhibits. Sam Leach was there to promote his new book *A Rocking City*, Allan Williams was selling Merseybeat souvenirs, a group of New York session men called The Fab Faux who played Beatles numbers were setting up their equipment, and Spencer Leigh was due shortly to interview various visiting celebrities.

Speaking to the dealers, the general opinion was that I should put the tape into Sotheby's but many of them thought I'd be lucky to hold on to it in view of the dubious means by which Bobby of The Voxtones had acquired it. The price they put on it ranged from £500 to £500,000 but I wasn't holding my breath.

When they opened the doors at noon, a flood of people charged through, amongst them members of the press anxious to interview me about the tape. I allowed myself to be photographed with it on the stall and told them I expected to place it in a forthcoming London auction.

While all this was going on, Tommy McKale and his brother Denis slipped into the hall and stayed within earshot of Nudger's stall.

Two o'clock came. The aisles were packed with punters. I was on edge. Any minute now I was sure the Harrimans would turn up – but would they dare attack me amongst all these people?

'Nothing?' mouthed Tommy McKale as he came past for what seemed like the hundredth time. I shook my head. He carried on walking. Nudger, meanwhile, was doing a brisk trade with the items on the stall.

It was 3.20 when Joey Harriman materialised from nowhere and stood in front of me. 'I've come for the tape,' he said, quiet menace in his voice.

I looked round desperately. Tommy was two aisles away, fingering through some magazines. I couldn't see Denis. Nudger was serving a man with bootleg CDs at the other end of the stall. There was only me.

'Not for sale, Joey. Sorry.' I looked past him expecting to see his brother, but of Frank Harriman there was no sign.

He put his hand in his pocket and I instinctively stepped back, but all he brought out was a photograph. A Polaroid. He handed it to me and waited for my reaction.

I glanced at the picture and was immediately hit by a feeling of nausea. It was Maria, still in her nightdress, bound and gagged, with a copy of the *Sunday Times* propped up on the pillow beside her to prove it had been taken this morning.

She was crying.

I remembered the look in Frank Harriman's eyes when I first met him at Altcourse prison and shuddered to think what he might do to Maria. And what about Roly? He wouldn't stand by and let anyone attack Maria. He wasn't on the photograph. Had Harriman killed him?

'Just give me the tape,' demanded Joey, 'and we'll let her go. Any funny business and you won't see her alive again.'

I realised I should have checked the street before I left Maria on her own. The thought that they might go for her had never occurred to me and I was furious with myself for not considering it. If anything happened to Maria it would be my fault. And what about the baby?

'I'm waiting,' snapped Joey Harriman, 'and it had better be the real one this time.'

I reached under the counter and picked up the John Lennon tape.

'How do I know that when your brother gets this, he'll let the girl go?'

'You don't.'

I made up my mind. 'I want to come with you.'

'Sorry. Not part of the plan.'

'Then you don't get the tape.'

I moved to put it back under the counter but Joey reached over, grabbed it out of my hand and wheeled away towards the exit.

'Tommy!' I shouted. McKale looked up quickly, saw my face and came running over. 'Joey's got the tape,' I told him. 'He went out of the far door.'

Tommy spotted Denis and waved him over. Nudger was still

sorting through CDs for his customer.

'After him,' commanded Tommy.

'You'll have to let him go,' I panted, as we thrust our way through the mass of people towards the exit. 'He's got Maria.'

'What?'

'Frank Harriman's got Maria tied up in her flat. He's a maniac, Tommy. He's already killed Albert Cronkshaw.' I'd made up my mind about that. 'Now he'll kill her.'

'No, he fucking won't,' said Tommy McKale grimly.

'That's him, getting in that car round the corner!' cried Denis. 'The grey Fiesta.'

'We'll have him,' said Tommy. 'This way.'

He ran down the Adelphi steps and leapt into a waiting green Jaguar XJ8. I didn't ask him how he'd been able to park on the service road directly outside the hotel but it didn't surprise me that he had.

I sat in the front, Denis jumped in the back and Tommy roared away before either of us had shut our doors.

The Fiesta was halfway up Brownlow Hill. Tommy stayed behind. 'I won't take him yet,' he said.

'Hadn't we better let him take the tape to his brother?' I asked.

'Won't make any difference. If he wants to ice her he will do.'

A chill went through me.

The Fiesta turned at London Road and headed down to the Pier Head and on to the dock road towards Crosby. Tommy kept his distance until we were well past the Atlantic and there were no other cars about.

'Right, are we all ready?' he said. 'Let's go for it.'

He slammed the automatic into a lower gear and the Jag practically took off as it bore down on the Fiesta.

'Are you going to stop him?' I asked.

'Stop him? I'm going to kill him,' and he roared alongside the small car, turned his steering wheel towards it and smashed the side of the Jag against the Ford's front wing. 'Big Alec's car,' commented Tommy. 'He won't mind the odd dint. It's usually bullet-holes.'

I could see the panic on Joey's face as he looked out of his window and realised what was happening. He tried to accelerate away but the tiny engine of the Fiesta was no match for the XJ8. He braked quickly but Tommy was ready for him and braked too. Joey put his foot down again and swerved onto the pavement but his front wheel caught the edge of an iron post and suddenly his car went sailing through the air to smash with a thunderous crunch against a solid wall of concrete.

And burst into flames.

'Bit early for Bonfire Night,' said Tommy, pulling to a halt and not making any attempt to rescue Joey from the conflagration.

'That's the end of the John Lennon tape,' I said.

'Sorry about that, Johnny. I didn't realise. You should have said.'

'It doesn't matter.' I probably wouldn't have been able to keep it anyway, and too many lives had been lost already because of it. 'I think we'd better be moving on – there's cars coming behind us.'

'You're right.' Tommy started the engine and drove quickly away. The Fiesta was still burning fiercely. I thought of Bernard Skidmore in the Parbold field. A similar end.

'One down, one to go,' said Tommy. 'Show me where your Maria lives.'

I directed him to Blundelsands and to the bottom of Maria's road. 'We're going to have to be careful,' I said. 'Frank Harriman's crazy.'

'Oh yes?' Tommy enquired. 'Well, Denis can sometimes go crazy, too. Especially when people upset him, so your man will be in good company.' He stopped the car and surveyed the road ahead. 'I reckon our best plan is to storm the place.'

'What if he's watching from the window?'

'He won't be. He'll be answering the phone. That's not by the front window, is it?'

'No, it's by the back window.'

'Good. This is what we do.' He handed me his mobile. 'You phone the house from the car and when Harriman answers, Denis and I will run across and smash our way in.'

'No need for that. I've got the key.' I dreaded to think what Maria's flat was going to look like afterwards but so long as Maria came out of it all right, what did that matter?

Tommy drove slowly up the road as I dialled. The ringing tone sounded, once, twice, three times. Why didn't he answer? Had he taken her somewhere else?

'Hello?' It was Maria's voice.

'Maria! Are you all right?'

Tommy and Denis leapt out of the car and ran up Maria's front path.

'Oh Johnny.' She started to sob, then the phone was grabbed out of her hand and a man's voice came on.

'Where's my tape?' The McKales quietly opened the front door and disappeared inside. 'I said where's—'

'Joey's got it,' I answered truthfully. 'Are you going to let my girlfriend go?'

He laughed horribly. 'What makes you think I'd do that?'

'Joey said—'

'Joey said,' he mimicked. 'What does Joey know?'

'Where's my dog?'

'Oh, that was a dog, was it? Not any more.'

I felt total despair. Roly dead. I'd saved him from starving only for him to end up killed by a madman. I'd have done better leaving him to rove the streets. Now he'd never wag that stump of his again.

Suddenly I heard a crash in the background and then Maria screamed. Harriman dropped the phone and shouted, 'Get back!' 'He's got a knife,' I heard Maria call out. There was the sound of furniture tumbling. A struggle then a ragged cry. 'You next,' I heard Harriman snarl.

I scrambled out of the car and ran towards the house, just in time to meet Frank Harriman stumbling out of the front door. He was covered in blood but he held a knife in his right hand and it was pointing at me.

'Come on,' he grated. 'Get me if you can.'

Something inside me snapped. All I could see was the photograph of Maria tied up in bed and a picture of Roly lying cold and lifeless in the kitchen. As Harriman launched himself at me I stood my ground and smashed my fist into his face, following it up with a left hook to the chin.

Tommy McKale staggered into view as Harriman slid to the ground. Tommy's jacket had been ripped open and blood was dripping from a vivid red scar along his cheek.

'Well done, Johnny,' he gasped out 'He's a tough bastard and no mistake, but at least he'll be dead before tea-time.'

'What do you mean?' And then I noticed that the blood that was all over Harriman was actually pumping out from his own arm.

'Main artery,' said Tommy. 'Hang on a few minutes before you call the ambulance, Johnny, or he could live. Give the bastard time to drain.'

But I had already pulled off my T-shirt and was wrapping it round Harriman's upper arm as a tourniquet.

'Why not let him bleed to death?' Tommy grunted, and spat. 'You'd save the taxpayer a fortune.'

'Can't risk you being done for murder, sunshine,' I said. 'Dolly's too old to run the club on her own.' I made sure the bleeding had been arrested.

'Better drag him into the house,' said Tommy. 'Don't want to frighten the neighbours.'

We carried him through to the lounge and dropped him, none too gently, in a corner. Chairs and tables were everywhere, two pictures on the wall were broken and a couple of ornaments lay in pieces on the carpet. Denis was sitting up in a corner, groggily rubbing his head.

I raced into the bedroom and there was Maria, still tied up, lying on the bed.

'Johnny, oh Johnny.' I ran to her and held her in my arms.

'Are you OK?' I started to untie the knots.

'I think so, but Roly . . .'

'He's dead, isn't he?'

'I don't know. That man hit him with a club and knocked him cold. I think he's still in the kitchen.'

I went to look, opening the door slowly, fearing what I might find. Roly lay behind the door, still as death; he made no move as I leant over him. I felt his wiry fur. He was still warm. Then I put my hand on his chest and felt a shallow rhythm.

'He's still alive!' I shouted. 'Where's the vet's number?'

'In the book. Mr Dunn. He's only five minutes away.'

I rang the vet, then ordered an ambulance for Frank Harriman. After that I managed to reach Jim Burroughs at home and, finally, I rang Detective Inspector Mike Bennett.

It was time to wrap the whole thing up.

Chapter Twenty-Six

Tommy and Denis McKale left before the Law arrived. 'We like to keep a low profile,' explained Tommy. Maria had bathed his face with antiseptic and the bleeding had stopped.

'It's only superficial – I've had worse,' said Tommy. 'Won't even make a decent scar to frighten off the undesirable punters.'

I said I didn't know prospective punters at the Masquerade were ever deemed undesirable, provided they could afford an extortionate entry fee.

Albeit dazed, Denis had recovered from the blow to his head that Frank Harriman had delivered, with the same wooden club that had felled Roly. Probably the same one, too, that had killed Albert Cronkshaw. Denis had been lucky.

'Thanks for coming,' I said.

'Always a pleasure to help you, Johnny.' Tommy grinned. 'You bring a bit of excitement into our dull little lives.' He looked across at Harriman, still lying in the corner. 'I've met men like him before, with those hard eyes. They make good soldiers. He'd probably have won the VC in Kosovo. Mad as a hatter, of course, but you have to be, don't you? See you around, Johnny.'

Mr Dunn was first to arrive. He examined Roly carefully. 'Concussion,' he said. 'No bones broken. He should recover fully.'

Even as he spoke, Roly began to stir. He looked up at me for a moment, then gave a weak smile before closing his eyes again.

'Let him rest, he'll heal better when he's asleep, and put him on a light diet for a day or two. I'll give him a painkiller and an anti-inflammatory shot to be on the safe side.'

The vet was followed closely by the ambulance, siren blaring. The makeshift tourniquet had stemmed most of the bleeding from Frank Harriman's arm but he was still unconscious.

'What happened here?' asked one of the paramedics.

'Cut himself shaving,' I said.

His colleague bent over the recumbent body. 'His nose is broken too and he's lost a lot of blood. He needs to be in hospital.'

I explained that we were waiting for the police. 'You'd better hang on until they get here.' Maria came through to the lounge, walking rather shakily. The paramedics checked her over after I told them what had happened. 'Shaken but otherwise fine,' they said.

Jim Burroughs was next to show up. 'Christ, it's like a hospital ward,' he said, taking in the paramedics and the walking wounded. 'So that's our Mr Harriman. Where's his brother?'

I'd almost forgotten about Joey. 'Had a bit of an accident,' I said. I described the car chase. Unfortunately, he had the John Lennon tape with him.'

'You're joking! After all this trouble, you've lost it?'

'Irrevocably, unless it can withstand a blazing inferno.'

'Bloody hell, there's been some carnage with this lot and no mistake,' said Jim. 'What's the latest death toll?'

'Four so far, five if Joey croaks.'

Jim nodded towards Harriman. 'Has he confessed?'

'To Cronkshaw's murder, you mean? No, but somewhere around this flat is a wooden club he used on Denis and Roly. I'm sure it'll be the same one he used to kill Albert.'

'DNA tests will sort that.'

'And his knife's somewhere in the front garden – probably the one he attacked me with in the car park.'

Jim looked across at the blood-stained Harriman. 'Bit careless with his belongings, isn't he?'

DI Mike Bennett arrived ten minutes later. 'This is becoming a habit,' he said. 'Who've we got this time?'

I pointed to the figure slumped in the corner.

'Frank Harriman, wanted for the murder of Albert Cronkshaw among other things.' There was always Maria's kidnapping, the break-in at Dale Street, cruelty to an animal and various assaults to throw into the pot as well.

'Have you any proof?'

'The weapon is in the flat. Forensic shouldn't have a problem.'

'I take it he needs to go to hospital?' Bennett asked the paramedics, who confirmed he did, and as quickly as possible. 'In that case, I'll get uniform to send along a man to guard him.'

'Any joy with Mrs Jenna and Mrs Harward?' I asked.

'I was coming to that. We picked them up last night, on the M20. They were intending crossing the Channel from Dover.'

'Have they admitted everything?'

'I don't know the details, Inspector Fletcher's dealing with it, but I believe they each tried to blame the other so I've no doubt we'll be able to put them both away for a very long time. They also incriminated Graham Bowlands, so he'll stand trial for the murder of Owen Jenna when we pick him up.'

'Do you think you'll be able to prosecute Doreen Harward for Bernard Skidmore's death?'

Mike Bennett wasn't optimistic. 'It won't be easy to prove, but the Edgar Marshall killing will stand up and, with the attempted murder of that young accountant . . .'

'Nigel Abram.'

'That's him. Not to mention her alleged attempted murder of Charlie Peyton . . . they'll enough to get her life.'

'Or ten years with remission,' I said bitterly.

Jim smiled. 'Johnny's in favour of execution.'

'By the way,' asked the Inspector, 'what happened to Harriman's brother?'

'Thereby hangs a tale,' I said. 'You didn't happen to come along the dock road, did you?'

Mike Bennett groaned and put his hand over his face. 'Don't tell me – that pile of ashes by the dock gates that used to be a car? The Fire Brigade are out there now.'

''Fraid so. He, er, missed the bend.'

'Of course he did. So where's this tape that all the trouble's been about? I want to hear it for myself. See if it's worth all the havoc.'

'Too late,' I said.

Jim explained. 'It was in the car, Mike, along with Joey Harriman. He'd stolen it from Johnny at the Beatles Convention.'

'I get it. So you were following him and he suddenly came off the road with you nowhere near him?'

'Like I said, he didn't make the bend.'

'It's a straight road, for God's sake.' But Mike Bennett didn't seem to want to create an issue out of it. 'You won't make your fortune from John Lennon after all, then?'

'No. I guess I'll just have to carry on being a detective.' Bennett did not look as enthralled at this as he might have done. After all, we *had* solved his case for him.

It was eight o'clock by the time everybody had left the flat. 'Should we go out to eat?' I asked Maria.

'No thanks, Johnny. I don't feel like anything after all this. In fact, if you want to know the truth, I just want to go to sleep.'

'You get back to bed then and I'll make you a hot drink.'

Roly woke up when I went into the kitchen. I boiled some hot milk for Maria and gave him a bowlful too. He drank it all. I stroked his head gently and he wagged his stump. 'You'll be fine, old chap,' I said.

'I don't want you to stay, Johnny,' Maria said when I took in her drink.

'Oh.' I felt deflated. 'Why?'

'I'd like you to go away and think about what you want to do.'

'You mean about . . . the baby.'

'If there is one. I haven't done a test yet.'

'Maria, I—'

She stopped me. 'I said, think about it. Commitment is a big step for you and you've got to do it properly. For a start, it would mean no more Hilary.'

'I see. You're right – it is a big step.'

'That's why I'm leaving you to sort yourself out and, when you've done so, whatever you decide, ring me.'

There was nothing more to say. I fetched Roly from the kitchen and he walked a little unsteadily behind me. I remembered then that my car was still at the Adelphi so I rang for a taxi.

Back home, I couldn't settle. I wanted to ring Hilary and talk to her about the situation but, of course, she was the last person I could do that with. Anyway, things with Hilary were in a delicate state too.

I gave Roly some food and made sure he was settled in his basket, then I walked across town to the Adelphi to pick up the RAV4.

The Convention was still packed. Some band was playing Beatles numbers too loudly in the back hall. I broke the bad news to Nudger about the tape and thanked him for letting me use his stall.

'One good thing, Nudger. I forgot to tell you, I've got the radio show back. I start tomorrow, usual time, six to seven.'

'Great, Johnny. I'll be listening.' He handed me a tape. 'Don't forget this. Your other tape.'

It was Bobby and the Voxtones, the one I'd promised to give to Charlie Peyton.

'Thanks, Nudger.'

I realised I hadn't eaten anything all day so I drove out to Harry Ramsden's, past the Albert Dock, for a plate of fish and chips, a few yards up the road from the European Carriages offices.

It was after eleven when I'd finished the meal but I didn't feel like going home. I went instead to the Bamalama Club, where the blackboard announced that Houndstooth Willie – 'Last of the Mississippi Cotton-Pickin' Delta Bluesmen' – was performing. I'd known Willie for years. His father might well have deserved the honorary title but Willie himself was born in the Dingle.

'I'm just waiting for John Lee Hooker to peg out,' he once told me, 'and I'll be the last of the old bluesmen left. Then I'll treble my fees.'

I went over to the bar and ordered a Scrumpy Jack. 'Hello, stranger. You've turned up at last,' said Shirley.

I remembered what Geoff had told me about her wanting her bedroom decorated. 'I always do in the end.'

'About my bedroom . . . do you want to come and look at it tonight?'

I did, and I wondered if, subconsciously, that was where I'd been heading all evening, ever since I left Maria's. Shirley was one of my havens when things got rough. Then I remembered Roly.

'My dog's ill. I need to go home.' Shirley waited. 'If you fancy coming back to mine . . . ?'

'OK.' She smiled a big, happy smile. 'You're on.'

I found a stool at the bar and watched Houndstooth Willie launch himself into 'Dust My Broom' He played better bottleneck guitar than anyone I knew.

Jonas came over to say hello.

'It's Willie's last night,' he said. 'I haven't told him yet. The youngsters, they want dance music and rap now. Only the old folk want the blues.'

'You do all right,' I said, looking round. The Club seemed busy enough to me.

'All old people though, Johnny. They die off, my club gets empty. I need the young blood.'

'Perhaps one or two nights maybe,' I suggested. I'd never been into rap music myself but then, it's a generation thing in the same way that Glenn Miller fans in the fifties could never get their heads round Elvis Presley.

'Have you heard the bad news about Kenny Leatherbarrow?' he said.

'No. I wondered why he wasn't at his usual place at the bar. What is it?'

'He had a stroke last week, he's in hospital.'

'Is it serious?'

'He can't talk and he can only move one finger. They say he bangs it on the bedsheets as if he's playing the drums but he can't keep in time.'

'He never could when he was well,' I said. 'I wouldn't worry about that. What are his chances of recovery?'

'Not good apparently. The boys are calling him 'Less Kenny' now because he's not really with us.'

When Jonas wandered away, Willie embarked on 'Moaning in the Moonlight', a number guaranteed to depress the senses more than a shipload of Valium, and I had another two hours of it before Shirley finished.

The Scrumpy Jacks helped and, at 2.00 a.m., I called a taxi and took Shirley back to my flat.

'In all the time I've known you, you've never brought me here before, Johnny. It's fabulous.' She went over to my white baby grand and belted out a Motown tune.

'I didn't know you could play piano like that.'

'Well, you're always saying I look like one of The Supremes but I can't sing so I've got to have something musical going for me.' She launched into the first few bars of 'Baby Love'.

Roly peered out of his basket and smiled weakly.

'You never told me you had a dog.' Shirley stopped playing and went across to stroke him. 'He's lovely. What's he called?'

'Roly.' I explained how he'd been injured.

'Poor boy.' She patted his head softly and he licked her hand.

I went into the kitchen and fetched a bottle of hock from the fridge. 'Drink?' I asked and poured us each a glass.

'Cheers,' she said, 'to my favourite landlord.'

'So how's your lovelife these days?' I asked her as we sat down together on the settee. 'Rodney's gone, you said.'

'Well gone. You know me, Johnny, I've had the odd guy here and there, but nothing serious. How about yours?'

'Mine's a nightmare.'

'Not again?'

I needed somebody to talk it over with and Shirley and I had been friends for years. And occasional lovers, of course, but that was almost an afterthought, although Maria probably wouldn't see it that way if she walked in now.

'Be careful, Johnny,' Shirley said, after I'd told her about Maria. 'Some people marry the wrong person and they end up spoiling it for both themselves and each other.'

I thought of Owen and Susie Jenna. On their own they were probably happy people, but together . . .

'Maria and I would get on well together married,' I said, 'as long as I could still see Hilary, that is. And vice versa.'

'I don't think it works like that.' Shirley ran her fingers through the back of my hair and I shivered.

'What about you? Would you demand a hundred per cent fidelity from a man?'

'I'm a realist, Johnny. Men aren't monogamous by nature. I know enough of the girls on the game to be aware of that. Even the faithful ones are usually only faithful because they don't have the opportunity or the offers.'

'That's very cynical.' But then I remembered Bernard Skidmore and Diana Loder, and now Dougie Loder with Bernard's widow. Not to mention Owen Jenna and his 'niece' and Susie Jenna with Graham Bowlands. Adultery, it seemed, made the world go round. Why did anyone bother getting married at all? Everyone was at it. It seemed Shirley was right.

I started to stroke her hair in return. 'I shouldn't be doing this,' I said, realising as the words left my mouth how crass they sounded. Especially as I carried on caressing her. 'It's taking advantage of you.'

'Nonsense. What are friends for? The trouble is, people want relationships to be all black and white and they're not like that. They're ever changing, like water in a river. The river remains constant but it's always different water. The trick is to keep afloat and take love where you can get it.'

I put my arm round her neck, pulled her face to mine and kissed her gently on the lips. 'I'm afraid, unlike you, I don't have black satin sheets,' I said.

She smiled. 'I'm easy. I can make do with fur.'

I led her into the bedroom.

'What we do is between you and me, Johnny, because we're friends and this is what we need right now. It doesn't affect how you care for Hilary or Maria. Or whether or not you want to marry either of them.' She grinned mischievously. 'Or both! Right?'

'Right. Wait a minute though, I am your landlord now, don't forget.' What was the rule I had about landlords not doing it with the tenants?

'Crap,' said Shirley, unzipping her dress and letting it fall to the floor. 'We're people, not labels. I'm not a barmaid, not a tenant, not a consumer. I'm me, Shirley.'

I laughed and put my hands on her firm black boobs.

'And tomorrow, Johnny Ace, you can go away and be a landlord, or a husband or a private eye or whatever you like.'

And come to a decision about Maria, I thought.

'But tonight,' she started to unbutton my shirt, 'tonight you're mine.'

'Hang on a minute.' I took a mini-disc from the bedside cabinet and slotted it into the portable hi-fi by the bed. 'Let's have some music.'

'That's a nice song,' said Shirley as she took off the rest of her clothes and pulled back the sheets. It was a plaintive ballad with acoustic guitar backing. 'Who's singing it?'

'Have a guess.'

'It sounds a bit like John Lennon. I thought I knew all his songs but I don't know this one.'

I smiled and climbed into bed next to her. 'You're right about the singer – it *is* Lennon. These are songs from *The Lost John Lennon Tape*. You won't hear these anywhere else in the world.'

'How come you've got them then?'

I ran my tongue against the lobe of her ear. 'It's a long story,' I replied.